When the Ocotillo Bloom

by

Linda LaRoque

This is a work of fiction. Names, characters, places, and incidents are either the product of the author's imagination or are used fictitiously, and any resemblance to actual persons living or dead, business establishments, events, or locales, is entirely coincidental.

When the Ocotillo Bloom

Published by *L.G. Smith Books*
Cover Art by *Diana Carlile*
http://www.designingdiana.blogspot.com

Publishing History
First Edition, 2007
Second Edition, 2009
Digital ISBN 978-0-9979908-2-9
Print ISBN 978-0-9979908-3-6

Published in the United States of America

Chapter One

Lynn paused in packing her toiletries and stared at the jar of face cream with unseeing eyes. "Abby, are you sure I'm doing the right thing traipsing off to God knows where this summer?" She'd been haunted by that question since receiving the letter from Seth Williams a week ago.

I'm pleased to inform you the job of...is yours...please be in Mesa Flats by...my son, Brian will meet you...to Ocotillo Ranch.

This was a big step for her, leaving her home for the summer, her safe comfortable environment. It was only natural for her to have doubts.

She glanced at her reflection in the full-length bathroom mirror and shuddered at the lackluster face staring back at her. Her complexion was no longer peaches and cream but sallow and washed out. She focused her gaze on the jar of expensive brand face cream she'd been using for years. The label read; *renew your skin's youthful appearance.* Yeah, right, it had sure done that. Shaking her head in disgust, she tossed it into the trash. She'd save money and buy her cosmetics at Wal-Mart from now on.

No, that wasn't quite true. Of all those summers, the last several had been spent floundering, wallowing in inactivity and isolation. Because of lack of exercise and outdoor activities, her health had suffered. She'd neglected friendships and her social life was the pits.

It didn't take a rocket scientist to know that sunshine and fresh air would return her skin's glow. Auburn hair that used to bounce and shine with vitality still looked pretty good. Probably due to the salon bought conditioner she used faithfully. She let her gaze travel the length of her body and snorted in disgust at the size of her butt. Okay, so she looked awful, but plans for change were in the forecast. Surely her posterior would shrink if she didn't sit on it all summer in front of the television working cross-stitch patterns.

For the past fifteen years, when school let out, Lynn Devry spent her summers relaxing, doing as she pleased. No, that wasn't quite true. Of all those summers, the last several had been spent floundering, wallowing in inactivity and isolation. Because of lack of exercise and outdoor activities, her health had suffered. She'd neglected friendships and her social life was the pits.

That was no way to live. If so, she might as well give up and jump in the wastebasket with that jar of face cream and the rest of the trash.

This summer she'd taken a job, and on a ranch to boot, a place that had dirt and smelly cow poop. She'd never been on a ranch in her life and knew nothing about cows and horses. Fear squeezed her heart. What had possessed her? She shrugged at her image in the mirror. Her reflection didn't know any more than she did. *God, I pray this isn't a mistake.* Oh, well, it's a done deal now. She would be indoors and far away from the animals. Lynn tossed the last of her toiletries in her cosmetic bag balanced on the edge of the lavatory. She zipped it closed and carried it down the short hall to the living room foyer where her other bags were parked by the front door.

Abby was bent over in front of the entertainment center stacking CD's in a small box. She straightened up and with one hand fisted on her hip, flipped her long blonde braid over her shoulder. "Mother, you know where you're going. It's West Texas, not Mars. Relax for once in your life. You'll probably enjoy the fresh country air if you'll just give it a fair chance."

Relax, huh? Lynn sat her cosmetic bag down with the others. She hadn't been able to do that in a long while. Oh, she put on a good front. But, that's all it was, a facade. And, it didn't fool anyone close to her.

Lynn couldn't resist teasing her daughter about West Texas. She suspected Abby thought the ranch would be a cure all for her mother's problems. Wouldn't that be wonderful?

"Well, it sounds like the middle of nowhere to me. Anytime you have to drive two hundred and fifty miles to reach a shopping mall, you're in the boondocks." She joined Abby at the entertainment center, unplugged her portable CD player, and carried it over to sit with her luggage.

Abby's face twisted with concern. "Mother—"

Lynn patted Abby's cheek. "Hey, relax, sugar. I'm teasing. You know how I like to talk and complain. I promise to give this experience a fair chance." She took the box from her daughter's hand and walked to the door with Abby on her tail.

"Okay, but remember, I heard that. You said, 'I promise.'"

Trust her daughter to remember her words and hold her to them.

Lynn opened the front door to find Art Wayne, her trusted friend and family doctor, standing under the overhang of her small stoop, his finger aimed at the doorbell. Of her pre-divorce social circle of friends, he and Loretta were the only two who stuck by her. They still saw Dan on occasion, but not often.

As a single, she just didn't fit in with the couples she and Dan had socialized with, but he and his new young wife did. The country club set welcomed his bride with open arms. Well, the socialites were welcome to the pair. She shuddered. Lynn was glad to be out of that pretentious circle, and out of Dan's controlling clutches.

Lynn's parents died when she and Dan were newly wed. With no siblings for emotional support, she'd have drowned without the shoulders of Art and Loretta to lean on.

She grinned as Art started and jerked his hand back. "Hey, Art, I didn't know you were coming by this morning. You're just in time to help load the car."

Art looked at the stack of bags behind her on the oriental runner atop the waxed wood floor and sighed. "Darn! I should've waited another ten minutes."

Lynn peeked around his large frame to see his car parked behind hers in the single drive. "Loretta not with you?"

"No, she's packing for our trip to Europe, but sends her love." The two were leaving next week and would be gone for a month. Lynn was surprised Loretta had been able to talk him into leaving his practice that long. Having a new partner probably helped. They would rent a car and tour every castle Loretta could locate, would even stay in a few that were now country inns.

He stepped through the arched doorway into the foyer and kissed Lynn on the cheek. "You know I couldn't let you leave town for the summer and not say bye."

Yeah, he'd pushed this summer job as hard as

Abby. He probably wanted to make sure she didn't change her mind, and see to it that she got out of town on time. She watched for clues of his intentions, but his eyes were on Abby. *Shame on you for being suspicious, Lynn.* It's only natural that he'd want to say goodbye personally since she'd be gone all summer.

Art hugged Abby. "How's my girl this morning?"

"I'm fine, Uncle Art." She smiled and melted into his embrace, swallowed in the folds of his suit coat and large body. He patted her back.

Since Art and Loretta were unable to have children, when the two couples became friends, two-year-old Abby adopted them and tagged them aunt and uncle. They'd been delighted and took their honorary title seriously. To Lynn and Abby, they were family and a Godsend.

Lynn picked up her cosmetic and carry-on bags and stepped outside onto the porch. Art followed with her two larger suitcases. He loaded them in the trunk and turned to take the smaller ones from her hands. Concern niggled at her mind. "I'm not too sure about that, Art. She's been acting strange this morning and won't tell me what's wrong. Keep an eye on her for me, will you?" Art looked startled and turned to Abby.

Abby rolled her blue eyes and shook her head, setting her long blonde braid in motion. She handed him the box of CD's and the portable stereo and glared at her mother. Hands on her hips, she sputtered. "I've been telling her all morning, I'm fine."

Art put his arms around Abby's shoulders and squeezed. "Quit your worrying, Mom. Your little girl will be fine. She's got a good head on her shoulders, so get in that car and hit the road." Abby raised her chin a notch.

Lynn threw her hands up. "Okay, okay, I'll let it go." Lynn hugged Art and walked with him to his car.

"Oh, damn, I almost forgot." Art pulled some papers out of his breast pocket and handed them to her. "You need to sign these before you leave, so I can fax them to Seth at the ranch this morning."

Lynn sighed. It was just like Art to wait until the last minute. He spread the papers on the hood of his Mercedes and handed her a pen.

She cocked an eyebrow. "Why did you get these and not me?"

"Because you don't have a fax machine and put down my fax number on your application."

Well, he was right about that. She looked down at the documents. "Art, you know I can't sign these without reading them first." Though just two pages, they were covered with print. It would take a while to plow through them, and she just didn't want to take the time. If she did, she'd be late arriving at her destination tonight. The thought of driving through the desert in the dark sent a shiver up her spine.

He drew back as if offended, then muttered, "I've read them. Trust me. They're just emergency release forms in case you fall off a horse or something."

She snorted. "Trust *me*, Art. It's not going to happen. I won't be anywhere near the creatures." Her on a horse? The idea was ridiculous. She'd never been on one and didn't plan to change history. Though the idea was intriguing—her riding across the desert at sunset. She dislodged the picture from her mind. She was afraid of the animals.

In a hurry to get on the road, she grabbed Art's pen

and signed a copy and returned to her car and stuffed hers in the side pocket of the carry-on bag in the trunk of her car. She'd read them that evening at the hotel in Marathon.

Slamming the trunk closed, she turned back to say goodbye, but Art was already in his car backing out of the driveway. He tooted his horn and with his arm out the open window, waved. "Have a good time."

Lynn returned his wave wondering why the rush.

Abby followed her around the car. They stood for a minute, studying each other. Her baby had grown into a beautiful young woman. She was so proud of her. Tears stung her eyes, and she coughed to clear the knot of emotion forming in her throat.

"Come here and give your mama a hug. I'm going to miss you." When they pulled back, Lynn cupped Abby's face and searched her eyes. No, she hadn't imagined it. Something was on Abby's mind, but she was determined to keep it to herself. Well, Abby was a woman. Lynn couldn't keep interfering in her affairs. But it was damn hard to keep her mouth shut and not try to finagle it out of her.

She tucked a wayward strand of Abby's hair behind her ear. Abby looked so much like her father, tall, blonde, and blue eyed. Even the expression on her face mirrored the one Dan used to wear when worried. She smiled ruefully. Thinking about her ex-husband no longer hurt as it once had. Thank God that part of her life was over. Their divorce had been bitter, but Dan had been fair and she'd come away with enough money to buy her small house in an older, but desirable, neighborhood in Fort Worth. The houses were stone or brick with manicured lawns and big old trees. Now if she could only restore her outlook on life and move on without looking back, she'd be happy.

"You know how much I love you, don't you?"

Abby nodded. She looked ready to cry and fell into her mother's embrace, arms locked around Lynn's neck. The girl was several inches taller than her five feet, four-inch stature, making her feel short. Lynn reached down and playfully swatted her on the butt. "Don't you cry now, or you'll get me started." Abby giggled, and Lynn held her baby close, rubbed her back, and then released her.

Abby sniffed. "I love you too, Mother. Be careful, now." She tried to grin, but her face twisted as she choked out, "You know, watch out for the other guy like you always tell me."

* * *

When Lynn left Fort Worth that morning, she chose the scenic two-lane state highway over the interstate. It was nice to not have to compete with the truckers for the passing lane. The wind they created blew her mid-size Ford Taurus all over the road. Native wildflowers lined both sides of the road. Red and yellow Indian paintbrush and Mexican hat dotted unplowed pastures, while violet snapdragons, purple phlox, and white angel trumpets grew among the rocks and along the fences.

Shortly after noon, with her stomach grumbling loudly, Lynn pulled off Texas State Highway 67 at a small town between San Angelo and Fort Stockton. She turned into the parking lot of Terry's Steak House. The sign boasted "Best Food in Town," and the crowded lot was encouraging.

Entering the dining room, she looked around

before locating a vacant booth. Unfortunately, it was in the smoking section. She slid across the red vinyl seat, adjusted her skirt, and then pulled a menu from between the sugar container and napkin holder.

She tapped her nails on the Formica tabletop as she studied the single sheet laminated menu. *Gee, now why am I not surprised? Let's see, I've got a choice of pan-fried, deep fat fried or chicken fried.* She stuffed the menu back in place.

A gum-popping waitress in tee shirt and tight jeans took her drink order, and then returned with a quart Mason jar of iced tea. Pulling a pencil from her topknot of hair, the rail thin woman cocked her hip and poised the pencil over her order pad. "What can I get ya, hon?"

Lynn smiled. *Well, what the heck, why not? When in the country, do as the natives do.* "I'll have the chicken fried steak with fries." She shuddered at a mental picture of fat clinging to her arteries. *Don't think about it.* Lynn added artificial sweetener and lemon from a plastic package to her tea, and as her tall spoon swirled the mixture around in the jar, she let her eyes slide around the room and take in the kaleidoscope of people.

Patrons of varying ages entered the restaurant, and most seemed to know one another, creating a loud family atmosphere. They stopped at booths and tables to chat and slap each other on the back on their way in and out. Some smiled at her in greeting as they passed. The place reminded of her a diner where she and her folks ate when she was just a girl.

The middle-aged waitress returned and plunked the overcrowded plate down before her. The size of a hubcap, the steak was enough meat for two and hung over the edge of the plate.

"Here you go, hon. Can I get ya anything else?"

Lynn smiled up at the woman and shook her head in awe of the meal before her.

"No thank you." Good grief, how could anyone eat this much food? She glanced at some of the male customers in their work jeans and cowboy boots. They probably did manual labor, and putting away a meal like this was easy for them. She snorted. Bet they didn't worry about the calories either.

The waitress sucked a small pink bubble back into her mouth, popping it, and gave Lynn a big smile. She laid her check in the center of the table. "Well, you just holler if you do now, ya hear?"

"Thank you. I will."

Lynn was pleased to note the steak was sirloin and home cooked, not one of those that come frozen, two dozen to a box. Tenderized, the meat was battered with milk, egg, and flour, and then fried until crisp and golden brown. The cream gravy was heavily peppered and looked and smelled delicious. And the fries were real, the kind made from a fresh potato that had been peeled and sliced. Ah, home style Texas cooking at its best, just like the sign read out front.

Breathing in the luscious aroma, Lynn sighed before popping a fry in her mouth. She felt a stab of guilt at the calories she'd be consuming. The skirt she wore pinched her waist reminding her of the weight she'd put on last summer. With a shrug, she pushed the guilt aside and tucked into her meal. The food was here. What would another pound or two matter at this point?

The dining room hummed with the low rumble of voices as cigarette smoke collected in a cloud near the ceiling. Obviously, the no smoking ban hadn't reached this small community. Voices and laughter echoed around the room making it hard not to hear individual conversations. Major topics of debate were the price of beef, how gas prices were hurting farmers, and warnings about some kind of infestation that was causing problems with this spring's tomato plants. All around the room clear plastic bags filled with water hung from the ceiling. She didn't have a clue what they were for.

Stuffed, with half her meal still on her plate, she paid her bill, visited the ladies room, and headed for her vehicle. She smelled like a dirty ashtray. Too bad she didn't carry cologne in her purse. All she had was evergreen air freshener for the car. Deciding she'd take stale smoke odor over that of a Christmas tree, she got in her car and drove next door for gas. Soon she was back on the road.

With Central Texas far behind her, the abundance of flora diminished as she drove deeper into West Texas. A sprinkling of wildflowers and prickly pear cactus with their yellow blooms dotted the landscape. But nature no longer dominated.

Beyond the ditches, oil pump jacks and gas compressors stood reign over land ruined by drilling. The ugly equipment was a stark contrast to the beauty of the cactus and the prairie and Chihuahua flax growing in the reddish brown dirt. The pungent smell of raw gas filled the air. Her lips formed into a silent, "yuck." How could people live with that smell all the time? Maybe it grew on them. As quickly as she'd driven into the offensive odor, she drove out, leaving the marred landscape behind.

Lynn rolled down the windows and let her auburn hair fly in the breeze. The weather was mild for late May, the temperature just below ninety degrees. The fresh air felt good on her face. Hiking her skirt above her knees, she turned on the floor vent to cool her legs. Unable to hear the radio over the road noise rushing in the open windows, she turned up the volume.

Enjoying the scenery and humming, hair bouncing as she kept time with the music on the car stereo, she tapped out the rhythm with her left foot. Relaxed and carefree for the first time in a good while, she decided maybe this trip was just what she needed. Unruffled by her off key voice, she joined Linda Ronstadt in song, belting out the lyrics of "Shattered". The outside wind blew into her face giving her voice a vibration effect. She laughed with abandon—she hadn't done this in years. Dan never liked her singing along with the radio. "Well, pooh on you, Danny boy!"

The landscape roughened with each mile, but the beauty was still breathtaking. Flat buttes spanned across the terrain. Atop the highest ones, wind turbines twirled generating electricity. They looked like something from outer space.

Her thoughts turned to her destination—Ocotillo Ranch. She looked forward to a long-needed vacation. Hopefully the ranch would live up to its name and be surrounded by the colorful plants she'd read about in *Texas Highways* Magazine. She'd been intrigued and couldn't wait to see them. The name made the ranch sound serene and romantic, not that she cared about romance.

Serenity sounded good though, especially after ten months with her hormone-driven students. Five hours a day she'd work for her room and board and the remainder of the time would be hers. If she finished early, she left early. With any luck, she'd enjoy her job as bread cook. Nothing was more relaxing than working bread dough in her hands and forming it into different shapes. After work she'd enjoy the facilities at the ranch, walking, swimming, and the exercise room. She'd like to rid herself of a few pounds.

At the thought of pounds, she felt a tug of guilt over her indulgence at lunch. Her skirt was cutting her waist. She loosened the top button and pushed her discomfort to the back of her mind. Maybe she'd develop new interest, even work out of the rut she'd been in for so long.

What would ranch owner Seth Williams be like? Probably old and bow-legged, a jolly sort of guy. Would he be one of those cowboys who chewed tobacco or dipped snuff? She shuddered at the thought. Spit cups were nasty, and men who felt the need to spit at every opportunity were disgusting. Almost like a dog marking its territory.

The Taurus rattled, and her body felt every bump in the road. She missed the quietness and smooth ride of the Volvo she'd driven before the divorce. No matter, she was grateful to have the dented four-year-old, tan Ford. It was reliable, and it was hers, free and clear.

She'd given up a lot of material things with the divorce. They didn't matter. But in those years of marriage she'd lost part of herself—the spontaneous child inside her, the happy, carefree individual who loved to have fun. She was grateful Abby had been able to see her that way before Dan's climb up the corporate ladder. He hadn't always been stiff and controlling. The money and prestige made him that way. And with each rung of the ladder, she'd changed as she'd tried to fit into the mold of the perfect wife that Dan expected.

Lynn's enjoyment in the drive dwindled bit by bit, then died like a snuffed out candle. She tensed and looked around trying to find a source for her changed mood. The scenery was beautiful and vast. She could see forever. It wasn't her environment that bothered her—it was the past. Her anticipation turned into concern.

My, God. What am I doing out here miles from nowhere? What the heck was she doing driving to the far ends of the earth for a summer job?

"I don't know. That's the problem," she muttered to herself. *Yes you do, Lynn. You're here to try to make a change in your boring life.* She was a grown woman, had faced this type of anxiety before, and could do so again. She forced her eyes back to the beauty beyond the roadside and tried to ignore the knot in her gut and the tightness moving up her chest.

Sharp tingling, as if being stuck with a million pins, started at her toes and traveled to her scalp as adrenaline pumped through her body. "Breathe deeply and slowly," she repeated. The exercise the psychiatrist taught her several years ago usually worked. "In through the nose. Out through the mouth. In, out...."

Grasping for something to distract her, she turned the stereo up and tried to sing with the music. It failed to distance her from the emotional war in her body. Moisture filled her eyes and blurred her vision. Her heart beating like a thrashing machine, she eased the car to the shoulder, shifted to park, and dropped her head back against the headrest. Tears squeezed through her closed lids and trickled down her face.

Grabbing a handful of tissues from the box on the passenger seat, she wiped them away. The pressure inside her was near the bursting point. She beat on the steering wheel and screamed at the top of her lungs, releasing some of the tension. The sound flew from her car window and dispersed in the vastness of the bare desert terrain. A couple of cactus wrens, startled by the odd noise, burst into flight from the yucca plant where they perched.

As Lynn watched them fly away and cautiously return to the plant, she resumed her breathing exercises. Gradually the fear eased, and her breathing slowed. Anxiety attacks and depression had plagued her for several years after her divorce. They'd strike, she'd ride the wave of despair, and then they were gone. She didn't have a clue what caused them, other than the psychiatrist said they were related to her depression. Medication helped for a while, but the coping techniques she learned were invaluable, and eventually she was able to get off the medicine. It had been over a year since she'd taken a pill.

What had triggered this one? She shrugged and shook her head. Probably the excitement of leaving home for her working vacation, making a change, or fear she wouldn't enjoy her stay. If she didn't like it at the ranch, she could always go home. So, what was there to be afraid of? Nothing, absolutely nothing.

She relaxed as the knot in her stomach gradually dissolved. Her tension eased, and she straightened in the seat. Breathing and pulse under control, she turned on her blinker, looked in her side mirror, and waited for a car to pass. A state trooper going the opposite direction slowed as he drove by, and then made a quick U-turn.

Oh, shit! She was ready to pull onto the pavement when the trooper flashed his lights and pulled in behind her. Heat flushed her body. In a stupor, she braked, turned off the ignition, and sat frozen, hands fisted in her lap. *What now, Lord?*

Lynn's chin began to quiver before the trooper unfolded his lanky frame from his cruiser. She watched from her side mirror as he closed the door. Tall, wearing a Stetson and reflective sunglasses, he took his time approaching her battered Ford. When he reached her window, she was snuffling like a baby.

"Ma'am." He tipped his hat. "You having car trouble?"

His eyes took inventory of her, her car, and the surrounding desert landscape. She supposed she did look suspicious parked to the side of the deserted two lane highway between Fort Stockton and Alpine.

She shook her head, setting her auburn hair in motion and tried to answer, but tears erupted. She gulped, her mouth opening and closing like a fish, then reached down to the passenger floorboard to grab more tissues. She froze at his sharp command.

"Keep your hands where I can see them."

Shocked at his terse order, and at his hand on the gun at his waist, she brought her hands up slowly, a wad of tissue in each. The young Hispanic man's lips twitched as he nodded. She grinned stupidly, Lord she must look like an idiot, and emitted a tiny, nervous giggle before mopping at her face. Her eyes flicked to his nametag, reading Espinoza.

"Ma'am, I need to see your license and proof of insurance."

Flustered, her fingers fumbled, and she had difficulty removing her license from the plastic window in her wallet.

Taking them both, he walked back to his cruiser.

You haven't done anything wrong, Lynn, so quit worrying. The thought did little to ease her mind as she watched the trooper through her rear-view mirror. He got in the vehicle, and she supposed he was looking at a computer screen, looking her up to see if she was a criminal.

When he returned, he removed his sunglasses, propped an arm on the roof of her car, and leaned down to her eye level. She looked into his eyes, noting the shade. Their brilliant blue surrounded by dark lashes softened his rugged appearance. How'd he get those with a name like Espinoza?

"Now, ma'am, what seems to be the problem? Are you in some kind of trouble?"

His kindness made her want to start blubbering again.

She blew her nose, mortified at the honking sound, and then wadded the tissues into a ball. "Really officer, nothing's wrong. I didn't feel well and pulled over. I was about to get back on the road when you flashed your lights."

He lowered his chin. His eyes narrowed slightly. "You were mighty upset."

"It's not every day I get stopped by the law. I'm too sensitive I know, but I was embarrassed." Lord, she wished her voice would stop trembling. At least her lips had.

He returned her license and insurance papers. "Well, everything seems to be in order. What's your destination?"

"I'm stopping in Marathon for the night, and then heading for Mesa Flats in the morning."

He studied her a while longer. Lynn wanted to fidget but sat still as his eyes probed hers. "Well," he rapped his knuckles on the roof of her car and straightened. "You be careful now."

Before she could thank him, he was striding back to his vehicle. He followed her for a couple miles before making a U-turn and heading in the opposite direction.

She sighed with relief, and the tension diminished. Her hands eased their hold on the steering wheel. She stretched her muscles and rolled her head to loosen the tightness in her neck, shoulders, and back. *Oh God, how humiliating.* Then she started laughing—so hard her belly ached, and she was wiping tears off her cheeks.

Voice deep, she muttered. "Keep your hands where I can see 'em, ma'am." She was grinning and cackling like a loon and thought for a minute she'd have to pull off the road again but finally got her giggles under control.

That's an experience I hope never to repeat. No way could she have told him she'd had an anxiety attack. Most people didn't understand, and he might be like her ex-husband. Oh, yeah. She'd be lucky enough to be escorted to the county hospital in Alpine for observation. Emotional problems and anxiety attacks didn't mean a person was crazy.

Chapter Two

Seth Williams, owner of the Ocotillo Ranch, leaned against the corral, his long arms folded across the top rail. He stared at the distant horizon, deep in thought. Reaching up, he whipped his weathered straw hat from his head, raked his hands through his dark, salt and pepper hair, and then settled the hat back in place.

His mind was on the new crewmember due to arrive that evening. Damn, Art. He'd called early this morning and left a message on the answering machine.

"Seth, this is Art. I'm afraid there is one little detail I failed to tell you about Lynn. Uh, you see, she thinks…and doesn't know…"

Shit. Mrs. Devry would arrive this evening, and tomorrow he'd have the dubious honor of setting her straight.

He'd hired her, without an interview, as a favor to his friend, Dr. Arthur Wayne. What had he been thinking? Seth shook his head. As usual, his heart ruled in situations like this. If Art thought working on the ranch would help her, that's what he wanted to do.

Well hell, my specialty is kids, not women.

Rubbing the tense muscles in his neck, he sighed in resignation. He owed Art a big favor; therefore, he'd do this for his friend. He needed a bread cook this summer, so it wouldn't be a problem unless she couldn't cook. Being a teacher, she'd at least be good with the kids. They were his major concern.

Seth, an adolescent psychologist, once had a large practice in Dallas, but hated the city and loved this land. When a friend suggested a summer camp for troubled kids, he went with the idea. He remembered how excited he'd been moving back. His three boys were thrilled at being able to live on the ranch. They'd ride their horses up to the highway, stable them in a lean-to, and catch the bus in to Study Butte for school. But his wife Barbara hated living so far from the Metroplex. He bought a fax machine, a computer, the works, everything she needed to work from home. They had the money where she could drive or fly to Dallas whenever necessary, but it wasn't enough. It wasn't Dallas.

He'd cancelled all of his plans for the summer camp, and they'd moved back to Dallas. Though he was unhappy, he tried without success not to show it. Barbara accused him of not making a dedicated effort. Two years later, he and Barbara had decided to separate and then divorce. Now, he was here and doing what he loved most. Unfortunately, he still loved Barbara, and he believed she still loved him. But, there was no middle ground for them and neither would make the ultimate sacrifice.

Every summer, he boarded children and teens with behavioral and social problems. It appeared this session he'd be dealing with a woman who couldn't manage her life. Well hell, he'd hired her but didn't plan to waste time worrying about her or playing nursemaid.

What was he saying? He respected Art's opinion. If Art thought he could help Mrs. Devry, he'd help her, in any way he could. But she wasn't an adolescent, nor was she a client. He couldn't treat her like one. She'd have to want to change, put forth some effort for a transformation to take place.

How much trouble could one woman be anyway?

On the ranch, kids and employees participated in a

strict exercise program. Plus, each camper had an assigned job in the laundry, bunkhouse, mess hall, or the stables. They also were required to take care of their horse and participate in various other activities to keep them busy and out of trouble.

Glancing down, he scratched his faithful companion's head, then squatted and with noses aligned, looked into the Lab's eyes.

"Whaddya you think, Sam? Can we 'whip her into shape?'"

Sam jerked his head up, catching Seth's hat with his nose knocking it askew. He backed up, and with a bark jumped into the air a couple times.

"Think so, huh?" He chuckled. "You have more faith in me than I do." He stood up and righted his hat. "Come on, boy. Let's go get our breakfast."

The yellow Lab fell in step beside him as they started for the dining hall. Sensing Seth's mood, Sam darted away, located a stick, then ran back, and with tail wagging, dropped it at Seth's feet and barked.

"Okay, okay. Just a couple times." To Sam, fetch cured everything. If only life were that simple for the rest of them.

He picked up the stick and threw it down the road toward the dining hall. Sam ran off in a streak of yellow, sending dust flying as he skidded past the stick before righting himself and coming to a stop. He dashed back and forth until Seth reached the steps of the building and had to go in.

Inside the dining hall, Seth grabbed a tray and went through the serving line filling it with Cookie's fluffy eggs and bacon. At a table, he eased his tall frame into the chair beside his son, Brian. He was a young man in his late teens, with gray eyes and dark hair similar to his own.

Seth reached for the pepper, and shook some on his eggs. "Brian, I need you to pick up a Mrs. Devry this evening in Mesa Flats."

Brian stopped eating, his buttered biscuit caught in mid-air. "Okay. What time?" he asked before taking a bite.

"Be there by six thirty. She's due at seven, but I don't want her waiting around alone if she arrives early."

Seth studied his canned biscuits with disgust before spreading them with butter. They were hard on the outside and soft inside. Monday morning they'd have real bread—home made. He hoped. At least the eggs were always good. He finished his breakfast and pushed his tray to the side.

"Who is she, Dad?"

"She's our new bread cook."

Brian released a long sigh, leaned back in his chair, and rubbed his belly. "Finally. It's a good thing she's coming. The crew's been complaining about being served store-bought bread three times a day."

Seth glanced at Brian, taking note of the stack on his plate. Humor laced his words. "Canned biscuits don't seem to be slowing you down any."

"You know me, Dad. I'll eat anything when I'm hungry." Mouth full, Brian took a drink of orange juice and swallowed. "I'm still growing, you know."

Seth shook his head. "Let's hope she's as good a cook as her application stated."

Brian looked from his dad to Jake. "Why would a teacher want to come out here to spend the summer?

You'd think she'd want to do something relaxing, like go to Hawaii or some other exciting place."

Jake laughed. "She'll probably be asking herself the same question before the summer's over. Anyway, not everyone has the same ideas of fun, Brian. You'd never catch me in Hawaii."

Seth's lips twitched at the thought of his stocky foreman lounging on the beach wearing a loud floral shirt and sipping a tropical drink sporting a paper umbrella and flower. A no frills kind of guy; Jake's drink of choice came in long neck bottles.

Seth went to the beverage table and refilled his coffee cup. When he returned to the table, he sat directly across from Jake. He said, "If you're finished, I need to talk to you. Privately."

"Sure. You want to go outside?"

Brian shoved his chair back and stood. He grabbed all three of their trays, stacking loose items on the top. "I can take a hint. I'm leaving."

"Thanks, son." Seth looked around. Most of the kids had eaten and left for their daily scheduled activities so they had privacy where they were. "We can talk in here."

"First off, I hired Mrs. Devry as a favor for Art Wayne. You remember me talking about him, don't you?"

"Yeah. He's your doctor friend." Jake arched his left eyebrow. His expression was one of uncertainty. "Does this mean she can't cook?"

Seth couldn't keep from grinning. His foreman was tired of hearing the wranglers complain about the canned biscuits, too.

"Art assures me she is a good baker. Of course,

since she's a good friend of his, he's probably prejudiced."

"If she can't, we may have a war on our hands," Jake said. "Your two boys will be on the front line."

Seth couldn't deny that Brian and Jared were pretty vocal about the food situation. The wranglers and staff weren't as comfortable voicing their opinions.

"You need to know, that even though Mrs. Devry is an employee, she has some personal issues she needs to deal with while she's here. I say *needs to* because she doesn't have a clue what kind of operation we're running here."

Jake whistled. "Uh, oh. That sounds like it could mean trouble."

Jake was a trusted employee, his assistant, therefore, he felt comfortable revealing Mrs. Devry's problems.

"Art says she's been depressed for a while, not clinically, but enough to affect her energy and her desire to get out and socialize."

"How does she make it through the school year? Is her job suffering as a result?"

"No. It seems she's an excellent teacher. She's fine during the school year because she has a routine. School and her students keep her busy." Seth was relieved to know that. Kids were important to him, and he didn't like the idea of a person teaching and not doing a good job.

"The summers are her problem. She sits around, sleeps too much, and doesn't get any exercise. Not that she does during the winter, but at least then she's getting out of the house."

"So, what you're saying is that Art thinks she'll do

well here because our strict schedule will help her develop self-discipline."

"Exactly. She's gained weight and is out of shape. It'll take a while to build up her stamina. Art's words were, he wants us to, 'Whip her into shape.'"

Seth could see Jake didn't believe he was serious. When the man realized he was, he burst out laughing. As a marine, he'd whipped a lot of young people into shape, maybe even a few women recruits.

Sobering, he asked, "What do you want me to do, boss?"

"Just be aware of the situation. Keep your eyes open. Let me know if you see any behavior that indicates her depression is worsening."

Jake nodded.

"I don't want you to think badly of her. In Art's words, 'She's a lovely woman, but she's floundering right now and needs our help.' He feels she's in a rut, one she can't get out of on her own."

"No, I won't. And, I'll try to forget what you've told me and not let it affect my first impression of her."

Seth knew he was lucky to have a man like Jake working for him. The man had integrity. He was tough and disciplined, but had a gentle side. He worked wonders with the kids and animals. Patient to a fault, Seth had never seen him lose his temper. Of course, his undergraduate degree in psychology helped too.

They walked out of the dining hall together.

"Oh, there's one other thing you need to know. Art left a message on my answering machine this morning." He was probably chicken to talk to him in person. "It seems Mrs. Devry didn't get a chance to read her contract before signing it, and she thinks this is a relaxing kid-free place. A dude ranch."

* * *

Saturday evening, Lynn drove into Mesa Flats, a small town of crumbling buildings, a post office, and a convenience store. A stop sign served as the major intersection that crossed a two-lane blacktop highway. Parked at an adobe building, with a carport wide enough to hold about eight vehicles, sat the white Suburban she'd been told to look for. Painted in red on the front door were the words Ocotillo Ranch.

In the dirt yard, a young skinny cowboy in his late teens played ball with a frisky golden Lab. Dust, stirred up from the chase, and flew around them. When she pulled to a stop beside him, he leaned in the window on the passenger's side and tilted his hat back on his head. Gray eyes crinkled at the corners as he smiled.

"Hello, Mrs. Devry." He pointed to the carport. "You can park in any slot. Then I'll get your bags."

She'd been told, in her letter of acceptance, that the ranch road was rough and often impassable without four-wheel drive. Given the choice of making the drive in her car or leaving it in town, leaving it seemed the best alternative. She pulled into the slot closest to the building.

The young man was at her door when she turned off the motor. He opened the door, removed his hat, and extended his hand. "My name is Brian, ma'am, Brian Williams. Seth Williams is my dad."

Seth Williams must've had his children late in life. She'd pictured him as an older man.

She returned his handshake and smiled. "Hello, Brian. I'm Lynn Devry. Thanks for meeting me." She glanced around at the deserted area. "I'd have been lost in this wilderness."

Brian started unloading her bags. When he finished, she rolled up the windows and locked the doors.

The Lab parked in front of her. Wiggling from head to tail, he dropped a ball on the ground at her feet. Tongue lolling out one side of his mouth, he whined, gyrated, and panted as he looked at her with hope.

"And this is Sam. If he bothers you, just tell him 'No,' and he'll leave you alone. He'll run you ragged if you let him. Silly mutt never gets tired."

Lynn squatted so she could look into the dog's face and scratched his ears. "Hello, Sam. Don't jump on me, and we'll be good friends."

He chuffed blissfully, and then nudged his ball closer to her feet.

She looked at the slobber-covered ball on the dusty ground. Sam nuzzled her hand.

"Sorry, mister, I'm not touching that nasty thing."

Brian loaded her luggage into the Suburban and opened the passenger door for her. Before she could climb in, Sam jumped in and sat on his haunches in the center of the front seat.

"I hope you don't mind, Mrs. Devry. He's used to riding up front."

"No, I don't mind." At least she didn't think she did. Grateful for the running board and the denim Bermuda shorts she wore, she stepped up and slid onto the seat beside Sam.

They traveled northeast and about five miles out turned west onto a dirt road—a road full of potholes. After a few bone jarring bumps, she grabbed the handgrip above the window and hung on for dear life.

"Sorry it's so bumpy, ma'am, but keeping this road free of ruts and potholes is next to impossible." He glanced over with concern. "I'll slow down if you want, but it won't be less rough."

She shook her head, wincing at the hole he just hit. "No, that's not necessary. And please, call me, Lynn." He smiled and nodded.

"I hear you're a teacher. Dad's a firm believer in education."

"He sounds like a smart man." It was hard to imagine what Mr. Williams would be like. His family must be important. From experience, she'd learned well-mannered young man like Brian came from caring homes.

"What do you teach?"

"Math at the middle school level." His face twisted into a grimace, and she laughed. "You don't like math?"

"It's not that I don't like it, I just have a hard time with it."

Her love of math made it hard to understand why others didn't enjoy it like she did. She knew some people struggled to pass.

"Are you in college, yet?" He didn't look old enough to shave.

"I start this fall. I'll go to the University of Texas at Arlington and live with my brother, Jared." He swerved to miss a pothole and then continued. "Jared and I'll help out on the ranch this summer. Dad can use the extra hands."

"How many brothers do you have?"

"There are three of us. I'm the youngest, then there's Jared and Brandon is the oldest. He lives and works in Dallas but comes home to the ranch every chance he gets."

Three boys? Wow, what a handful. "Has your dad always ranched?"

"No. He's a practicing psychologist. Hated living in the big city—missed the wide-open spaces."

They hit a rut that jerked the vehicle sideways. Lynn released a squeal of alarm as Brian turned his attention to controlling the suburban. "Sorry about that." He shrugged and shot her a grin. "Anyhow, in the summer, he runs a camp for kids. In the fall and winter he ranches."

Lynn's eyes narrowed in confusion. Did he say kids? "I thought this was a dude ranch."

Before he could answer, Sam started yipping and whining causing Lynn to jump as his front paws kneaded the seat in agitation. "He's spotted something outside," Brian explained with a chuckle.

Lynn glanced to the wide-open spaces. Seeing nothing, she looked back to Brian as he spoke. "It's hard for him to stay still when he spots a jackrabbit. He's used to hanging his head out the window and barking—scares them to death. Of course, if he caught one, he'd probably just play with it."

At Sam's bark, she looked, catching sight of his target.

What on earth? "That rabbit's got the longest ears and legs I've ever seen."

"That's a black tail jack rabbit. Its ears keep it cool in the desert heat." He dipped his head and blushed. "They're called jackrabbits because their ears resemble those of a jackass."

Lynn smiled and swallowed the urge to laugh at his

embarrassment.

They traveled in silence. Brian concentrated on driving as Lynn tried to keep from hitting her head on the roof of the SUV.

They'd been climbing for a couple of miles and now began a slow descent.

"We're almost there. We'll reach the ranch at sun set."

Around a bend in the road, Brian stopped and pointed to the left. "See there? You can see the ranch in the distance. Isn't it beautiful?"

Ocotillo Ranch sat in a basin. The setting sun glinted off roofs of clay tile and brushed the white adobe in a blush of color. In the fading light, it was impossible to distinguish where the landscape ended and the buildings began. Ocotillo plants could be seen for miles. They were ugly during the winter, but in the spring tiny green leaves appeared at each thorn to camouflage its threat and protect the glorious red-gold bloom that topped each stalk from predators.

In the distance, a strip of turquoise sky dropped behind the mountains as darkness lowered from above. She absorbed the breathtaking view. It was the most beautiful sight she'd ever seen. The warmth of the color below radiated up, wrapping her in its warmth.

"Yes, it is," she exclaimed with awe. "I can see how the ranch got its name."

"You know about the ocotillo?"

She sighed and nodded. "I've read about them but have never seen them in their native environment. What a shame they aren't in bloom today." She would have loved to see the basin washed with color from their flowers, a "sea of red."

As they drew closer to the ranch, she had a better view of the main house. U-shaped, a verandah ran along three outer stucco walls. Spanish arches outlined windows, and French doors stood sentry on each side of the massive carved double front door. The house, surrounded by native plants, gave the impression it had sprung up among them.

Brian pulled the Suburban to a stop in front of a long, narrow building about a hundred yards from the main house. The building appeared well tended and made of freshly whitewashed adobe with a clay tile roof.

The minute the Suburban door opened, Sam leaped across her lap and shot out of the vehicle like a bullet.

Pressed against the seat back, Lynn was grateful he bypassed her lap. "Bye, Sam," she yelled. He ran in a short circle, woofed, and loped toward home.

Brain laughed. "He saw Dad sitting on the veranda. As much as he likes to go with the rest of us, it's Dad he wants to be with."

Lynn watched the dog disappear into the night. She could see lights on in the house they'd passed so could just make out Sam's destination. Darn, wish she'd gotten a look at Mr. Williams. Oh well, she would soon enough.

Grabbing her cosmetic bag and a suitcase, she walked to the steps and waited. Brian followed with the rest of her luggage and led the way into the dark room. The door wasn't locked. He flipped a light switch located just inside.

"Granddad built these back in the forties, and Dad redid them about five years ago. I think you'll be comfortable."

Her eyes scanned the room. The floors were warm Saltillo tile, the furniture rustic but comfortable looking. In the tiny kitchen area sat a 1950's turquoise Formica dinette with matching chairs. Turquoise canisters were lined up on the counter. She peeked into the bathroom. *Oh, my, gosh.* It had an old claw foot tub, just like the one her granny used to have.

A spicy aroma filled the room reminding her she hadn't eaten in a while. Brian turned on the kitchen light and peeked in the oven of the apartment size stove on the far wall.

"Maria, our housekeeper, left you some supper. She'll have a plate in the oven for me at home," he added with a grin.

"Thanks, Brian. I know you must be starving. I can manage on my own from here on."

"Are you sure, ma'am?"

Giving his shoulder a pat, she said. "I'll be fine. You go on and have your dinner." She walked him to the door.

He turned back. "Dad wants you to have time to get settled tomorrow, but would like for you to meet him at the ranch house at noon for lunch. Maria will fix something special for you."

"Oh, I don't want her to go to any trouble on my account."

With a grin, he adjusted his hat. "No trouble. She enjoys doing for everyone. Spoils us something awful, or so Dad says."

He waved and with the agility of youth, bounded off the porch. In two long strides, he was in the Suburban, then roaring down the dirt road.

Before unpacking, she took her dinner from the

oven. It was a spicy soup made with beef, hominy, tomatoes, and some type of noodle. It burned her mouth but the plate of sliced fruit she found in the refrigerator soothed it. The combination was delicious.

A short time later, curled up in bed with relaxing music, a large cup of coffee, and a romantic suspense novel, she sighed with contentment and settled in to enjoy the book.

Just as she got to a good part in her book, she remembered the papers she needed to read. Darn. Guilt tugged at her conscience. She should've looked at them last night, but she'd forgotten. Something about those papers bothered her.

She glanced at her carry-on bag sitting on one of the kitchen chairs. They'd just have to wait. She'd read them first thing in the morning while drinking her coffee. What could one more day hurt?

An hour later, having read the same paragraph three times, she dog-eared the page in her book and set it aside and turned off the CD player. The room dark, she snuggled down in the bed. She let her eyes adjust to the room and could see strips of light through the curtains from the low beam pole light outside. It was just enough light to get to the bathroom. But for the low hum of the window unit air conditioner, it was quiet, something totally foreign to a city girl. She'd just dropped off when a scream split the air. Her eyes flew open and she froze, listening, waiting. When she didn't hear activity from the adjoining cabins, she thought she'd imagined it. Then she heard it again, farther away this time. It sounded like a woman's scream, but she knew it wasn't—it was the cry of a panther, bobcat, or whatever they called the animal in this part of the country. Goose bumps popped out on her arms and she shivered. Dang, she hadn't considered the possibility of wild animals.

Chapter Three

The sound of young male laughter lifted Lynn out of a light sleep. She burrowed into the pillow and tried to ignore it. As the boy's words intruded, she found herself, one eye open and one ear cocked, listening.

"Hey, Julie, when're you gonna let me feel those cute little tits of yours?" asked an unidentified male.

Lynn's heart skidded to a halt at the insulting remark.

"I wouldn't mind grabbing a handful of your tight little ass either," he continued with a snicker. Male laughter and jibes followed the crude remarks.

"Tim, you're disgusting," cried an indignant young girl, presumably Julie. "I wouldn't let you near my horse, you creep, much less me."

Girls shrieked in outrage and flung insults while the boys encouraged Tim to continue.

Fully awake now, Lynn's protective instincts surfaced. If she didn't know better, she'd think she was back in Fort Worth watching the kids in the schoolyard after lunch. But she wasn't, she was on a ranch in West Texas. Tossing back the covers, she stood up, muttering, "Well, I never." She stomped across the floor and flung open the door. Looking through the screen, she stood hands on her hips, ready for battle.

At first she could only stare in open-mouthed shock. Kids were everywhere. Not the baby goat kind, but the kind with flippant mouths and attitudes, the kind that tried her patience for nine months out of every year.

She stared at the cluster of young teens causing the commotion outside her door. The group of about twenty hadn't noticed her and continued to hurl insults.

Hell. She surveyed the crowd again. That's the only place she could be. *I've been thrust into Hell.*

Slumping against the doorframe she mouthed. *Forgive me, Lord, for I must've sinned big time. My mouth has gotten out of hand lately, but to toss me in with these hormone driven adolescents is a bit harsh, don't You think?* "I promise to do better," she pleaded. *Remember, Lord? This is my summer break from school.*

Maybe this was a dream, a nightmare. Her students were always popping up in the scary ones. Like the time her classes had gotten so big she'd had to teach in the auditorium. If she pulled her hair and it didn't hurt, she was dreaming, if it did... Chuckling, she reached up, grabbed a handful of hair, and yanked.

"Ouch!" She rubbed her scalp. This was no dream. The teenagers were real, as was the argument.

Pushing away from the doorjamb, she watched in a state of disbelief as Tim made an obscene gesture to Julie. Julie, a petite blond with long hair pulled back into a ponytail, shrieked in outrage. From personal experience, Lynn knew not to interfere unless absolutely necessary. Kids needed to solve their own problems when possible. But this was sexual harassment and not to be ignored or tolerated. Of course with gang activity becoming so prominent, there was a fine line drawn and trying to intervene before either party crossed the line was vitally important.

Tim was a well-built nice-looking kid with auburn hair pulled back and tied at his neck. His face, dominated by a large nose, was sprinkled with acne but well scrubbed. At the moment, it happened to be red from Julie's insults and rising anger. Too much testosterone, caused by adolescence, was playing havoc on Tim's emotions and personality. He was building up for another ugly remark.

Lynn stepped out onto the porch allowing the screen door to slam with a loud, whack.

"That's enough, Tim. I suggest you shut your mouth before you land yourself in deep trouble."

Twenty heads swiveled in her direction.

Forty eyes gaped at her in surprise, as she stood barefoot in baggy seersucker pajamas. She could just imagine what her hair looked like. It always stood up at odd angles around her head in the mornings.

Laughter erupted, some unrestrained while others politely tried to hide their grins and amusement. It didn't faze her. She'd been made fun of by kids for years, and those that tried to manipulate her by poking fun had learned it didn't work.

She waited. Tim's snickering stopped when he realized it had no effect on her. He puffed out his chest. "Who are you to tell me what to do?" He stood stiffly, hands fisted at his side waiting to see if he won this round.

Ignoring the disrespect and his question, she gave him her stern schoolteacher "I mean business" glare and continued. "I'm just an employee here, a new one at that. But I can guarantee that if you don't do what I asked, I'll find a way to make you wish you had." Her eyes never left his face. "You apologize to the young lady, and then get about your business."

Her gaze swept the entire group. She made flapping motions with her free hand—the other remained fisted on her hip. "All of you. Move it. Now!"

The majority of the group disbursed. A few stragglers hung back and moved with Tim. "Not you, Tim. We're waiting. You have something to say to Julie."

Tim grudgingly mumbled an apology to Julie and shot Lynn a dirty look as he turned and stalked off, his body stiff as a board.

Julie waved and said, "Thanks," then ran to catch up with her friends.

Lynn went back inside, shut the door, and looked at the clock. It was only seven forty-five. What had she gotten herself into?

* * *

The roadway outside Lynn's cabin was as busy as Interstate 35 in downtown Fort Worth during rush hour. Kids talked, laughed and shouted, horses trotted by, plus she heard the occasional roar of a vehicle. She expected to hear a police siren or the blare of a fire truck at any minute.

At nine o'clock, grumbling in irritation, she threw back the covers and sat up on the side of the bed. With both hands, she scratched her head then finger combed her upended hair back into a modicum of order. She sighed in defeat. After she'd put a stop to the disturbance out front, she'd tried to go back to sleep but did nothing but stare at the ceiling.

She stood and stretched, then made her way into the bathroom. She wanted to find out what was going on outside. Why all the kids? Brian mentioned a camp for kids but surely they didn't house them close to the adults. Brian must have taken her to the wrong cabin.

The smell of bacon and other breakfast foods hung in the air, tickling her nostrils. Her stomach grumbled in appreciation. She pulled the curtain back and peeked through the blinds over the front window. The dining hall was across the road, but she didn't want to get out just yet. She put on a pot of coffee, showered, and ate a couple slices of toast, mentally thanking whoever had stocked her refrigerator and cabinets.

Lynn took her cup of java outside and sat in the rocker at the end of the porch. Filtered morning sunlight warmed her skin. The slatted overhang, made of dead ocotillo stalks, kept the direct sun at bay. She sipped the dark brew and looked beyond the ranch buildings at the rugged landscape that had been carved out by glaciers millions of years ago.

What had settlers thought about this parched land when they'd first glimpsed it? Lynn could see herself two hundred years ago riding on the hard wood seat of a covered wagon, poke bonnet shielding her skin from the sun as her children squabbled in the back. She could hear herself saying to her husband, "You spent our entire life savings on this...this dry worthless pile of rocks?" Setting up house out here would be hard grueling work. Certainly not a job for the faint at heart.

A loud cheer rose from the group at the pool drawing her eyes back to the road. Her gaze dropped from the Mesa to top the valley floor where the pool overflowed with kids of various ages having swimming lessons. At the shallow end, they congregated in groups in waist high water repeating the motions of their teacher. At the high board, on the far end where the water was deepest, a group stood in line waiting their turn to dive.

A young girl, as if carved in stone in the forward dive position, balanced on the edge of the board. A young man below the board talked to her giving her instructions and encouragement. It was too far away to hear what he was saying, but as his lips moved, he used his arms for emphasis. The girl looked down at him and shook her head. Gesturing with his hands, he clapped and said something else.

Her friends egged her on by chanting, "Go Jen, go Jen, go Jen." Jen stood rigid, then repositioned herself and dove. As she broke the water, her legs fell back over her head. Lynn smiled. Jen surfaced, a huge grin splitting her face. The onlookers cheered and whistled. Lynn whooped and danced a victory jig. Coffee sloshed over the side of her mug, and she skipped back a step or two to keep it from getting on her clothes. She looked around in embarrassment. Thank goodness she wasn't observed.

She plopped back down in the rocking chair and breathed in the fresh, pure air. Pure that is, except for the occasional whiff of manure and the pungent aroma of some type of plant. A gust of wind lifted dirt into the breeze, twirled it, and then scattered it about again. Though warmer, the air felt cooler on her skin than the sticky humidity of the Metroplex—that metropolitan sprawl made up of Fort Worth, Dallas, and a large number of smaller cities.

The nicker of horses drew her gaze toward the barns and corrals. She sat her coffee cup by the chair, stepped off the porch, and set off down the road. Halfway there she realized she'd made a mistake in her choice of footwear. With every step, her sandals filled with sand, and she had to stop to shake dirt from her shoes. Squish, shake, squish, shake. Oh boy, she must look ridiculous.

* * *

"Seth, you got yourself a tender foot for sure this time." Ben, one of his young cowhands, laughed as he nodded his head in the direction of the woman headed toward the stable.

Seth stopped brushing down his favorite horse, Chester, and watched the woman approach. He had to admit she did look out of place.

"She's wearing a shirt with fringe and silver conchos all over it. And, look at those sandals." Ben's eyes never left the woman. His grin threatened to crack his face.

Seth shook his head. Ben didn't know when to keep his mouth shut. He had to agree, her outfit looked ridiculous. From his trips to Fort Worth and Dallas, he knew women dressed like that because it was the style. But who in their right mind would wear sandals in all this dirt? Had she never been to the country before?

Around him, the other men were making similar remarks and laughing at the woman's expense.

"That's enough," Seth ordered. "You know how I feel about that kind of talk. How can we teach these kids to be tolerant of the differences in others if we don't provide a good example?"

He glanced around the barn to make sure those within earshot understood. It took a great deal of effort on his part to keep the rumble of laughter that bubbled in his chest from erupting.

"The lady is our new bread cook. If one of you runs her off, you'll be on Cookie's hit list. If you're smart, you'll make her welcome."

They nodded and turned back to their work, everyone except Ben, the youngest male in the group.

He continued to stare, his face a mask of tomfoolery.

Sally, one of the few women hands on the ranch, glanced from Ben to Seth and, with a smile, winked. Seth grinned in response and nodded. He left Chester's side, walked over to Ben, and clapped him on the shoulder.

"Ben, I want you to show Mrs. Devry around the ranch before lunch."

He had to bite his lip to keep a straight face at Ben's expression of horror. All humor vanished, and his face paled for a fraction of a minute and then reddened.

"Uh, uh…Boss, I sure would like to do that for you but I've got a pile of chores to do this morning."

Ben fumbled with the hat he'd yanked off and worked it around in his hands. Seth knew he was trying to think of a way out of this predicament.

"I'm sure you do, but tell Sally what's so urgent, and she can assign it to some of the older boys."

Seth smiled at the young brunette who worked at spreading ointment on the forelock of a quarter horse called Buttermilk.

"But, Seth, I…," pleaded Ben.

"No buts. Take my jeep and have her at the ranch house by noon."

He tossed Ben the keys and walked into the shadows of the barn. Chester nickered at his approach. "Chester, you think that boy will ever learn?" The big horse tossed his head as if to say no and snorted. Seth laughed. "Me neither."

Two years ago Seth had asked Ben to show Clara, the dessert cook, around the ranch. The older woman had latched on to the boy and mothered him to death every opportunity she got. Ben pretended he didn't like her fussing, but he soaked the love up like a sponge. His mother left him when he was a baby, and his father spent more time drunk than he did at being a father. Ben was a fierce protector where Clara was concerned.

By the time he arrived at Seth's camp, Ben had been through the legal system and was in danger of being lost to society. It had been a tough summer, and for a time Seth didn't know if he'd be able to salvage the boy or not. When Ben finally realized Seth didn't intend to give up on him, he started conforming. Seth would never forget the look on Ben's face when he told him he had a place here on the ranch if he wanted it when he graduated from high school. Now he was one of his best hands and good with the kids. Helping these kids meant the world to him.

From the shadows of the barn, Seth watched Ben; hat in hand, amble up to the woman that looked so out of place standing in the dirt yard. He couldn't hear their words, but as Ben greeted her, Mrs. Devry's face broke into a wide smile. As Ben explained his instructions, she tilted her face up, listened intently, and then nodded in agreement. Shoving his hat back on his head, Ben led the way over to the jeep, opened the door, and helped her in.

Before he could start the motor, Sam bolted into view and jumped into the back seat. Mrs. Devry turned around to greet the dog, giving him a good scratching behind his ears. Sam, tongue lolling from his mouth, basked in her ministrations.

Seth tilted his hat forward and scratched the back of his neck. She was hard to figure. From her radiant smile, you'd never know she suffered from anything. No, that wasn't fair. Many people experiencing depression hid their feelings.

With a chuckle, he shook his head at the memory of her outfit, especially the sandals. The term "city slicker" fit her to a T.

He wondered how much information Art had given her. How would she react when she learned the truth? She would be furious—dude ranch indeed.

* * *

Promptly at noon, Ben pulled the jeep to a stop in front of the ranch house. Sam jumped out and trotted to the shade of the verandah.

"Here we are, Mrs. Devry. Let me know if I can do anything for you while you're here." He walked around to help her out. She took his offered hand and patted him on the arm.

"Thanks, Ben. I appreciate that, and thanks for the tour."

With a shy smile, he tipped his hat. "My pleasure, ma'am."

As if on cue, one of the double entranceway doors opened and an attractive Mexican woman in her late fifties stepped out onto the veranda.

"Hello, Mrs. Devry. Welcome to Ocotillo Ranch." She took Lynn's arm and drew her inside where cool air washed over her.

"I'm Maria, Seth's housekeeper and nanny to those three boys of his." She grinned and shook her head at the snorts and sounds of outrage from the males in the other room.

Maria's dark eyes flashed with interest as she talked. Her beautiful skin, smooth and olive in color, framed graying dark hair pulled back, braided, and twisted into a roll at the base of her head. A touch of red lipstick, the only make-up she wore, enhanced her lovely features. Lynn liked this warm woman and immediately felt at ease.

"Here's the bathroom, Mrs. Devry. You take your time freshening up. Seth will meet you in the hall when you're finished." Cheeks dimpling, she winked, "I better get back and make sure those heathen boys haven't gotten into the food."

"Thank you, Maria," she said, chuckling at the teasing remarks of the housekeeper. "I feel like I've got an acre of dirt caked on my face. And please, call me Lynn."

Maria smiled and nodded.

When Lynn exited the bathroom, a tall man approached and extended his hand.

"Welcome to Ocotillo Ranch, Mrs. Devry. I'm Seth Williams." Gray eyes trimmed by thick black lashes twinkled as he smiled in greeting.

Confused, Lynn stared at him with a dropped jaw. He didn't quite fit the mental picture she'd formed in her mind—he was too good looking.

With a mental shake, she snapped her mouth shut and extended her hand. "Hello, Mr. Williams. I'm pleased to meet you." Smile shaky, she lifted her chin and studied him as he scrutinized her.

Approaching fifty, Seth Williams was tall, dark, and finely honed. He wore denim jeans and a chambray shirt that emphasized his body, muscular and fit from work and exercise. Just under six feet, he stood and carried himself with an air of confidence and command.

This man expected respect and most likely got it. His dark hair, with its salt and pepper effect, added to his good looks. A native Texan, his deep voice dripped with the typical drawl—as smooth as warm molasses. Steel gray eyes missed nothing as he assessed her.

Still in possession of her hand, Seth studied her features. She was attractive when she smiled. Her hazel eyes crackled with intelligence and curiosity as she inspected him. Her skin was pretty but with some fresh air and exercise, it would glow like peaches and cream. Auburn hair, cut just below her ears framed her face and bounced as she moved.

Releasing her hand, he took her elbow and escorted her to the table. Flustered for some reason, she ducked her head as she slid into the chair he held for her. He couldn't help but notice the redness of her neck. Had he done something to embarrass her? He didn't think so. She's probably just shy.

Brian sat at the table next to his older brother, Jared. "You know my son, Brian."

Brian grinned in welcome, which she returned before looking toward the other young man.

"This is my middle son, Jared. He's home from college for the summer."

"Nice to meet you, Mrs. Devry."

She nodded. "You too, Jared."

He sat at the head of the table and Maria started serving the food. "Their older brother, Brandon, works and lives in the Dallas area."

Seth sometimes forgot that he was a fortunate man. Brandon had graduated from college with honors, held a good job, and seemed happy with the life he'd mapped out for himself. It looked like Jared and Brian would follow in his footsteps. Whatever they chose to do in life, he wanted them to enjoy it, to be happy.

He placed his napkin in his lap and cleared his

throat. "Just in case I forget to tell you guys on occasion, I'm proud of you."

Both boys looked at each other in astonishment. Jared elbowed Brian.

"Did I hear Dad just give us a compliment?"

"Yep, I believe you did, big brother." Each sported a grin as wide as their plates.

He stifled a chuckle. "Don't let it go to your heads. I didn't say you were perfect."

The room buzzed with lively conversation as the boys traded quips with each other and Maria. Lynn seemed to enjoy their exchanges as her eyes lit with pleasure, and she laughed when they teased each other. They were lucky to have Maria. All three boys adored her, and she loved them in return. She'd worked for his folks before he took over the ranch. Not wanting to start over with another household, she'd stayed on. She was like family.

When she finished serving, Maria took her place beside Lynn.

"Jared, return thanks for us."

"Yes, sir."

As they ate, Lynn studied the two boys. With his thin, lanky frame, Brian stood taller than Jared whose body was stocky and compact. She wondered if Brandon was another carbon copy of his father. And where was Mrs. Williams?

The meal consisted of a delicious taco salad with guacamole, and side dishes of tortillas, rice, beans, and fruit. The guacamole was luscious, creamy and without the onions and tomatoes often found in the dish at the Tex-Mex restaurants she frequented.

The men were generous in their praise of the food.

"Yes, Maria. It was delicious. Best guacamole I've ever eaten."

Maria beamed and promised to give her the recipe.

Jared leaned back in his chair and rubbed his full belly. "How about we do this again next Sunday, Dad?"

"How about we don't?" He turned to Lynn. "We take all our meals in the dining hall."

Maria patted her arm. "We wanted you to feel welcome, Lynn."

Flustered, she said, "Oh, you shouldn't have gone to all this trouble for me."

"It was no trouble." She nodded at the boys. "These two need to practice their table manners on occasion anyway. This was a good excuse."

Seth shoved his chair back from the dinner table. "Mrs. Devry, if you'll come to my office, we'll discuss your schedule."

He held her chair as she rose from the dinner table.

Following him from the room, Lynn struggled to keep her eyes off her new boss—off his well-built butt in particular. His well-worn jeans encased his muscular backside and legs like smooth fitting gloves.

Horrified at the direction of her thoughts, the red from her burning ears moved forward to her cheeks. *What is the matter with me?* She hadn't been so drawn to a male part of the anatomy since junior high. Well, he was a good looking man and darn sexy. His love for kids, his own included, made him even more so to her.

To hide her blush, she sat in the chair across from Mr. William's desk and pretended to adjust her sandals.

He settled into the chair behind his desk and removed papers from a legal size folder. Behind him, bookshelves held pictures of his three sons. Several photos included a glamorous dark haired woman. The boy's mother, she presumed. One shot included the entire family. Mrs. Williams was a stunning woman— Mr. Williams, arm around her waist, hugged her to his side. The boys grouped around them in a variety of poses. None of the pictures were of her alone or with just Seth. That was odd since the woman was so photogenic. And she was everything Lynn wasn't, sophisticated, elegant, and beautiful.

The room was all male. Big comfortable pieces of furniture dominated. A colorful rug accented the desk area with its two chairs in front. Western prints depicting harsh land and hardworking cowboys hung on the walls, and a potted plant sat in the corner by the French door. If there was a Mrs. Williams, she didn't interfere in this room.

Not that she cared. She didn't need a man, and he wouldn't be interested in her. Men were nothing but problems. She'd learned that lesson the hard way from the jerks she'd dated in Fort Worth. Conceited, insensitive clods were interested in one thing and it wasn't her cooking.

"Are you feeling all right?"

She nodded, hoping her face wasn't still red. "I'm fine." Thank goodness her hair covered her ears because they were hot and probably blinking. She was cursed with ears that indicated her degree of embarrassment or anger. When she wore her hair shorter, her students used them as a yardstick to determine when they'd pushed her patience too far.

"You look flushed." Shaking his head, he added, "Probably got too much sun riding around today without a hat." He rose, walked to the corner of the room, and returned with two packages, one a hatbox. He sat them in the chair beside her. "These arrived for you."

"Thank you. I ordered jeans, boots, and a hat before leaving Fort Worth, and had them sent directly here."

He nodded. "Good. It's important to wear a hat at all times around here. The sun can make you sick before you know what hit you."

Lynn nodded. She knew the dangers of heat exhaustion and heat stroke. Anyone who went out in this heat without a hat and long sleeves was a fool. She didn't consider herself one. The fact that she had earlier today didn't count. She didn't know she'd be riding around the countryside in a jeep.

Seth studied her as she inspected the return address on the boxes. Pride evident in the way she held her body, but her rigid posture conveyed tension and restrained control. It probably helped her maintain discipline in her classroom. In his office, it made her seem uppity.

A bit overweight, a nice looking woman, she'd be attractive if she lost thirty pounds. Ah, hell. She was attractive now, just not his type. She had too many problems. And he wasn't in the market for a woman.

He glanced at the picture on his desk of Barbara and the boys. A knot formed in his belly. He drew his gaze from the picture back to Mrs. Devry. Odds-on she'd never fit in on the ranch and be a burr under his saddle all summer.

From Jake, his foreman, he'd learned she knew how to control teenagers. She'd stepped in and put a stop to the near fight between Tim and Julie that morning. Jake had chortled at the telling. Evidentially the ruckus woke her because she stood on the porch of her cabin in pajamas, hair standing on end. Arms folded across her breasts, her stance dared them to talk back. She had backbone and spunk—two commodities needed around here.

Another plus for Mrs. Devry was his dog Sam's response to her. Animals, like small children, had good instincts about people. And Sam, without a doubt, liked Mrs. Devry. It was going to be interesting to see how she managed a horse. Amused at the thought, he ducked his head to hide his grin, and then turned his attention to the matter at hand.

He cleared his throat. "How's your cabin? Do you have everything you need?"

"The cabin is lovely. It's very comfortable. Uh, I do have a request, however." She looked down, as if unsure.

He looked up in surprise. It was their nicest cabin.

"I think I was put in the wrong cabin by mistake. There were so many kids traipsing back and forth this morning. They were so loud I was unable to sleep." Pausing to inhale, she relaxed. "Anyway, I thought this was a dude ranch for adults."

Oh, boy. *She's not going to like what I'm about to tell her.* He paused to collect his thoughts. "Lynn." His forced smile felt like a grimace. "May I call you Lynn?" She nodded assent. "Mrs. Devry is so formal and please, call me Seth. Everyone does, even the kids."

He leaned back and folded his arms across his chest. "You need to understand something. This is a working ranch, as well as a camp, dude ranch, whatever you want to call it. But, it's for kids, troubled kids. Work here begins early in the morning."

Reaching for her folder, he glanced at it and nodded. "As a matter of fact, you'll report to work at five a.m. so the hands can start coming in for breakfast at six."

Leaning forward, his eyes locked with hers. "We believe that to rise early, work hard, play hard, eat properly and turn in early are basic life skills training for these kids. Most of these kids don't have decent role models at home. I expect you to be a good example."

That said, he leaned back in his chair and relaxed.

Lynn felt her jaw drop. She grinned and shook her head. "Five o'clock in the morning?" Her laugh set her hair in motion. "You're kidding me, right? I never get up that early, not even during the school year, and especially not in the summer."

She waited for him to comment. He didn't. Her grin wilted. "Can't you find a job for me that starts later in the day? I'm not much good in the mornings."

"Sorry, that's not an option. As our baker, we need you for breakfast, and the other shifts are full."

"But this is my vacation," she groaned. "Three months out of the year I get to sleep late in the mornings, relax, and take a nap if I want to." His face was void of all sympathy. He didn't have a clue what she was feeling. "Look, I love my job as a teacher, but it takes a lot out of me each year, and I need time to re-energize." His expression didn't change. *He isn't interested in what I need or want. After all, I'm just the hired help.*

Leaning farther back, he propped his booted feet, crossed at the ankles, on an open drawer of the desk and steepled his hands on his chest. "Look, I'm sorry this isn't what you expected, but we're running a business here. You've signed a contract for a job as bread cook for the breakfast shift. That means you work six days a week from five a.m. until ten a.m. Longer if you can't get the work done in that amount of time. The rest of the day is yours as long as you fulfill your planned activity time with the kids. And your scheduled exercise."

Planned activities and scheduled exercises? In your dreams, cowboy. She wanted to laugh but felt she better reserve judgment until after his explanation. "What do you mean by scheduled exercise and group activities?"

His boots hit the floor. Turning two sheets of paper around, he positioned them side-by-side so she could read them.

"You'll start with water aerobics and work up to swimming ten laps of the pool every day. Our swim instructor, nicknamed Duck by the kids," he never understood how they'd come up with that name, "Will monitor your time and let me know if you are not fulfilling your contract."

Some employees balked at the required exercise plan, and he'd fired several because they refused to cooperate. It was tyrannical on his part, but necessary. Ranch life was hard, and weakness caused accidents. Not that accidents didn't happen on occasion, but he wanted his crew to be physically prepared to handle it. All of his employees were trained in CPR and several were trained EMT's, plus they had a RN on staff.

He tapped the other paper. "And this is your schedule for working with the kids. You need to get in six hours a week."

Stacking the papers and stapling them together, he handed them to her. When she didn't take them, he laid them on the desk within her reach.

"Of course, you're welcome to spend as much time as you want interacting with the kids. Lord knows they need as much attention as they can get."

Lynn sat, stiff as a statue, and didn't move an inch. "I'm afraid there's been a terrible mistake." This was the craziest thing she'd ever heard of. Nowhere on the face of this earth had she heard of a job requiring its employees to participate in an exercise program. Her chin was trembling, and she saw the uncomfortable, panicked look that flashed in Seth's eyes.

Her voice shook as she spoke. She began slowly, choosing each word with care. "I was told you owned a dude ranch, an adult dude ranch. And yes, I knew I'd be working, but this is not what I had in mind. I came here to get away from dealing with kids every day. I love them, but I need some time away from them to relax and rest—prepare myself for the coming school year." As she finished, her voice reached a crescendo. "And if you think I can swim ten laps of that pool, you're crazy."

She stood, prepared to leave. "I think I better head on back home. You can find someone else for this job. I can do without the torture."

He stood, strode around the desk, and faced her. "I'm afraid that's not an option. I'm sorry you were led to believe this was a dude ranch for adults, but I can assure you it wasn't by me. Furthermore, I'm running a business here, and you signed a contract and can't break it for six weeks."

"This was Art's doing, wasn't it?" Her breath

hitched. "And my daughter's?"

Seth nodded. "I don't know about your daughter's involvement, but Art knows the situation here."

She seemed at a loss for words for just a second. Tears glittered in her eyes. "You can't keep me here," she said, voice cracking. She chewed her lips to stop their quaking.

He rubbed the back of his neck to ease some of the tightness in the tendons. Man, he hated this. He would wring Art's neck the next time he saw him. He leaned against the desk, arms folded across his chest. "No, I can't. However, I would expect that someone with your job history would have a strong work ethic and be honorable about the commitments you make. Is that what you teach those students of yours? Make a promise and then break it?"

How dare he insinuate she had a low work ethic? She wanted to yell at him and list her credentials, but that would serve no purpose so she kept her mouth shut. His gray eyes locked with her hazel ones. He shook his head, mouth tense. "Look, I'm sorry if you were misled by Art and your daughter." He threw his hands up. "But I had nothing to do with it. I didn't know you'd been misled until yesterday."

So Art had duped him, too. Lynn almost felt sorry for him.

"Lord, what a mess." He raked his hands through his hair. "I have to have a bread cook, so I'd appreciate it if you'd stay. You'll be happier if you accept and make the best of this situation until I can find a replacement. Then you can leave with a clean conscience."

Hands fisted on her hips, she drew herself up to her

full five feet, four-inch height. "Is that so? Just six weeks. You act like that is no time at all. Well, I've got news for you. It's forever to me. Oh, I'll fulfill my contract, but I can guarantee you're going to regret it."

"Look, I'll advertise for a replacement right away. When I find one, you can leave."

She said nothing, just glared at him, as she tried to keep from crying.

His shoulders sagged. "You're all I've got, Lynn. Consider my position here." Lynn tried but could only see how tied down she'd be for the next few weeks. "I know you're upset. Give yourself a couple of days. You may find you like it here." To break the tension, he added, "Dinner is from five to six at the cook house. It's a fun time around here. All the hands will make you feel welcome, especially Cookie."

She grabbed the two schedules off his desk, wadded them into a ball, and threw them, hitting him square in the chest.

"That's what I think about this job and your schedules."

He caught the wad before it hit the floor. His jaw tightened. She took a step back. Snatching her packages off the chair, she turned and headed for the door.

"You start work at five sharp in the morning. Don't be late. I'll drag you out of bed if I have to."

Back rigid, she strode out the open French door. She heard him release a string of curses at her exit. Refusing to look back, she marched down the road to her cabin.

Seth watched her go. Dammit. The woman was going to be trouble.

Chapter Four

Lynn peered at her swollen face in the mirror, the lids so puffy the irises almost hidden. *You look like you've been on an all-night drunk.* And she felt like it too. *That's what you get for crying half the night.*

Her head throbbed. With a groan, she found the Tylenol in the medicine cabinet and took two. She looked at the pills in her hand and added two more and washed them down with a glass of water.

When she'd reached her cabin yesterday after lunch, she'd read the contract. There, in bold print, was the agreement Seth had reinforced verbally. The job was for the entire summer, but her signature proved she'd agreed to stay at least six weeks, or until a replacement could be found.

Those two snakes, Abby and Art, knew what was in that contract. It's a good thing they were miles away right now. If she got her hands around their necks she'd squeeze until their forked tongues fell out. That's why they didn't give her time to read it before she left. Now that she thought about it, she hadn't imagined the look of remorse she'd seen on Art's face.

Moisture sprang to her eyes. With an angry swipe of her hand, she muttered, "All right, Lynn, we had this discussion last night. Buck up, get over it, and move on—no more of this weepy business." Crying wasn't the answer. Getting even was.

Her stomach growled, but the thought of eating made her queasy. She stepped out onto the porch. Still dark, the cool air was fresh and filled with the soft scent of animals and desert foliage. It wasn't an unpleasant smell, just different from city smells. She gazed up at the black cloudless sky, amazed at the number of stars. They looked almost touchable.

It was time. Taking a deep breath, she stepped off the porch. She might not want to be here, but her work ethic was strong. Seth had read her correctly in that department. Abby and Art didn't know her as well as they thought. And before the summer was over, she'd prove it. If they thought she'd stick around here and dance to their tune, they had another thought coming.

Her watch read four fifty-five a.m., still the middle of the night for people with good sense.

Inside the cookhouse two men joked with each other as they worked. They both stopped when she entered. The large, balding man with a salt and pepper beard rushed over. Dressed in white from head to toe, he wore an apron wrapped around his abundant waist and tied in front. "Mrs. Devry, we're plum tickled to have you join our crew."

Before she knew what was happening, he grasped her hand and led her behind the serving counter. With a swift, deft motion, chattering all the while, he wrapped her in an apron similar to his own. He beamed at her. "Everybody calls me Cookie and this fella is Pete. He's our meat cook." The tall, skinny man waved to her.

"He usually doesn't work mornings, but wanted to be here to meet you. So he's cooking the bacon while I catch up on some other chores. Anyways, it'll give me more time to show you the ropes."

Pete poured her a cup of coffee and handed it to her with a shy smile. She accepted the hot brew with gratitude.

Cookie asked. "You sleep all right, Mrs. Devry? That cabin's a beauty, ain't it? The nicest one on the ranch."

Pete added, "Ain't this the most awesome country you've ever seen?"

The two men chattered away, filling in the awkward spaces, not expecting a response and not waiting for one. Could they tell by looking at her face them she was about to crumble?

Their kindness made her throat constrict. Surely Seth wouldn't have told them about her reluctance to stay and why? She'd die of embarrassment if he had. Slowly she shook off her worry. Their talk eased her discomfort and before she knew it, she was laughing.

Cookie showed her the bakery station and gave her a recipe for biscuits. It made eight dozen. "You let me know when you're ready to use the big mixer."

Within thirty minutes both she and her workstation were a mess. Flour covered the counter and parts of the floor making it slippery. But, she was ready to use the mixer.

Clucking like a hen, Cookie bustled towards her broom in hand. He swept the flour up into a small pile. "Can't have messy floors in here, Lynn. They cause accidents."

She nodded. It was because of this darn headache. "I'll be more careful." Accidents in the kitchen were nothing to scoff about. She felt the same way about her kitchen at home.

Cookie showed her how to operate the industrial size mixer.

Adding the liquid, she started the mixer on low as he watched.

"Looks like you've got it. Don't over mix. The dough hooks will finalize the mixing as they knead the dough. As soon as the dough is smooth, stop the mixer."

She nodded. "I can do this. It's similar to my mixer at home only bigger."

"Just remember, this machine is powerful and can be dangerous. Be careful and call if you need me."

With a smile and pat on her back, he was gone.

After kneading, she turned the dough out onto the floured wooden counter and broke it into sections to roll out.

Cookie appeared at her side. "Here, let me show you a quick way to cut these." Instead of using a biscuit cutter, he took a sharp knife and cut the dough into squares.

"See, it's fast and there's no waste. Now, just three more batches and you'll be ready to start the yeast rolls."

"You've got to be kidding," Lynn sputtered, wiping her flour-covered hands on her apron. "That's enough biscuits to feed an army."

A lock of hair fell from under the bandana she'd tied around her head to keep hair away from her face. It kept flopping and tickling. With the back of her hand, she pushed at it, but it wouldn't stay put. She caught herself blowing air upward in an attempt to keep it out of her way.

"Yep. That's pretty much what we're feeding here. The hands require plenty of hardy grub and the kids eat their fair share."

Cookie laughed at the expression of shock on her face. "Don't worry. You won't have to fix quite as many yeast rolls."

At six fifteen, she slid the first five pans out of the

oven. Cookie started the waiting wranglers through the breakfast line. Though fifteen minutes late, no one complained.

At the appearance of Seth's commanding appearance in the food line, Lynn bristled. She waited for him to comment on their lateness, but he didn't. He pinched a bite off the top of a flaky biscuit and popped it into his mouth. As he chewed, a grin as big as Texas spread across his face. "Excellent biscuits, ma'am. I see Art didn't lie about your baking skills."

Lynn snorted and turned her back on him. Arrogant man. She'd like to make a few special biscuits just for him. Wonder what he'd prefer, arsenic or hemlock? When she looked again he was gone.

Hustling back and forth from counter to oven, she finished the additional batches and waited for the last pans to come out of the oven. Satisfied, she looked around the workstation at the mess she'd made.

"I better get this mess cleaned up before I start the yeast rolls," she muttered. But Cookie took her arm, led her from behind the serving counter that separated the kitchen from the dining hall, to a table and insisted she eat some breakfast.

"Okay, I'll eat, but no eggs please. I don't think I can face one this morning." The clatter of trays and cookware was replaced by the rowdy hum of children's voices. Evidently Evidentially Seth believed meal times were for socializing as conversations and laughter flew around the room. Her eyes sought their fearless leader. He sat amid a group of teenage boys, laughing at the antics of one. Her respect for him grew a notch. She admired a man who enjoyed the company of kids.

Seth watched his new bread cook. Her face was

flushed from the heat of the ovens and the hard work of rolling out biscuits. If she were tired now, she'd be dead when she finished kneading bread dough.

He leaned back in his chair, folded his arms across his chest, and looked around the room. It was going to be a good day. The wranglers were well fed and happy. Lynn's face lit with pleasure at their compliments. And she deserved every one. Her biscuits were some of the best he'd eaten. He considered going back for two more, but didn't want to experience another glare like the one she'd shot him as he went through the line. Probably because of the big grin he'd had on his face. Flour was smeared on her cheek, and a glob of dough clung to a strand of her bangs that had escaped the bandana she wore to hold her hair back. Damned if she didn't look cute.

Lynn finished her breakfast. When she glanced up to see him watching her she stiffened. Ignoring him, she stood and walked back into the kitchen.

By the time Lynn had three quantity size batches of yeast rolls shaped and ready to rise again, she thought her arms would fall off. A sharp pain traveled up her back and shoulders, and throbbed at the base of her skull. The heat inside had risen. She felt like a well-done pop over as sweat trickled between her breasts. She probably looked like one too the way she filled out the white apron.

She was rolling her shoulders to ease the pain when a spry, older woman waltzed into the kitchen. The chatty atmosphere turned downright raucous. She caught Lynn up in a tight hug.

"Hi, hon. You're just what this ranch needed. Another woman to help keep these old men in line."

Snorts and expressions of disgust echoed around the cooking appliances.

She released Lynn and looked her over. "In case you haven't figured it out yet, I'm Clara, the dessert cook."

Lynn clasped her hand, grateful for another woman's company. "Hi, Clara. I'm Lynn. It's good to see another woman's face."

Clara nodded. "You met Maria, yet?"

"Yes, at the main house yesterday."

Her head bobbed. "Good, good. Several afternoons a week, we meet for iced tea and cookies. First chance we get, we'll come by your cabin and chat."

Before Lynn could respond, Clara bustled away.

In her sixties, Clara was a wiz in the kitchen. In no time at all, she had piecrust rolled out ready to top peach cobblers.

At eleven thirty, Lynn's station was spotless and she could leave. As she hung her cleaning rags over the sink to dry, she heard the rustle of paper and turned toward the sound. Cookie gave the top of the brown paper bag a final fold and thrust it into her hands.

"First day, and all, I figure you're too beat to wait around for lunch."

Lynn smiled at the thoughtful gesture and turned away, certain she would never open the bag. Food wasn't a priority right now—a bath and her bed were. She hadn't taken two steps when she heard him whisper.

"Good job today, Lynn." He wrapped a long arm around her shoulders and gave her a gentle squeeze.

She felt a surge of warmth at his sweet gesture.

Before she reached the door, Clara called out.

"I'll be by this afternoon to pick you up for water aerobics, Lynn. The girls are all anxious to meet you."

Yeah, and she just bet Seth was anxious to see if she followed his dictates. She was going to nickname the man Hitler.

The minute she entered the cabin, she started stripping, leaving a trail of clothes across the floor. In the bathroom, she turned on the water to the tub and walked back to the living area to adjust the small window air conditioner. Back in the bathroom, she caught her reflection in the mirror and laughed; surprised she had the energy to do so. Her face was smudged with flour and a glob of dough in her bangs drooped from under her bandana. She glanced down at the pile of clothes on the floor. The apron she'd worn had saved her jeans and shirt from the flour, but they were so sweaty they couldn't be worn again.

She sank into the water, releasing a long groan of pleasure. Easing lower into the tub, she wet her hair and then shampooed and rinsed the goo out. Too tired to soak, she washed quickly, dried off, put on her cotton robe and fell into the unmade bed. Within minutes she was fast asleep.

* * *

The cool tile of the bathroom floor soothed Lynn's hot skin. A moan of misery escaped her lips as she fought the nausea that moved over her in waves. With each pulsing throb, her head expanded as if it rose up off the tile before settling again. Somehow, she'd made it to the bathroom, but had lacked the strength to remain on her knees and wait for the inevitable heaving to begin again.

From her position below the toilet bowl, eyes

scrunched against the light that felt like a knife piercing her brain, she measured the distance to the tub and the washcloth hanging on its side. Its dampness would feel so good on her face. Her stomach lurched at the thought of trying to reach the tub, which increased the tempo of the pounding in her head.

She wanted that wet cloth. She needed that wet cloth.

Forcing her body into action, she rolled to her left side, threw out her right arm, grabbed the washcloth and rolled onto her back, all in one motion while throwing the cloth over her face. She lay still, willing her body to stop shaking and the nausea to recede.

There was a pounding on her front door and someone called her name. Tears stung her eyes.

"Go away. I'm sick." Her voice barely rose above a whisper. *Oh, God, my head.*

At the sound of her voice, a dog started barking. It was Sam. With his keen senses, he knew that something was wrong.

"Please, go away," she pleaded. Then it grew quiet. The next thing she heard was the crack of splitting wood.

* * *

Seth's mood was murderous as he stomped across the road to the guest cabins with Clara, twisting her hands, following in his wake.

"I know she's in there, Seth, but something's wrong. I just know it. And Sam knows it too. Look at him."

Agitated, Sam paced back and forth, whining, in front of Lynn's door. He started barking when he saw Seth.

Swearing he was going to wring the woman's neck if she'd caused all this commotion over nothing, Seth bounded up the steps to Lynn's door.

A terrifying thought seized him. Surely Art would've told him if she was suicidal. Gasping for air, he slowed his breathing to calm himself. Of course he would. Art wouldn't keep something like that from him. He pounded on the door hoping maybe she just hadn't heard Clara, but he didn't get a response.

Since he didn't have a key with him, he backed up and kicked open the door, cursing under his breath as the wood-facing split.

Making a mental note to keep a running tab for Mrs. Devry, he grabbed Sam's collar and ordered, "Stay."

Inside the darkened room the air conditioner hummed. He looked around. The bed was unmade and rumpled and clothes littered the Saltillo tile. A paper sack sat on the kitchen table. Lynn was nowhere in sight.

A groan came from the bathroom. A chill raced up his spine. He approached the partially open door and tapped lightly. "Lynn, you all right in there?"

"Please, I'm sick. Go away."

Pushing the door open wider, he peered inside. The sight that greeted him stopped him cold. Lynn lay on the floor with a wet washcloth covering her face. The robe she wore gaped, exposing the creamy fullness of one breast. Her skin was beautiful.

Seth felt a stab of desire and swore under his breath. *Get a grip, man, the woman is sick for God's sake.* Bending, he adjusted the robe.

"What's wrong, Lynn? Did you fall?"

"Migraine."

At her word, Clara, who'd been peering over his shoulder, pushed him aside and bent over Lynn. "Oh, you poor thing. You just hang on. We're going to make you comfortable. Seth, let's get her in the bed."

Clara, crooning words of comfort, helped Seth get Lynn into bed. Clara opened a dresser drawer and pulled out a white cotton gown trimmed with pink ribbons. Working together, they slipped it over her head then managed to remove the robe from under the frilly nightdress. Lynn tried to help as Clara worked her arms into the sleeves while he held her steady. Lynn was like a rag doll in his arms. Her face was pale and her riotous auburn hair swirled around her head emphasizing the lavender shadows beneath her eyes. Feeling strangely vulnerable at the woman's suffering, Seth eased her back against the pillows and settled the sheet around her.

He reached out and let his hand brush her cheek in a comforting caress. "Try to relax. I'll check on your medicine."

Her response was a whisper. "Thank you." She grabbed at his arm. "Medicine in bathroom. Took both at noon."

Seth patted her hand. "Okay."

Clara moved about the room picking up clothes and putting them in the hamper.

Sam hadn't stirred from where he'd been ordered to sit outside, but howled in distress because he couldn't come in.

"Lord, Sam, you're giving me a headache." To shut him up, Seth brought him in to the rug beside the bed. "Sit. Stay." Sam sat with his neck stretched as far as it would reach trying to nuzzle Lynn.

Clara patted his head in sympathy as she laid cool rags over Lynn's face and neck. "She's going to be okay, Sam. Don't you worry."

She smoothed the covers over Lynn, and brushed the hair back from her forehead. "You just try to relax, honey. We're going to get you some relief."

Worry tore at Seth as he watched from the foot of the bed.

Cookie had pulled him aside at lunch. "Boss, I think you ought to know, Lynn's face was all puffed up this morning, like she'd been crying."

The stress from her long drive, finding out she'd been duped by her loved ones, and then the crying had probably been too much for her body to handle. He knew a large number of people suffered from migraines, but this was the first he'd witnessed. Hopefully it would be the last.

Lynn's fists were locked on each side of her head gripping handfuls of hair. Moaning, she pulled. What the hell was she trying to do, pull it out by the roots?

He'd never seen anyone suffer like that, and watching her agony made him damned uncomfortable. There must be something they could do for her pain.

Taking his cell phone into the bathroom, he closed the door and put in a call to Art in Fort Worth. He'd just about given up on getting an answer when Art picked up.

Seth rubbed the back of his neck. Worry was giving him a headache. "Art, thank God. Man, am I glad I caught you."

"Seth? Is that you, Seth?"

"Hell yes, it's me, Art." He heaved a sigh, sat

down on the toilet lid, and dropped his head into his hand.

"What's wrong? Has something happened to Lynn? She's only been there two days!"

"Hold on, Art. She's not hurt, but she's suffering from a migraine. It looks like she might have thrown up earlier as she was on the bathroom floor below the toilet bowl when we found her."

He hadn't known what to think when he saw her laying there. And here he'd thought she might be putting on an act just to get back at him.

"What can we do to give her some relief? She took both medicines at noon."

"She can have both again now and repeat in four to six hours," said Art. "She hasn't had a migraine in a long time. I wonder what brought this one on."

"Dammit, Art, what do you think? She was angry and hurt when she learned this wasn't a dude ranch for adults and that you and Abby hadn't revealed the true nature of this job. As a matter-of-fact, I'm rather pissed about the matter myself, but I'll take that up with you later."

Seth heard Art's groan through the phone.

"What's she doing with all this medicine if she hasn't had a migraine in a long time?"

"If you'd ever had one you wouldn't have to ask. Actually, it's a safety net."

Made sense to Seth. If he'd ever suffered like the woman in the next room, he'd never go anywhere unprepared.

"We totally screwed up, didn't we, Seth? She's never going to forgive us for this."

"Yeah, afraid you did."

"I guess she's determined to come home then."

"Yep, she wouldn't be here now if it wasn't for the contract you had her sign unread. Fortunately for me, she'll stay until I can get a replacement." Seth cleared his throat. "I'm hoping she'll decide to stay all summer."

"Really? Think there's a chance?"

"Probably not," said Seth. "She did a fine job today and is well liked by the others. Let's not give up yet." He hadn't given up on anyone easily before and he wasn't going to start now.

"Yeah, well, she's a fine cook. You know I wouldn't have encouraged you to hire her if she wasn't."

"Well, thank goodness for that, old friend."

"I'm really going to owe you after this, aren't I?"

"You can count on it."

"Loretta and I are leaving on our trip tomorrow. My associate will know how to reach me."

"Will do. Have a good time. Lynn will be fine."

He wished he felt as sure of that as he sounded, but hated to worry Art further. Seth needed his head examined. Why on earth had he let himself get mired in this plot?

Switching off the cell phone, he slid it back into the pouch he wore on his belt. In the medicine cabinet, he located the bottle labeled Midrin and shook out two of the maroon looking capsules, and then added one tiny orange pill from the bottle labeled Phenergan. Art's instructions echoed what was written on the label. He filled the glass in the toothbrush holder with water and carried it and the pills to Lynn's bedside.

Sam had worked his way from the floor to the bed.

He started to order him down, but noticed Lynn wasn't shaking as much. She had turned her face into his coat and her hands gripped handfuls of his hair. His coat was so short it looked more like handfuls of his hide. Sam lay still but raised his head and wagged his tail when Seth walked up.

"Guess she's not hurting you, pal."

He sat the glass on the nightstand. "Lynn, you want to sit up and take these pills? Art said it was safe to have two more now and another two in four hours."

He perched on the side of the bed and lifted her back off the pillows. Trembling, she leaned into him. His hand instinctively clasped her shoulder pulling her a little closer. She put the pills into her mouth. Seth handed her the glass of water, she took a drink and swallowed with care, then waited a minute. It must have settled in her stomach all right because she took another drink and handed him the glass. He eased her back down

With a weak, "Thank you," she closed her eyes and reached out to Sam.

"Lynn, I sent Clara to go change clothes and eat supper. She'll be back in a minute and sit with you a while, until you feel better. When she leaves, Sam will stay here with the door cracked, so he can squeeze through. If you need me, just tell him, 'Go get Seth,' and he'll understand."

"Be fine by self." She loosened one hand from Sam's coat, patted him, and then grasped his hide again. "Got Sam." Sam's tail thumped the bed.

Seth grinned, marveling at how Sam responded to her. Yep, his dog liked this woman. Even tanked up and half drunk on those pills, she was as cute as could be.

Hell, maybe when she got over this feeling sorry for herself bullshit, she'd be all right.

Could he blame her for being upset? Hell no, he wouldn't take being lied to, even by one of his best friends. He'd make damn sure the conspirators didn't make the same mistake twice. Seth moved across the room, and sat on the sofa waiting for Clara.

He better get someone to replace Lynn in the morning. Dang, the men would be disappointed, including him. Cookie had nothing but praise for Lynn's first day on the job.

"You should've seen the pleasure on the men's faces when they bit into her biscuits." He'd chortled and clasped his hands over his abundant belly. "She might get a proposal of marriage before the week is over."

Seth laughed at the idea. Who would it be? If it weren't for Maria his money would be on Jake.

Chapter Five

She lay still, waiting for the pounding to begin. It didn't. *Thank you, God!* Thin slivers of light stabbed through slits in the curtains. They widened as they penetrated the room, softening the darkness. Someone had left the front porch light on. Looking down, she could make out Sam on the rug by her bed. With care, she tilted her head to see the alarm clock. It read 4:05 a.m.

Sensing she was awake, Sam padded over and put his paws on the bed. She closed her eyes pretending sleep. He stuck his nose in her chest. Chuckling, she patted him on the head.

"Didn't fool you, did I, buddy? Don't know what I'd have done without you last night."

Or Seth and Clara. She flashed a glance toward the sofa. Clara was gone. Good. I hope she didn't stay too late. Dammit! It was embarrassing for them to think of her as sickly. She blushed at the thought of Seth seeing her in her nightgown. She looked down at the full cotton garment. Oh, well, it's not like it was sheer or sexy. No need to dwell on it.

She hugged Sam and then scratched his ears and neck as she looked into his chocolate eyes.

"I bet you're thirsty, boy. I sure am."

He twitched and hopped back to sit on his haunches. A low "ruff" rumbled from his throat.

"Okay, I'm coming."

To test her condition, she gingerly sat up on the side of the bed. When her head didn't hurt, she turned on the light. Her stomach felt all right, as a matter of fact she was hungry. She stood and waited a moment before leaving the bedside.

In the kitchen, she turned on the overhead light, located a bowl and filled it with water for Sam and a glass for herself. Sam lapped his up while she drank hers down.

"You ready to go home, fella? I bet you're hungry."

He trotted over to the door. Or what remained of the door. Lynn looked at it in stunned silence. It was completely separated, the doorframe still intact on the hinge side. What on earth had happened? She vaguely remembered hearing a crash when Seth and Clara entered yesterday afternoon. He'd had to kick the door in. She giggled as she imagined Seth's irritation at having to force his way inside. It was his just reward for holding her to the contract.

"See ya later, Sam." She tried to move the door that sat partially over the opening. Before she could, Sam squeezed through and bounded down the road in the early morning darkness.

She made tea and toasted two slices of bread. Though hungry, she'd go easy on the food for a few hours.

Searching through the closet, she came out with her favorite tee shirt. Pink with the logo *World's Greatest Teacher* printed across the front in bright purple, it was a surprise gift from her students on her last birthday. Grinning at the memory, she headed out the door.

When she entered the dining hall, Cookie and the others stopped working and stared. Cookie, acted surprised and not pleased as he bustled toward her.

Brow wrinkled, he emphasized each word with the large tongs in his hand. "Seth said you wouldn't be in this morning, Lynn. You go right back to your cabin and rest."

She grabbed an apron and tied it around her waist. "I'm fine, Cookie, really. Actually I feel good. You know it's weird, but when my head hurts as bad as it did yesterday, once the headache's gone I usually feel great. Strange, huh?" And it was the truth. She never ceased to be amazed at the extreme difference.

He stood with his hands on his abundant waist.

"Well, if you're sure. But, if you start hurting again let me know."

"I will." She made on X on her chest, then reached up and patted him on the cheek. "I promise."

She poured a cup of coffee, took a deep whiff of the rich brew, and sighed.

When the last batch of biscuits was in the oven, Lynn fixed a plate of one biscuit with butter and jelly and two slices of bacon. No need to push her luck. She could always eat more later.

She sat down across the table from Ben. With him was a rough looking older man in his late fifties.

Ben looked up, a shy smile on his freshly shaved face.

"Mrs. Devry, this is Jake, Seth's assistant and ranch foreman. If you ever need something and can't find Seth, Jake's the man to see."

"Hello, Jake. I'll remember that."

Jake's gaze didn't leave her face as he assessed her. She must have measured up as he nodded and extended his hand.

It was big, warm, and covered with calluses as it engulfed hers in a firm handshake. "Good to meet you Mrs. Devry. How are you feeling today?"

"I feel much better and please call me Lynn. You too, Ben."

Lynn studied them surreptitiously as they ate and talked about the kids and ranch business between bites. She didn't think Ben was quite twenty as his face still held some baby fat. It didn't have the honed look of manhood. The sun had added blond streaks to his brown hair, complementing his sky blue eyes.

Her gaze turned to Jake. From Ben's demeanor, the "Yes, Sirs" and "No, Sirs," he obviously admired and respected him. Jake wasn't a handsome man. His face appeared somewhat flattened, like it had been smashed. But he was attractive in his own way. It could be the way he held his stocky body or his air of self-confidence. His hair was gray and short like a marine drill sergeant's. It wasn't hard to imagine him snapping to attention and barking orders. His eyes were a contradiction though, brown and as soft as a puppy's.

Jake looked around the room then turned to her. "You did a fine job of handling Tim the other day."

"How did you know about that? Did Julie come talk to you?" She was surprised Julie would tell anyone.

"No, Julie wouldn't tattle, but I heard their exchange."

"Oh, I'd meant to let Seth know about the situation as I'm sure he would want to talk to the boy. I guess I forgot."

"It's understandable, you've had a lot on your mind since you arrived. I let Seth know and he had a long talk with Tim later that morning."

Lynn nodded. "Good." Consequences were most effective when delivered as soon as possible. Of course there had been occasions in her teaching career when she'd postponed the inevitable just to heighten the suspense. Kids didn't like that worry time and it was often more effective than other discipline tools.

She took several sips of her coffee then sat her cup down.

"Well, he obviously wants Julie's attention but doesn't know how to get it in an appropriate way. Can't help but feel sorry for him. He doesn't have a clue why she's repulsed by his behavior."

He rubbed his chin, and his eyes twinkled with humor.

"I sure hope he figures it out soon. He's shoveled more horse manure than any two kids put together." With a wry twist of his mouth, he added. "I'm tired of having to supervise the smelly work."

"Why is Tim here on the ranch? I realize this isn't your ordinary camp, but what kind of problems do these kids have?"

"What I've told you is not confidential, just general run of the mill discipline problems. But the reasons behind their behaviors are private and only Seth can discuss those with you."

"Oh, I can respect that."

Jake stood and stacked her tray with his.

Lynn smiled. "Thanks."

"You're welcome."

They walked toward the kitchen area where the dirty trays were deposited. "By the way, Seth wants you to come to his office after dinner tonight. Said he'd pick you up in the jeep at seven p.m."

Lynn stood and stared at his retreating back. Seth's office tonight? Dang, she didn't know how she should feel about that. Maybe he wanted to show her a running total of her bill for damages. No, he probably wanted to explain the rules concerning the kids.

"Come on, Sonny, you can work faster than that." Pete was emptying paper from the trays into a trashcan before letting the conveyer belt take them inside to the dishwasher. "Look at Sue. She's getting twice as many done as you."

He patted the young girl on the shoulder. "Way to go, sugar. You keep working like this and Seth may give you a raise."

The little redhead grinned with delight and when Pete turned his back she stuck her tongue out at Sonny.

He mouthed, "Brat," but Lynn noticed he picked up speed in emptying the trays.

Several other kids were carrying small buckets of soapy water and wiping down the tables. When the kids had kitchen duty, they cleaned countertops and washed pots and pans. The older ones were allowed to use the commercial dishwasher, but it was the only piece of equipment they could operate. They were on a three-week rotation. Cookie and Pete supervised their work.

Most of the kids were in their teens, though a few looked about eight years old. An older teen or adult watched the young ones at all times.

As she shaped yeast rolls, she watched the younger children. A little guy, sitting slumped in his chair, looked ready to cry. The other kids teased and shoved him around. One kid in particular took food off his tray, and hit him when their counselor wasn't looking.

She'd just about had enough when a young woman grabbed the bully by the back of his shirt collar and moved him down by her. Guess the counselor saw more than Lynn realized. She sighed with relief.

By shift's end, she had rolls shaped and set to rise and her work area was clean. Hallelujah! She could call it a day.

* * *

"I really don't think this is fair or necessary. What does it have to do with my job?" She knew, Seth had explained that day in his office. His rationale made sense but that didn't mean she had to like it or accept it joyfully.

It wasn't that Lynn didn't like to swim. She did, but resented being ordered to do something.

Clara ignored her mutterings. "Maria will be at the pool today, as will some of the wrangler's wives. Most of them work on the ranch too."

Lynn ignored her. Shoulders slumped, head down, she dragged her feet along the packed earth path to the pool. *Good grief! I probably look like one of my pouting students.* At the thought, she picked her feet up. How many times had she told her students, "Pick up your feet?" She often thought they did it just to get a rise out of her.

Clara presented a colorful picture in her bright floral swimsuit. For an older woman, somewhere in her late sixties, she appeared to be in good shape. Thin and wiry, she was flat chested and almost butt-less.

If her figure lacked curves, her personality lacked for nothing. Happy and talkative, she studied Lynn with her brow wrinkled. "Are you sure you're up to this, Lynn?"

"Yeah, I'm fine."

Though tempted, she resisted the urge to lie and say she felt sick just to get out of swimming. She couldn't bring herself to do it.

"If you're fine, lift your head up and quit pouting."

Startled, Lynn glanced up to catch the older woman's lips twitching.

"You'd think you were going to the executioner's block instead of for a swim."

Surely she didn't look that bad. She snorted. *Oh, hell, Lynn, just get to that pool and get it over with.*

By the time they reached the pool, Lynn was drenched in sweat. It was a good thing she'd slapped on a heavy coat of sunscreen. If the thermometer outside her door hadn't read one hundred two degrees, she'd swear it was one hundred ten. That's what it felt like on her black swim suited butt. Since it protruded, the sun had direct access.

Clara's loud yell startled her. "Hey, Duck, this is your new student, Lynn Devry."

He waved from the small office building and Lynn grudgingly waved back.

Clara explained. "Lynn, you can swim any time you want to, except during lessons, but the kids will be here. The men come for an hour right after us." Then she turned her attention to Duck, the swim instructor.

Glancing down at her white, slightly hail damaged legs, Lynn decided once a day would be fine with her. She knew how she looked in a swimsuit, and she didn't need any critical remarks from smart mouthed teenagers to remind her.

And she definitely wouldn't be here when the men were in the pool. That's all she needed was for Seth to see her in a bathing suit. At the thought, she peeked around to make sure they weren't being observed. Boy, she'd love to catch a glimpse of Seth in his swim trunks. Wonder what kind he wore? Surely not one of those Speedo things. Nah, he probably wore one that fit like boxers. She bet he looked sexy as hell. He would be tanned with a sprinkling of hair trailing from his chest down to his... *Stop that, Lynn. You are not interested in that man, or any man for that matter.*

Lynn dropped her towel and kicked off her flip-flops. She went to the shallow end and walked down the steps until the water reached her knees. Shivering, she inched her way deeper. It was freezing! How could it be this cold when the air was so hot?

About midway down the pool, Clara and the others dove in or jumped in feet first. Shaking off and slicking back hair, they urged her to take the plunge.

When she was waist deep, she looked over to see Duck standing by the side of the pool watching her slow descent. Duck was a bronzed hunk of a young man. Near six feet, he was slim with dark hair cut close to his head. His eyes were as blue as the water, and crinkled when he smiled as he was doing right now. Wow, he's gorgeous and has a healthy set of teeth. Why couldn't he be sullen and rude? Then it would be easy to dislike him. After all, he'd be following Seth's orders and spying on her.

Suddenly he yelled, "Cannon ball," and jumped into the pool with his body drawn up into a ball. Before she could react, she was drenched.

Sputtering, Lynn sank.

"Just hold your breath and jump in next time," he said matter-of-factly. "It's much easier that way.

Clara and the other women chatted away. Duck joined them in what appeared to be a daily ritual of sharing witticisms. He kept up a steady flow of teasing as the ladies bobbed up and down in the water trying to warm up.

Duck turned to Lynn and flashed her a grin.

She snorted. *Don't even think about it. I'm not that easy to win over.* She did allow her lips to turn up a tad at the corners, but that didn't mean she was going to like him. Okay, she'd be civil, but she was here under duress and he knew it, so she'd not play nice-nice to make his job easier.

The class started with arm stretches and leg lifts to warm up their muscles. They progressed to exercises for the arms—arm circles, windmills, and front and backward handclaps.

After a variety of weird named exercises, more like contortions, Side Scissors, Bicycles, Donkeys, and Up and Down the Wall, she wanted to voice her opinion of water aerobics. It was a joke. They were so easy they couldn't be doing much good.

Finished, they were given time to work with weights made of Styrofoam. When Duck brought them out, she giggled and resisted the urge to ask, "Think those are heavy enough for you?"

Later, she was grateful she'd kept her mouth shut. She could feel the pull on her arm muscles caused by forcing them through the water. It felt good but if not careful, she'd be mighty sore the next day.

Clara and the others tossed their weights onto the pool deck and started their laps. Lynn continued to work with the weights. When the other ladies finished and exited the pool, she climbed the steps with them. She'd stepped into her shorts when Duck poked his head out of the pool office and yelled.

"Mrs. Devry, I'm sure you don't want to forget your laps."

"Oh shit" she muttered under her breath. He must have eyes in the back of his head or could see through wood. She raised her voice to be heard. "Two laps today. Is that right Duck?"

"No, I believe it is ten laps." He leaned out the window of the small building where swim toys were kept. "However, we'll start you with four, and you can rest between if necessary. I'll help you keep count."

"You're too sweet," she muttered sarcastically.

Twenty minutes later, legs aching and shaky, she hauled her tired, limp body out of the pool. She couldn't swim one full lap without having to stop and rest. She slid her feet into her flip-flops and started home with her towel wrapped around her, clothes in hand. Getting dressed required too much energy.

Duck walked out to meet her as she passed the hut. "You did well today, Lynn. It'll get easier. In no time at all you'll be swimming those ten laps with no problem."

Not stopping, she waved bye and stifling a groan, muttered, "Yeah, yeah," and continued to drag her feet along the path to her cabin. Her knees shook so she feared they'd crumble under her weight.

She'd gain strength over time. What irked her was not being given a choice. That burned her butt.

She was just about to cross the road to her cabin when movement to her left caused her to look that way. Seth stood, bent at the waist with his forearms propped on the porch rail of the dining hall watching her. Was he checking to make sure she went through with the exercise? *Well, of course, Lynn.* He wouldn't be standing in this heat for nothing. She wouldn't be surprised if he'd brought out a lawn chair so he'd be more comfortable. The arrogant man. He waved, a big smile on his face.

Furious, she turned her head and with her nose in the air, marched toward her cabin. The sound of his chuckle rumbled her way. The infuriating man had the gall to smile at her after checking up on her. He didn't even have the decency to be sly about it.

She'd just opened her newly repaired door when he yelled, "Pick you up at seven."

* * *

Lynn was waiting on the porch when Seth drove up. He reached across the seat and shoved the door open for her. *Guess we can assume this isn't a date.* She jumped in and had no sooner settled her butt in the seat than he took off. Dirt flew up around them. It didn't take them two minutes to reach his house.

When he pulled to a stop in the circular drive, she said. "I could've walked this short distance."

He grinned. "Yeah, but it may be dark on the trip back you'd have to be careful where you stepped."

"Oh, horse manure and stuff?"

"No, snakes."

"Oooh, I appreciate the ride."

Opening her door, he stepped aside to let her out. "Figured you would." He took her elbow and walked her to the veranda.

"Better say hello to Sam so he'll let us work."

They entered his office through the French doors off the portico. She sat down in a chair facing his desk and scratched Sam's ears. Seth kept walking. "I'm getting coffee. You want some?"

"Sure. One sweetener."

After having his ears scratched, Sam was content to

lie down at her feet and doze. Her eyes lit on one of Seth's pictures, the one where their young sons surrounded him and the lovely Barbara. Picking it up, she studied it closely noting how much Brandon, the oldest, favored his mother. She'd just put it back when he returned and sat a mug for her on the corner of the desk. Its surface was covered with folders and for the first time Lynn noticed the large locked file cabinets.

While she was looking at them, Seth was studying her. She flushed under his gaze. "You appear tired. I'm sorry to drag you out like this, but didn't feel you were up to this conversation Sunday afternoon."

"How do you know I am now?"

He chuckled. "Good question." He watched her over the rim of his mug. "Instinct, I guess. Let me say first, I admire the way you handled Tim and Julie Sunday morning. Jakes says you're great with kids, and I trust his judgment."

She nodded.

"And, I respect an employee who comes back from feeling like you did Monday and puts in a full day's work without complaining."

"I—"

He held up his hand. "And lastly, you make damn good bread."

She was curious. "And which of those characteristics would you say is most important?"

His stormy gray eyes didn't blink. "In the order I listed them. I realize you don't plan to stay and wish you'd reconsider, but..."

He waved away her attempt to answer. "While you're here, you need to understand that you do not talk about any student's personal history with anyone but me, alone or in group meetings. All information is confidential and kept that way. Staff members do not at any time discuss a child's case among themselves. Doing so is cause for dismissal. Many of the college students working as counselors are working on board certification in psychology. An incidence of failing to provide confidentiality could ruin their career."

"But I'm not a counselor, I'm not likely to know anything." This was a little more responsibility than she wanted.

"Yes and no. Ideally you were hired as a bread cook but you will also spend time with the kids. You need to be prepared to handle any situation that arises."

He picked up a folder. "Take Tim for example. You already know something about him by observing him interact with Julie. It probably wouldn't surprise you to know that he comes from a male domineering and abusive home."

Lynn dropped her head. "No, I can see how that could be."

"I'll be talking with Tim several times this week and hopefully we'll come up with a plan to change his attitude."

Lynn sipped her coffee and thought for a minute. "At one point that morning I was afraid Tim might hit Julie." She met his eyes.

"You're right to be afraid and be prepared. But Tim has never exhibited violence toward any of the girls though Lord knows he and some of the boys have tussled a time or two.

"We're not designed to handle kids with mental disorders, just kids with behavioral problems we think can be changed with our methods. These kids have been in counseling for a year before they come here. They're hand selected for what this camp has to offer."

She was relieved. It lessened the level of responsibility a fraction.

"Also, I'm a psychologist, not a psychiatrist, so none of these kids are on medication. The only medicines allowed at camp are acetaminophen, allergy medications, and such as that, and they're under lock and key with our staff nurse."

He tossed a thick bound pamphlet across the desk. "This tells you what all we can offer the kids here. When we get time, I'll take you on tour of our facilities. You may even want to take part in some of the activities yourself."

Chapter Six

"Lynn, when are you gonna quit giving Duck so much misery? It's not fair. He's just doing his job." Maria sat on the sofa in Lynn's cabin, Clara beside her.

"Yeah, I know. I'm just being pig-headed. It's hard to give in and admit that Seth is right about the need for exercise. And, I don't like being told I have to do something."

It was the end of her second week on the ranch. Familiar with her job now, she actually finished early and was free until water aerobics in the late afternoon. She liked the people she worked with and felt comfortable cutting up with them. And she'd made friends. Some afternoons, like today, Maria and Clara stopped by and she'd make a pitcher of iced tea.

In truth, the day after her first class, she'd been so sore her pain had been hard to hide. It hadn't been just the laps, either. The exercises and weights she'd thought were ridiculous did more than she'd imagined. But, it got easier each day. She still wasn't ready to admit that being at the ranch was good for her. That Art and Abby's reasoning for misleading her was sound.

She tested Duck at every opportunity to see if he kept up with her laps. Drat his hide. If she skipped one lap, he noticed. But, at least Duck wasn't bored. He had to stay on his toes to keep up with her efforts to cut corners.

Clara rolled her cool glass across her forehead. "You know, Lynn, only healthy folks survive out here. The exercise helps to keep us that way, otherwise the ranch wouldn't run as smoothly." She glanced around the room. "It's not like we're living without modern conveniences. We have comfortable quarters, three meals a day, and get paid. Why complain about a little exercise?"

Clara sipped her tea and looked at Lynn with one eyebrow cocked. "Get caught on the range just once with a lame horse and you'll understand why it's important to stay fit out here. If you survive, that is."

Maria's brow furrowed as she shook her head. "I don't understand what makes you dislike Seth so."

"I don't dis—"

"Don't tell me that. You pick on Duck to get back at Seth," said Maria. She lifted her chin and peered down her nose at Lynn. "Because you know you can't get away with picking on Seth."

Lynn gasped. "That's a terrible thing to say. Duck and I enjoy harassing each other." She looked from Maria to Clara.

When Clara didn't comment, Maria continued. "He's a good man, and a fine looking one too. Haven't you noticed?"

Lynn snorted. "Of course I've noticed. I'm not blind, or dead, for that matter."

Maria would just not let up. "Maybe you're attracted to him and that's why you act the way you do."

"I am not attracted to him." Not much, anyway. Lynn glared and shook her finger. "Now, don't you two try any matchmaking." She took a drink of her tea. "Anyway, he may be good looking, but he seems to have it in for me. I don't think he likes me."

"Well, I don't guess your pleasant attitude to being here would have anything to do with it," muttered Maria. "You know, it's not his fault that he can't get someone to replace you right away."

Over two pitchers of tea and a plate of cookies, they'd loosened up and shared portions of their lives. Lynn explained the circumstances of Abby and Art's deception. Both women were sympathetic, but didn't feel the outrage that she did.

Lynn muttered. "You're right, but—"

"This tea is sooo good, Lynn. It's got something different in it, but I can't figure out exactly what. Do you have a special recipe?" Clara sipped, closed her eyes and smacked her lips. "I know there's peppermint, but there's something else."

Lynn rose from the bed where she'd been sitting and walked into the kitchen. She opened a cabinet door, picked up a bottle and waved it in their direction, then winked. "I put just a tad of peppermint schnapps in it to enhance the flavor."

Both Clara and Maria sat on the sofa with their feet propped on the coffee table. As if on cue, in one motion they sat up, their feet hit the floor with a "plunk."

"What?" they chorused.

Maria covered her mouth. "Oh, my Lord. Seth doesn't allow alcohol on the ranch when the kids are here." She looked at her empty glass. "If he finds out he's liable to fire all three of us."

Clara eyed her glass, and then shook her head. "Nah. He can't afford to fire all three of us at one time. He'd just warn us and set us to mucking out stalls."

They cast sideways glances at each other. Maria started giggling. When Clara chimed in with her braying laugh, Lynn choked on a mouthful of tea sucking half of it up her nose.

When Lynn could talk again, she shrugged. "We'll

just have to make sure he doesn't find out about our little tea party. What he doesn't know won't hurt him." Trying not to laugh, she looked them in the eye. "We won't make it a habit."

All three women grinned in agreement and Lynn poured them another glass from the pitcher.

Clara stood. "I want to make a toast." They tapped glasses. "To the health benefits of peppermint!"

* * *

Lynn liked to take Sam on a walk after work each morning. They usually stopped for a while to watch the kids on their horses.

The younger kids were taught to groom their horses, to examine their tack and how to properly sit in the saddle. Eager to learn, they worked hard to please. Smiles spread across their dusty faces when one of the wranglers patted them on the back with a, "Good job, cowboy."

Chue, the corral boss, checked the kids grooming their horses. From the way the kids looked up to him, they might have thought he was God himself.

An older Mexican man, he wore a wide brimmed hat and fancy boots with the highest heels she'd ever seen. They narrowed and angled toward the sole. How he managed to keep his balance, especially the way the heels were shaped, was a mystery to her. Thin as a rail, he limped as he walked.

His disposition was notorious when it came to the horses and the tack. Both kids and wranglers alike knew to take care of both or they'd get a tongue-lashing. Though his temper was fiery, he had a tender heart.

Lynn left the corral and walked over to watch the horses in the pasture. Chue had never spoken to her personally so it came as a surprise when he walked up and joined her at the fenced area. She nodded in greeting, waiting for him to speak.

He just tipped his hat and stood, chewing on the end of a matchstick, watching the horses as though looking for one in particular. In silence, they studied the animals.

"You bout ready to pick out a mount, gal?"

"Who, me?" Glancing around, she didn't see any other "gal," and said, "No, I don't think so, but thanks anyway."

"Why not? You been here over two weeks now, nigh on three. It's time you got in the saddle." He took off the big hat and used it as a fan, then plopped it back on his head.

"I don't know how to ride. Actually I'm scared of horses, but I enjoy watching the others ride."

A horse trotted up to the fence and studied her with interest, blowing hot air out its big nostrils.

She jumped from the fence and stumbled.

Chue grabbed her elbow. "Whoa, gal, don't back off. She's just curious about ya."

He pulled a sugar cube out of his pocket and held it out to the brown spotted mare. The horse approached Chue with caution and sniffed the treat in his hand. Shaking her mane, she rolled her eyes and turned away.

Chue laughed, slapping his knee as he did so. "That crazy horse. She don't like men one bit. Ain't that a hoot? Won't even take a treat from one."

His reaction to the animal's disdain was so funny Lynn giggled.

He handed the cube to Lynn. "Here, you give it a try."

Lynn stepped back and shook her head. "I don't think so. Who's to say she'd like me any better?" She shuddered. "She might bite me."

"Naw, horses aren't meat eaters and Seth don't keep any mean horses around on account of the kids. Come on give it a try."

He placed a sugar cube in her palm. "Just hold it out and let her come take it."

The horse did seem to like her. They studied each other. She wasn't pretty—actually she was downright unattractive. It looked like someone had thrown bleach across her back, making white and gray spots across the brown. Of course, the horse might not think much of her looks either.

What did she have to lose, other than a finger or two? Chue knew all about horses and if the horse bit her, he'd save her before she lost too many fingers. She eased her hand across the fence.

"Talk to her," Chue coaxed. "Softly and in a gentle voice."

Voice cracking, Lynn crooned, "Here, girl. You want some sugar?"

The mare looked her straight in the eyes before sniffing her and the offered treat, breath teasing across her palm. Whiskers and hot air brushed her hand as the horse took the cube.

Lynn jerked back, laughing with delight. "That tickled."

The horse sniffed her shirt and butted her chest looking for more sugar. Lynn turned to ask Chue for more but he'd walked away. The western tune he whistled growing fainter by the second.

Garnering her courage, she reached up and touched

the mare's head. When the horse didn't jerk away, Lynn continued to rub. The animal's coat felt silky under her fingertips.

"You're a sweet girl and you've got excellent judgment in people. I don't blame you one bit for disliking men. They're a sorry lot. Us girls have to stick together." She continued to stroke and pat, reluctant to put a stop to this new experience.

"I think I'll call you Beauty. How do you like that name, girl?"

As though giving her approval, Beauty nickered in reply.

From inside the barn, Seth watched and smiled at the exchange between the woman and horse. Lynn's laugh had been one of joy when the mare had tickled her looking for more sugar. At her pleasure, laughter had rumbled up from his chest. He'd choked back the noise knowing she'd be angry if she thought he was spying on her. Then she'd tossed her head back. Her face kissed by the sun, was radiant and beautiful, and he'd wished desperately for the smile to be for him.

* * *

The next few days, if possible Lynn avoided Seth. Though she didn't have a clue why, it was hard for her to relax around him. She wasn't angry with him any longer. She didn't resent being on the ranch, actually she enjoyed it, her exercise regime, and working with the kids. If Art asked her though, she'd never admit it to him.

As usual, dinner on Saturday night was a gala affair. Tonight kids, staff and wranglers would dance.

Cookie came from the kitchen area, clapped his hands, and ordered. "Let's get these tables moved back."

Cowboys and kids alike rushed to do his bidding. Seth plugged in the jukebox at the far end of the room. Most of the songs were old country western favorites but a few modern tunes had been added for the kids.

The first number up was country. Kids around the room moaned in unison. Laughing, she was tapping out the rhythm of the Texas two-step when Jake appeared before her and made a courtly bow. He held out his hand. "May I have this dance, madam?"

She stood and dropped a curtsy. "Yes, you may."

A good dancer, Jake twirled her around without missing a step. She had a hard time keeping up. On the last swing, she turned and plowed into Seth's chest.

"Oops! Sorry." He grabbed her shoulders to steady her. Heat moved up her body making her cheeks burn.

With a nod to Jake, Seth took Lynn's arm and led her over to some chairs against the wall. Seth had watched Jake and Lynn dance from the sidelines. They looked good together and she had no trouble keeping up with Jake's fancy two-step. He was popular with all the ladies. It'd be a shame for Lynn to develop a crush on him and the feeling not be returned. Not that Jake would ever hurt any woman intentionally. But, he was known for playing the field. The one woman who had a chance of snagging him was Maria.

Was Lynn attracted to Jake? He shook the thought away. It was none of his business. "Would you like a glass of lemonade?"

"Sure."

Seth returned with two cups, handed Lynn hers and drank half of his in one gulp. As he watched the activity on the dance floor, Lynn's eyes roamed his profile. He had a strong chin that tilted up a little on the end, his nose was slightly crooked and he had prominent cheekbones. She wondered if he had Indian ancestry. How would he look with long hair, a strap tied around his head? Damn sexy—like one of the heroes on the cover of a romance novel, his chest bared displaying rippling muscles.

Seth chuckled at Jared's attempt to teach Julie the two-step. He turned and caught her studying him. Too late for her to turn away and act casual, their eyes locked. The silence was awkward for a minute. She was damned pretty with her face flushed, her hazel eyes sparkling. He cleared his throat thus breaking the spell.

"Lynn, I'd appreciate it if you'd ask some of the boys to dance. We're short on females and they need partners."

With a hand, she fanned her cheeks. The slight breeze felt good but didn't lower her temperature. *Oh, please, don't let my face be red.* "Sure. Be glad to."

"Great." He nodded toward a group of boys. "There are your first targets."

He stood, took her hand, and escorted her over to the young men. When they approached the three boys, talking stopped. They shuffled their feet and looked down rather than make eye contact. "Guys, have you met Lynn?"

"No, sir." He introduced them and Lynn shook each of their hands.

"Guys, you know the rules. No standing around in groups talking. Since we need more female partners, Lynn is going to help us out."

The three friends didn't appear excited about the idea, but Lynn didn't give them the chance to scatter.

She took the arm of the tallest boy. "May I have this dance, sir?" Before he could say no, Lynn had him on the floor laughing and struggling with a waltz. Seth realized the woman was a natural at putting people at ease.

Lynn danced her way through the group of boys and realized she was having a blast. It was fun to watch the kids move from one partner to another. They relaxed and had more fun with one of the staff. Dancing with their peer's added pressure they weren't sure they were ready for. And most of the cowboys were great dancers. They moved her around the room with as much enthusiasm as they exhibited when roping a calf.

As soon as the jukebox stopped, there was a race between the adults and kids to program in the next songs. Pete joined her and laughed. "Kids can't stand too much country. Have to add some of that modern, wild stuff." When a disco beat blared from the speakers, Pete threw up his hand. "Excuse me, I believe I'll sit this one out."

Laughing, Lynn glanced around the room and noticed the famous three with their heads together again. Grinning, she moved across the room and stopped in front of the tallest boy again, he backed up.

"Oh man. Do I have too?" His buddies grinned at his discomfort.

"Don't worry, guys, I'll be dancing with each of you again." Their faces sobered. "I tell you what. I'll make you a deal. If I see you dancing with one of the girls, I'll leave you alone. But, if I see you standing around…" She shrugged.

Resigned, casting glances back to see if she watched them, the boys moseyed over to where the girls sat and each asked one to dance. Lynn watched for a moment to see how they managed the steps. She'd learned the camp provided lessons on Tuesday and Thursday nights. All campers were required to attend a class at least once a week. For kids hesitant to touch each other, they did the disco number justice.

Well, that wasn't so bad. She'd actually had a good time. Pooped, and out of breath, she got a glass of lemonade and fell into a chair.

Lynn glanced up to see Seth walk toward her. He snagged a chair and turned it with the back facing her before straddling it. She shifted in her seat. Seth's expression was serious, brow wrinkled. His gray eyes looked into hers for a minute.

He leaned forward with his arms crossed on the chair back.

"I've been spending a lot of time with Tim."

Lynn nodded and waited for him to continue. She crossed her legs and tried to look relaxed. His closeness made her fidget. He was so darn male and tempting to a woman who'd been lonely for a number of years. Until the last few weeks, she'd have denied missing male companionship. Now she missed it more than she wanted to admit.

Seth didn't understand Lynn's nervousness around him. He wanted to reach out, take her hand, and sooth her like he would a skittish filly. The direction of his thoughts drew him up short. Horrified that she might have seen his appreciation in his eyes, he plowed forth with his mission.

"I'd like you to teach a class to both the boys and girls on *etiquette*. It'll give you an opportunity to enlighten the boys on what is proper and acceptable behavior around girls, and what is not. I'd like for the girls to learn how to be a lady in a variety of situations like how to accept or turn down a date and other courtesies."

"Etiquette is not exactly my *forte*."

Seth's lopsided grin produced a dimple in his right cheek. Her heart lurched. His smile was downright deadly. She resisted the urge to touch her chest in the region of the flutter. He was too attractive for his own good. It wasn't often a man had a nice looking outer package combined with a fine inner one too. The recipe was lethal, but she wasn't going to bite. He wasn't interested in her. According to Maria and Clara he was still hung up on his ex-wife. Furthermore, she'd be leaving as soon as he found a replacement.

"Not exactly a math assignment, is it?" His stormy gray eyes studied hers. "Would it be too much of a problem, putting the material together?"

"No, I can manage well enough,"

His grin transformed his face, smoothing out his honed features. Now that she thought about it, she hadn't seen him smile much since she'd been here. The responsibility of running this ranch and the camp must be a heavy load.

"Great. Let me know when you're ready and I'll put it on the calendar." He stood to leave.

He couldn't go yet. She needed more particulars.

"Wait. Do you want them in the same group or separated?"

Brow wrinkled, he thought for a moment. "I'll let you make that decision. If you need help, you only have to ask."

He'd walked a couple of feet when she called out.

"You can go ahead and schedule it for the middle of next week if you want."

Stopping, he turned back, his expression uncertain.

"You can be ready that soon?"

"Yeah, it's just another lesson plan. Something I'm used to doing on a moment's notice, all teachers learn early in their career."

* * *

The *etiquette* classes for both the boys and girls went well. Sally, the cute brunette wrangler, helped her with the boys' class. When she walked into the room, they stopped talking. In her snug fitting jeans and tee shirt, her long braid swaying to the rhythm of her hips, the guys watched her progress as she made her way to a chair. She sat down on the front row, tossed her braid over back over her shoulder and turned her attention to Lynn. As if on cue, they moved as a group, falling over each other trying to sit on the front row near her.

Undaunted by their adoration, Sally was all business. Each boy escorted her, offering her his arm, seating her at the table, and walking her to the door. They role-played how to ask a girl for a date and how to act if she turned him down. When the discussion turned to how to show a girl you liked her without being too obvious, they were all ears. Lynn watched their faces as Sally explained how "not to treat" a girl. It was as though she had flipped on a light switch for Tim and one other boy. They had no idea their methods were repulsive.

When the girls filed into the dining hall, their eyes lit on Brian, and the whispering and twittering began. Brian, embarrassed to his toes, had been recruited to escort the girls as they role-played various date scenarios. Amid giggling, hip swinging and strutting, they vied for his attention. Lynn heard the words, "he's too cute" several times.

Somehow they managed to get through the role-play activities. Quiet and attentive, they listened to polite ways to turn down a date, and firmly rebuke unwanted physical advances. Brian was a perfect gentleman, a true testament to his father's teaching and example. Lynn was amazed at the reach of the man's influence. When had she started viewing Seth as the ultimate male role model? If she and Dan had a son, what kind of man would he be? She doubted he'd he hold a candle to Seth's boys.

* * *

The following morning, Seth stopped in the food line. "Lynn, if you get a minute, I'd like to talk to you."

Her heart jumped in anticipation, but she kept her voice calm. "Sure. I'll be ready for a break as soon as these go in the oven." What was this about? Was it something to do with the *etiquette* classes? She snorted. Probably her next assignment.

She sat her breakfast tray down across from him. He glanced up and waited for her to get comfortable.

"For the next two weeks, on Tuesdays and Thursdays, I'll be taking the younger kids on nature hikes. I'd like you to go with us."

"All right. What time?"

"Meet us at the corral as soon as you can get away. I'd like to leave by ten thirty at the latest." He looked at her t-shirt and pointed with his fork. "Be sure to bring a long sleeve shirt to cover your arms. Wear your hat, tennis shoes and put on lots of sunscreen."

"Do I need to bring a water bottle?"

"No, we'll have canteens and sack lunches."

She nodded and started on her breakfast of eggs, bacon, and biscuits. As she ate, she watched Seth interact with his campers. Kids stopped by to speak to him on their way out. Even Tim, the kid who'd mucked out more stalls than any two guys put together, stopped. Seth's large hand gripped the skinny, underdeveloped one in a firm handshake and clasped Tim's arm with the other.

"Hey, Tim. I hear we may make a cowboy out of you yet."

"I'm tryin'."

"That's all we ask, is do your best." Still in possession of Tim's hand, he gave his arm a squeeze. "I'm proud of you."

The boy blushed scarlet, and with a trace of a smile, nodded. He shot Lynn a glance and left.

Her throat tightened. That young man needed love and acceptance in the worst way. Thank God he was under Seth's influence. Here he'd learn to obtain it in an appropriate way.

"By the way, I hear the classes went well yesterday."

"Yes, they did. After we got their attention, that is. The girls swooned over Brian and in the boy's class, and when Sally walked in, I thought we'd have to scrape tongues off the floor."

His laugh rumbled up from his belly through his chest, and echoed around the room. The others looked around to see what was so funny. Soon, she found herself joining in.

He patted his chest. "That's the best laugh I've had in ages." Stifling the urge to continue, he coughed and shook his head. "Our Sally is an attractive young woman, isn't she?"

"Yes, she is."

"Didn't think she'd work out at first. Thought I'd have to knock a few heads together, but it didn't take her long to set the men straight. She's a good hand and the men respect her."

Then he reached across the table, his hand covered hers and he added, "You're doing a good job, Lynn."

* * *

That evening, Lynn settled in bed and reread Abby's letters. She'd been tempted to return them unopened, but fool that she was, she couldn't resist knowing what her daughter had to say.

Expecting pleas for forgiveness, the girl acted as if she'd not done anything wrong. Didn't even have the courtesy to sound guilty. Just, "Hope you're having a good time…"

A method of retaliation brewed in her mind, but the plan wasn't firmed up yet. She had more research to do.

One of the older wranglers made jewelry out of things in nature. She'd been intrigued to see necklaces made of deer droppings. The droppings had a hole pushed through the center, were dried and painted with acrylic paint and then strung on nylon string. They didn't smell because they were coated with polyurethane, which formed a seal.

Yes, Abby's little bombshell would be first. Then it would be time to work on something for Art. He didn't even have the nerve to write.

She'd let Abby stew a few more weeks. Thinking about Abby's little surprise, she started laughing. It bubbled out until she flopped back on the bed howling and holding her stomach, tears rolling down her cheeks.

Chapter Seven

"Listen up, you guys. Check your equipment and make sure you have everything." Seth knew from past experience these younger campers would forget something if he didn't drill it into them. It wasn't such a big deal for this short trip, but he wanted to develop good work habits early so the long hikes would run smoothly. "Everyone got their hat and a long sleeved shirt?"

He glanced at his watch for the second time and looked down the road. Where was Lynn? He didn't want her to be late for this new experience. It amazed him how she'd made a place for herself on the ranch so quickly. If she didn't stay, her absence would leave an obvious gap.

Seth was grateful she hadn't said anything more to him about quitting. It was a good thing, too, because he hadn't advertised for a replacement. He wasn't proud of the unprofessional over sight, but he wanted her to stay the entire summer, for the kids as well as for herself. That was all he was willing to admit to justify his actions.

He checked his cell phone for battery charge and glanced at his watch again.

"Yoo-hoo! Hey, Seth, I'm coming."

He looked up to see her rushing down the road at a brisk walk. When she reached them, he gave her a minute to catch her breath.

Surrounded by a group of youngsters hopping up and down like jumping beans, Seth smiled a welcome over their heads. His smile was contagious and Lynn couldn't resist answering it with one in return.

"Listen up, hikers. This is Mrs. Devry. She's going to be a part of our group today. If you girls need anything, she'll be glad to help you."

Lynn waved. "Hi, guys, just call me Lynn."

They smiled and chorused, "Hi, Lynn."

Corby sidled up to her. She gave him a friendly hug. "Hi ya, Corby. You gonna carry me up the trail if I tucker out?"

Laughing at her joke, he threw his arms around her waist and squeezed. "I'm glad you're going with us."

Before she could respond, he ran to join his friends.

Lynn heard a growl and turned toward Sam. Zane, the resident bully, was making faces and snarling noises at the dog. Sam growled at the threat. Just as Zane, growling and with hands curled like talons, started toward the animal, Seth clasped his shoulder. Jerking to attention, Zane straightened his face and shoved his hands in his pockets.

He looked up at Seth, blue eyes all innocence. "I didn't do nothing to him. He growled at me."

"We'll talk about it this afternoon, Zane, before your swim, so don't leave with the others." He nodded in the direction of Ben. "Go stand with Ben. I'll join you in a minute." Zane stalked off and Seth watched the boy's retreating back until he reached Ben's side. At his approach, Ben looked up and caught Seth's signal, then he wrapped an arm around Zane's shoulder and bent down to say something to him.

Seth turned back. "Let's get this strapped on before these kids decide they have to go to the bathroom again and we're late leaving here."

He held the backpack while she slipped her arms through the straps. They stood facing, toe to toe, as he adjusted them.

Struck dumb at his closeness, she merely nodded. A whiff of aftershave reached her nostrils as she stared at his wide chest. The view elicited a variety of feelings—longing, desire, fear. The dark hair curling above the buttons of his blue chambray shirt intrigued her. If she reached up and brushed it with her fingers, what would it feel like? Would it be soft or coarse? She fisted her hand to still the urge to find out.

Her eyes flicked up to see him watching her. He held her gaze for a moment, then cleared his throat and gave the straps one last tug. "Comfortable?"

"Yes, thank you." God, she was making a fool of herself. Seth would think she was an idiot. That, or worse yet, that she had the hots for him.

He removed a canteen from a fence post of the corral and hung it around her neck and left arm. As she adjusted it, he turned back to pick up the rifle that leaned against the corral.

"What's that for? Wild animals?" The idea made her heart lurch. "I thought I heard a panther scream my first night here."

"You probably did, but there're none where we're headed. On occasion they come down around the corrals at night, but Chue always has someone on guard." Expression somber, he touched her shoulder. "Don't worry. They won't come around us. With as much noise as these kids make, you won't find an animal within a mile. I carry a .22 rifle in case we run across rattlers."

A shudder ran up her spine. "You mean rattlers, like in snakes?"

His lips twitched at her reaction. "Yes, but they

rarely cross our path. I wouldn't shoot one unless it was a threat." He studied her face. "I'm a crack shot and I'm always prepared for the worst. Got a snake bite kit in my pack."

"Oh goodie. That's reassuring. Here we are miles from civilization. If someone got bit they'd be dead before reaching the hospital."

He gripped his cell phone. "If anything happens, I'll have a helicopter here within thirty minutes. And with a snake bit kit, you actually have a lot longer than that to get professional care. Relax and enjoy the day."

"Yeah, as if that were possible." Rattlers! Sheesh! She'd love to get Art and Abby out here for this one and see how relaxed they'd be.

They headed west at a leisurely pace, their line winding up the well-worn trail. It wove between prickly pear cactus, scraggly grass, rocks and small bushes with green leaves that emitted a distinct odor. *And Art thought I'd enjoy this? Maybe I'll take him one of those stinky bushes for a souvenir.*

Before the path started to climb, Seth stopped by an ocotillo plant. Its bare stems towered over him. He pointed to one of the long stems.

"It looks dead, but photosynthesis is taking place along its length. You know what photosynthesis is, right?" Heads bobbed. "When it rains, small green leaves appear, and in the spring a red flower tops each stem."

One of the boys reached out to touch a stem. Seth stopped him. "Be careful, it's covered with thorns to protect it from predators."

Lynn froze as Seth's eyes made contact with hers and held. Was he trying to tell her something? She bristled. Surely he wasn't comparing her to that thorny plant. Maybe he was warning her he was a predator. As if confirming her thoughts, he nodded and smiled, then turned his attention back to the kids.

Heat rose in her face and she turned away. The arrogant ass. How dare he?

"Because the stems of the ocotillo are easy to root, many people use them to make a living fence."

One of the girls spoke up. "Ah, you're kidding us, right?"

"I'm serious. They're beautiful when they're green and in bloom. Can you imagine a green, blooming fence?"

"Wow!"

"Awesome!"

"Neat!"

He ushered them back to the trail. They bunched around him. "Have you noticed the porch roof at the cabins where Lynn lives?" Some nodded while others shook their heads. "It's made of dead ocotillo stems." He caught Lynn's glare. "Isn't that right, Lynn?"

Lynn didn't have a choice. She had to answer or appear rude to the kids. She turned to face them.

"Yes, Seth is right. It's nice because it keeps the direct sunlight at bay, but allows air to circulate."

He moved out of the huddle and started up the hill.

"Come on, guys. Let's move on. I'm ready to see what Cookie packed for lunch."

Afraid she'd step on a snake, Lynn took each step with caution. Kids passed her by and before she knew it, she was at the back of the line. She stepped on a loose rock and stumbled. Ben caught her arm before she fell.

"Relax, Mrs. Devry. We won't see snakes along this trail. I haven't since I've lived here. With Seth up there, if one was around, he'd see or hear it first." Blue eyes twinkled, his grin making him look like one of the baby-faced kids. "But I imagine anything near this trail has scattered by now. We're making more noise than a convoy of tanks. We just have to be prepared."

Yea, she probably did look stupid. At least she wasn't tapping two sticks together to scare the snakes away. That scene from *The Parent Trap* never failed to tickle her.

Ben's young face sobered. "Chill out and enjoy the view."

She snorted, but made an effort to relax and look around.

Who could enjoy looking at rocks and dust? Aw, that wasn't fair. To be honest, the terrain was compelling, wild and raw, yet beautiful in its own way. In the distance, the mountains appeared stark against the blue sky. Cumulus clouds, looking like odd shaped cotton balls, dotted the blue adding texture. If she weren't so bent on watching for snakes, she might enjoy the scenery. And to add to her discomfort, the flat path now started to climb. The muscles in her legs ached.

The backpack had been light when she first put it on, but it grew heavier by the minute. It cut into her shoulders and the canteen strap irritated her neck. You'd think all that exercise in the pool would've prepared her for this trek. Why was she killing herself swimming laps if she couldn't even take a little hike?

Ben hadn't broken a sweat. His breathing was even, not stressed like hers.

"How much further 'til we reach the spot where we'll picnic?"

He stopped and looked around. "About another mile, maybe less."

"You're kidding, right? I thought this was a short hike."

"It is," he said. "This one is only four miles total. We'll work up to twelve miles by the end of the summer."

"Well, I'm not sure I'll live that long," she retorted. Ben chuckled at her mutterings.

Not only did her legs hurt, the muscles in her rear end burned too. This was great exercise but right now she would give anything for a cool place to sit. The backpack felt like it was loaded with rocks. She stopped to catch her breath and allow her screaming muscles to rest.

At points along the trail, Seth called a halt to show the hikers different plants, a ground squirrel's burrow, and mule deer droppings. He stopped beside a plant with dagger like leaves.

"This is a soaptree yucca, part of the agave family. The early settlers used its roots to make soap. The Mescalero Apaches used the mescal agave to make sandals, twine, sewing needles, thread, and liquor from its fermented sap."

With every step, the straps of the backpack cut deeper into her flesh. If her arms dropped from her shoulders and fell by the wayside, she wouldn't be surprised. They could pick them up on the way down. Sweat rolled down her back and between her breasts. Her nylon bra stuck to her skin, cutting into flesh and became more of a nuisance by the minute. The darn thing didn't breathe, so how could she?

She gave up trying to ignore the pinching contraption, grabbed and yanked it into a more comfortable position. Problem was it took more than one yank. To anyone looking, she must've resembled a contortionist. At the first opportunity it was coming off.

Snatching her hat off, she stood and used it to fan her face. She lifted the wet hair plastered to her scalp. A slight breeze drifted by and felt heavenly on her damp overheated skin. Ben was waving for her to catch up. Garnering what little energy she had left, she slapped the hat back on her head and trudged on. To think she'd complained about the laps. At least there she was cool and comfortable. She'd do three times her normal amount of laps to get off this mountain.

Finally, after what seemed like hours, they reached the top of the rise. When she joined the others, they were setting up for lunch.

Seth smiled and pointed to a small boulder where she could sit. On her rock, she struggled to slow her breathing. A stunted mesquite tree cast a small amount of shade across her.

Seth walked over, hunkered down and studied her closely. She knew her face was beet red from exertion.

"How're you holding up?"

With a nod, she muttered, "Fine."

"You feel dizzy, have a headache, nauseated?"

"Nope."

He pointed to the canteen in her hand.

"Drink plenty of water. It should be empty when we return to the ranch."

"Okay." She didn't have the energy to say more.

Seth removed her pack to get the lunches from

inside. *Thank you, God.* She rolled her neck and shoulders to loosen the tense muscles.

Seth and Ben started handing out lunches. As they did, they checked the kids to see how they were holding up in the heat. She was too tired to move. Thank goodness they didn't ask her to help.

Dirty, but still in high spirits, the kids chatted as they ate. Some sat on rocks while others removed the long sleeve shirts from around their waists and sat on them. Corby came over and sat by her.

Zane sat apart from others with a sulky look on his face. She felt sorry for him. He'd behaved well on the hike. Of course with Seth at his side, he didn't have much choice.

"Zane, why don't you come over and sit with us? Corby and I could use the company."

Corby grimaced but straightened his face when Lynn nudged him.

Zane shook he head and muttered, "Naw, I don't want to sit with sissies."

"That'll do, Zane. No name calling." Seth's voice wasn't loud, but firm.

Zane turned his back and continued to eat. A lump lodged in Lynn's throat. What had happened in this child's life to make him aggressive and defensive?

Lynn's breathing slowed as she looked out across the desert terrain. The chattering of youngsters, interrupted occasionally by the base of a male's voice, lulled her as she ate. Corby finished eating and left to join the other children.

Cookie's ham sandwiches made with thick slices of ham with mustard, tomatoes and lettuce were the best she'd ever eaten or aching muscles and the fresh air made her taste buds think so. She was licking the juice from her orange off her fingers when Seth stood and called for their attention.

"Before we leave, pick up every piece of trash and put it in your used sandwich bag. That includes the lettuce and tomatoes you've tossed on the ground."

"Yuck and gross," echoed around the camp as kids picked up dirty, discarded pieces of food.

Seth had the kids lined up ready to go. He cast a look her way that said, "We're waiting." When she didn't rise from her rock he walked over.

He sat on his haunches in front of her, a look of consternation on his face. "Do you need help getting up?"

Head tilted up, she shaded her eyes with her hand. "How about I sit here a while longer and bring up the rear?"

He reached out and felt her forehead and cheeks.

At his touch, her temperature shot up ten degrees. His work-roughened palm against her skin was electrifying. God, she hoped he couldn't hear the tempo of her heart.

"All right. Just don't sit here too long. Don't let us get out of sight."

The minute Ben passed from sight, she moved behind the small mesquite tree and reached up under the back of her shirt. Thank goodness her Aunt Dot had taught her how to take a bra off without removing her blouse. She unhooked the bra, and in less than a minute the offending garment was off and stuffed into the backpack.

With a sigh of relief, she looked down to check out the nature of things. *Uh Oh.* Her nipples were visible through the t-shirt. *Well, hell. I'm not putting that contraption back on.* She slipped into her long sleeve shirt, buttoned a couple buttons, and nodded in satisfaction. Her breasts jiggled when she walked, but the shirt hid most of the movement. She'd just stay behind or stop when anyone looked her way.

The trip down was much easier. The kids were hot, tired, and ready for a swim and left with their counselor right after turning their canteens in to Seth and Ben. Zane waited a few yards behind Seth, looking unhappy to be excluded from the swim. When she turned in her items, Seth said, "Thanks for helping out, Lynn."

She flashed him a tired smile. "You're welcome." Waving, she turned and headed for her cabin.

She changed into her swimsuit. Maybe she could talk Duck out of laps today because she'd already done the equivalent of seven days' worth of laps on that little jaunt up the hill. It wasn't likely, but it wouldn't hurt to ask.

Several hours later, exhausted from her laps, she noticed a small package propped against her door. It had no address so it couldn't have come in the mail. It was a brown paper sack folded and tied with string. She ripped it open, put her hand inside, and squeaked in embarrassment at what she found. Her bra. And included with it a note from Seth.

Lynn, next time, put this in your pocket. Ben may never recover from the shock of finding it. Try cotton. Maria has several catalogues you can borrow.

It was signed, Seth.

She felt a rush of heat and groaned. Seth had touched her bra. Oh, shit! He doubtless looked to see what size she wore. No, he wouldn't do something like that. Yeah, right. He was a man, wasn't he? *How can I ever face him again?*

And Ben. The poor kid would probably never speak to her again. She could just see his neck and face turning red. *Oh, Ben. I'm so sorry.* Where was her head? Why hadn't she stuffed the thing in her pocket?

* * *

The next day, Clara waved her cookie in the air for emphasis. "Lynn, the Fourth of July is the most exciting event of the summer. It's a chance to dress up and flirt with a handsome man." She poked Maria with a bony finger and wiggled her eyebrows.

They sat around Lynn's kitchen table discussing the upcoming July celebration. Lynn, studying the cotton underwear in one of Maria's catalogues, snagged another fresh baked peanut butter cookie. She'd eaten more cookies in the past month than she usually ate all summer long and hadn't gained an ounce. As a matter of fact, her jeans were a little loose in the waist and butt.

Maria snorted. "You see any handsome men around here, you let me know." Uncomfortable, neck flushed, she got up on the pretense of refilling her tea.

Clara winked at Lynn. "Anyway, there'll be all kinds of games and activities scheduled for the afternoon, with a barbecue dinner and dance that evening."

"It's a shame we won't be able to have fireworks this year." Maria sat at the far end of the sofa, out of Clara's poking range.

Some ranchers conducted controlled burns on their land to encourage plant growth. It was too dangerous this summer, as were firecrackers. Because of the dryness, the county Fire Marshall had declared a ban on all burning.

Clara believed Jake had taken a shine to Maria, and from the intensity of Maria's blush, Lynn suspected the feeling was mutual.

"Who all will be here? How many people are you talking about?" asked Lynn.

"There'll be a hundred to a hundred and fifty people," piped Maria. "People from neighboring ranches and Mesa Flats will be here. It's an annual event, and most folks around here wouldn't miss it for the world."

Lynn knew that several of the wranglers and towns' people had put together a band and would provide the music for the dance. They called themselves the Buckaroos. Sally played the fiddle and was lead singer. Both Brian and Jason sang and played guitar while Pete, the meat cook, played drums. Some of the kids would perform with them. They were ecstatic because they had their first gig.

* * *

Lynn stood at the pasture fence stroking Beauty's neck, watching the work going on around her. Special efforts were being made to make the ranch sparkle. Weeds were pulled or cut down, banners were strung on the buildings and across the road, and one of the barns was being made ready for the dance. Sam sat at her side. She leaned down to scratch his ears. "What do you two think about all the commotion?" she asked the two animals. "Are you looking forward to this shindig?" Beauty nickered while Sam wiggled in place and woofed.

Lynn sighed, breathed in the fresh air and listened

to the sounds of the crickets as the sun dropped, leaving a small strip of light behind her. Who would've thought that she could be this content? She hadn't had another headache. Nor had she experienced another anxiety attack. To be honest, she hadn't had time for any as she was constantly busy and on the move. At night she fell into bed and slept like a rock until four a.m.

She crossed her arms and propped them on the fence rail. Chin resting on her warm flesh, she thought about the past week. She'd attended one of Seth's anger management sessions and watched him interact with the kids. They discussed healthy ways to vent anger. What he said made sense. It also made her evaluate her plans for getting back at Art and Abby. Yes, they were childish, but harmless and she planned to see them through.

As an observer at a fear facing activity with the teenagers, she'd whooped and cheered as each one reached the top and stepped on to the platform. Seth had laughed at her enthusiasm and said, "We'll have you up there in a week or two." The man was dreaming. If she could control her fear enough to try to climb that twenty-foot wall, she wouldn't have the strength. Then she'd have to get back down. Sliding down a rope from that height was a tad too exciting for her.

Her face had lost all its humor, and she shook her head.

He'd grinned and nodded. The arrogant man. It wasn't going to happen. She was stronger now, but... She shuddered and put the issue from her mind.

She was pleased with her progress, but her resentment toward Abby and Art still rankled. Letters from Abby rolled in but she hadn't answered a one. It was childish on her part, but she didn't care. She wasn't giving an inch until she had to. Which would be soon. Abby's gift would be ready before long, just in time for the July Fourth gala at the museum.

Shorty, a colorful cowboy bent from hard work, was making the gift. Skinny as a rail, he had trouble keeping his jeans up and hoisted them as he walked. He reminded Lynn of that cowboy, Roy Rogers' sidekick. What was his name? Gabby Hayes? If she didn't find a way to keep her jeans up, she'd look just like him.

"Come on, Sam. Let's get back. It'll be dark soon."

The sun had almost disappeared behind the mountains when Seth left the barn. He watched Lynn and Sam as they returned from their walk. Sam sensed his presence, woofed, and ran toward him.

Seeing Seth, Lynn stopped for a moment, waved and then remembered her bra. Yikes! She ducked her head, swirled, and headed toward the dining hall.

"Lynn, wait a minute. I have something for you."

Puzzled, and slightly concerned, she turned and waited for him. He held out a small brown paper package. "This is from Shorty. He said you'd asked him to make some jewelry for you."

A smile split her face. "Yes. Thank you." Eyes bright with pleasure, she looked down and ran her fingers over the twine bow. "I'd hoped this would be ready in time for the July Fourth celebration." She held it against her chest.

Her behavior was a mystery. He'd never seen anyone get excited about Shorty's deer dropping jewelry. Who would've thought she'd be interested in seeing it, much less having some of her own? Who knew what made women happy? Evidently, he didn't have a clue. Tourists in Mesa Flats bought the jewelry as conversation pieces. Sort of like the pet rock. Maybe that's what she planned to use it for.

"Are you looking forward to the celebration?"

"Yes, I've never been to a barn dance before." Her eyes sparkled, matching the excitement in her voice. "It sounds like great fun. Everyone is working hard to get things ready. Cookie's had me baking extra loaves of bread for days to put away for the dinner. Is there anything else I can do to help?"

"Not that I know of, but I appreciate the offer. I'll let Jake know you asked. He may have something for you."

With her previous attitude, she'd be the last person he'd expect to offer to help. Though she kept to herself, Maria and Clara being exceptions, she handled her job well and hadn't reneged on her exercise routine. Duck said she grumbled about the laps, but she hadn't complained to him.

As she leaned against the fence rail to watch the grazing horses, her shoulders just reached the top rung. Her arms folded across the wood rail, she propped her chin on the wrist of the one hand. He joined her at the fence, keeping a comfortable distance. She was still somewhat skittish around him, and truth be told, being near her made him feel things that needed to stay buried.

"I've wanted to know, Lynn, if you're comfortable here?"

She turned her head toward him.

"How's the cabin?" If the smile on her face was any indication, she liked it. The knowledge pleased him.

"My cabin is perfect. I couldn't ask for anything nicer if I'd designed and decorated it myself." Turning away from the fence, she stuffed her free hand in her pocket and arched her left eyebrow in question. "Are you aware that the kitchen is a collector's paradise? In the city, people are paying outrageous prices for some of the items in that kitchen."

"Really? Like what?"

"Like all those Fiesta Ware dishes, the Pyrex and plastic canister set."

My, my, wouldn't Barbara be disappointed to learn that she'd tossed out something people collect.

"You don't say. My ex-wife wanted new things and when Mom and Dad turned the ranch over to us, she sent it all down to the cabins."

Barbara was a modern woman. She liked the fast-paced city life. He couldn't imagine her collecting anything as trivial as kitchen items. Not that she was a snob. She wasn't, but those things didn't interest her. As a writer, she loved books. Now, he could see her collecting sets of the classics.

"Is something wrong?"

His mind jumped back to the present. "No, no. Just wool gathering."

"You should know, though, that the dishes contain lead and shouldn't be used often." She cast him an innocent look. "Were you trying to give me lead poisoning?"

"You're kidding me, right?" Lord, he hoped so. Those dishes were in several other cabins.

"Yeah, I'm kidding, but not about the lead in the dishes."

Damned if she wasn't enjoying his discomfort. Her

eyes glittered with humor as she held in her laughter.

"I'll get something to replace them right away. Throw those away."

Holding the package to her chest, she thrust out her chin. "I'll do no such thing. They're worth a lot of money, well, maybe not a lot but some, and make beautiful display pieces."

The shoe on the other foot now, she didn't realize he was teasing her. She was cute when she got her hackles up.

"Don't worry about replacing them, I eat most meals in the dining hall. If I have a cup of coffee, I use one of the mugs I borrowed from Cookie."

"Good. But I'll send over some new dishes just in case. Someone else will be in that cabin before long and may not know about the lead in them."

That thought didn't make him happy. He liked having her occupy the cabin and didn't look forward to someone else moving in. As to why he felt that way, he couldn't say. He just did.

"Stack the others to the side. I'll send a box over. And make sure the others are gathered up also."

At her frosty look, he threw up his hands. "Don't worry. I won't throw them away. Maria can find a place to display them in the house."

Nodding, she turned her gaze back to the pasture. They stood in silence for a moment enjoying the view.

"How's your swimming coming along?"

"As I'm sure you already know, it's going well. I'm building strength and resistance and can swim eight laps now."

Still a little testy on the subject of exercise, are we? Seth chuckled, but not loud enough for her to hear. He couldn't forget the haughty look she'd flashed him the day of her first water aerobics class. She'd thought he was spying on her and was mad as a wet hen when actually he'd just stepped out to enjoy the view.

She crossed her arms over her chest and shifted her weight, cocking her hip.

"Don't think that just because things are going well that I intend to stay." She looked down, breaking eye contact. "This place isn't bad, but it's not exactly what I had planned for my summer. I hope you've advertised for someone to take my place so I can go home."

Hell, he thought she was beginning to enjoy the ranch. No way would he admit that he hadn't. His omission by silence rankled his pride and conscience.

"I've not had any responses yet. Actually, I'd hope you'd change your mind and stay on." He took his hat off and sat it on a fence post. "You're doing so well. The kids are crazy about you and most of the staff is too. The others would be if you'd just relax and enjoy yourself."

"How can I relax? I know the day I arrived they were making fun of me. They watch everything I do now just so they can laugh if I make a mistake."

He grabbed his hat and slapped it against his leg. "They do not. Sure they joked some that first day, but you have to admit, you did look out of place." He'd never forget the sight of her in those sandals and a shirt decorated with fringe and conchos.

She snorted and shot him a look that said, *"Drop dead."*

He couldn't hide his grin. "Have they laughed at you since?"

She didn't answer, just froze him with her glare.

Hell, talk about the cold shoulder. She had it down to the ice cube.

"No," said Seth. "I know they haven't. Sure, they know you're a city slicker, but they enjoy seeing you learn our ways." He looked her in the eye. "And they love your breads. I do, too." And he liked having her here. Dammit. He did and hated like hell to admit it.

When she didn't take the bait, he added. "Hey look, so what if they like to tease? You've got to learn to dish it right back at them. They all appreciate a good laugh so give 'em a hard time." He chuckled. "They'll be so shocked you had the nerve, they'll be speechless for a few days." He massaged the muscles in his neck. Dammit, he didn't understand this woman. "Why are you so anxious to get away from here anyway? As well as you're doing, I'd hate to see you leave." Stretching to his full height, he took a deep breath and continued. "You have a lot to offer these kids, Lynn. They look up to you. What kind of an example are you if you just give up?"

Out popped that chin again. If she weren't careful, it would freeze that way.

"I'm not giving up. I was brought here under false pretenses. If I stay, Abby and Art will win." Eyes swimming with tears, she looked away. "They've hurt me. I've got to show them they can't treat me this way."

Seth resisted the urge to put his arms around her and comfort her. He knew she'd suffered, but he'd also seen her start to bloom. And it had pleased him immensely. This woman got to him for some reason. She reminded him of the ocotillo—so prickly and dry but with such potential for beauty. Her outer shell was beginning to peel away revealing her strength and character. As much as he hated to admit it, he'd been drawn to her from the first. And as much as he disliked Art and her daughter's methods, they'd had her best interests at heart.

Shoving aside his thoughts, he cleared his throat. "I understand you're hurt and mad, but if you quit, you'll be the one who loses. Don't let resentment keep you from becoming a better woman, one that is self-confident and healthy."

"How can you or anyone else know what is best for me? Why does everyone think they know more about me than I do?"

Not waiting for an answer, she spun around and marched toward the dining hall.

Without turning she shouted, "Get me a replacement."

Seth shook his head as he watched her stride away. He felt sick at heart because he couldn't convince her to stay. Not for just the ranch and the kids, not for just her baking skills, but for....

Slamming the door to her cabin, Lynn stomped across the room, dropping the package on the sofa as she went to sink in the kitchen. She got a glass from the cabinet and filled it with tap water, drinking it down before taking a breath.

Seth's words about winning and losing had hit home. Maybe he was right, but she'd never let him know she thought so. She felt vulnerable where Seth was concerned. He stirred feelings in her she didn't want to face.

He was right. She was doing better, felt better, looked better, and in much better shape physically. But she could join a swim class at home and continue what she'd been doing here. The track at school was a perfect place to walk. People walked there every day. Why couldn't she be one of them? Yeah, right. The same reason she hadn't been all the years she'd been at that school. It was lack of motivation.

She looked at the package on the sofa, her gift for Abby. Grinning, she untied the package to reveal Shorty's creation, a three-strand bead necklace thirty inches in length. Alternating beads in colors of purple, azure blue, and silver were strung on thin nylon thread. She clapped her hands over her mouth. This was perfect. The three strands would move against each other and tangle. Handling them would cause the color to wear off, and eventually small flecks to flake off, leaving the bead bare. She'd told Shorty to use a non-permanent paint and not to seal them before stringing them.

He'd argued. "But the paint will wear off on your clothes, Miz Devry, look dirty and stink."

When she'd convinced him this would be the perfect gag gift, he'd bobbed his head in appreciation and given her a toothless grin. They'd had a good laugh.

"You got more spunk than I gave you credit for, ma'am."

Now the problem would be getting them to Abby intact and making sure she wore them to the gallery showing. Darn. If only she could be there to see her daughter's expression when she discovered she'd mingled with Fort Worth's elite, decked in their precious stones, wearing deer shit.

Chapter Eight

"Lynn, you've done more than your share," said Cookie. "With the loaves you put away earlier, we've got enough bread to feed all of Presidio County."

Lynn snorted. "Ha. From what I hear, the county is huge and from your bragging, it sounds like everyone within a three hundred mile radius will be here."

But Cookie was right. Loaves of bread covered every surface in the kitchen and dining hall. Clara and Pete had both slicing machines going. The sliced bread went into large plastic storage containers to be carried out when it was time to eat.

Cookie flapped his apron at her like he was shooing chickens. "Go on. Get on out of here and get prettied up for the dance. And wear your boots, not some of those fancy city shoes that'll get ruined."

Lynn saluted. "Yes, sir!" On impulse, she leaned over and kissed him on the cheek.

He blushed and blustered. "Get on with you now."

Laughing, Lynn charged out the door and headed for the corral. The mood for the July Fourth celebration was festive and contagious. Excitement welled in Lynn's chest as she walked down the road to watch the activities. Chue and some of the older wranglers were giving horseshoe-tossing demonstrations. Teenagers and children alike watched in awe as the shoe hit and twirled around the metal stake. Ben, with the help of Tim and Jared, supervised a volleyball game. Ben was referee and appeared unruffled by boos coming from the losing team.

Shouts and laughter drew her attention to the potato sack race. Seth and Jake were competing, and though a close race, Jake was ahead. The kids jumped up and down like jumping beans. Both men fell, but Jake's head was over the finish line. Laughing along with the kids, she glanced at Seth to see him watching her. He grinned and motioned for her to join them. Shaking her head, she decided she better make herself scarce. She didn't want to be pulled into a game that would leave her dirty and bruised. Anyway, it was time to start getting ready. Lynn was anxious for the barbecue and dance to begin.

As she preened in front of the mirror, she noted that her stomach and butt were firmer, and her once flabby arms now looked almost sleek. Her rear and upper thighs still carried negligible signs of hail damage, but overall she looked trimmer than she had in years.

The change in her appearance was empowering. She hadn't believed it possible, but Art and Abby had. Drat their hides. It was getting harder to stay angry with them.

What to wear? She rummaged through her closet and pulled out a mid-calf denim skirt. Her red silk tee shirt would look good with it, but she hadn't worn it in years without a jacket to cover the lumps and rolls it hugged. She slipped it on, enjoying its smooth texture against her skin. Since her middle had toned it fit nicely She tucked it into the skirt grinning at how great it felt not to be self-conscious about her body.

Her hair had grown longer than she liked. She pulled it up on the sides and fastened it on top of her head with a clip. She applied powder and lipstick, put silver teardrop earrings in her ears, and slid a silver cuff bracelet on her arm. Around her waist she fastened a belt that resembled woven hemp. It hung down the front of the skirt, ending in tassels.

"Don't look half bad for an old lady," she said to her reflection. Her boots gleamed from the polishing she'd given them the night before. She pulled them on over the cotton socks she'd ordered from Maria's catalogue. The cotton panties and bras really made a difference while out in the heat but tonight she'd been unable to resist wearing the red nylon and lace set she'd added to the order. She wanted something silky and sexy to show off her body, even if it was for no one but herself.

Outdoors traffic was heavy as people walked down the dusty road to the tables set up for supper. The sun was descending, and within an hour would give a candlelight glow to the area.

Nearing the large barn, she saw that people were everywhere, talking, eating, laughing and joking. Cookie barked orders at Pete and several cowboys as he supervised the replenishing of food.

From the serving line, Seth watched Lynn walk up the road. She seemed totally unaware of the admiring glances she received, a strong contrast to the mocking ones she'd received her first morning there. In the long skirt, her hips moved with an enticing swing. Each step she took caused her breasts to tremble beneath the flame red silky type top.

He gulped loudly then glanced around to see if anyone had seen the appreciation in his eyes. It wouldn't do for people to think he had a thing for Lynn, especially with Maria and Clara. The three women had become close friends. Thankfully their eyes weren't on him, but on Lynn.

As Seth watched, Clara and Maria caught Lynn's eye and waved to her from one of the tables, motioning to the seat they'd saved for her. Waving back she started through the line a short distance behind him.

He sat his plate down next to the place Clara and Maria had saved for Lynn and went back to the beverage table for drinks.

Seth reached the table just as Lynn sat her plate on the table. She turned to go back for tea.

"Here you go, Lynn. I picked up an extra." He put the glasses down, held her chair for her, and then sat down beside her.

"Thank you." When he sat down, their shoulders brushed. The closeness seemed to make her uncomfortable. She sat straight and leaned to her right trying to give him more room.

"Pretty tight quarters, huh? Relax. If we bump each other around, we'll survive."

Her lips formed a smile, defining the dimples in each cheek and her high cheekbones. Tonight she wore lipstick. The peachy shade brought out the color of her eyes. For the first time he noticed the shape of her mouth. It was fuller than Barbara's, the bottom lip heavier.

Hmm, very kissable lips.

He could imagine what it would feel like to kiss her and explore that bottom lip with his tongue. Shit! Where the hell had that thought come from? His gaze moved up and their eyes locked for a second. She glanced down.

She could still be mad about their last talk, but he didn't think so. She just wasn't used to close contact. Would she be happy to know he'd put a notice in the

Odessa and Midland papers the next day? If getting back at Art and Abby was more important than her health and well-being, so be it. She could go home soon.

As usual, the beef was tender and he'd slathered on plenty of Cookie's famous barbecue sauce. Seth took a bite and savored the spicy beef. When he finished chewing, Lynn was watching him with a soft expression. God, she had beautiful eyes, ones a man could get lost in. He swallowed with difficulty. If he wasn't careful, he'd be a lost man and that couldn't happen.

"Cookie makes the best barbecue in the world, don't you think?" Lord, he was floundering here. What had happened to the teasing woman who'd bought some of Shorty's jewelry? He glanced at her tanned neck noting it was bare of jewelry. He wondered why she wasn't wearing it.

"How do you like our celebration so far?" She stared at him, her fork midway to her mouth as if she hadn't heard him. "Lynn? I asked if you're having a good time."

A flush crept up Lynn's neck. Oh, Lord. Had he done something to embarrass her? Had she noticed his stares of appreciation? She was lovely tonight, actually pretty with that blush rising on her face. And smelled better than nice. Her scent wasn't heavy like the perfume Barbara wore, but light and subtle, leaving a tantalizing whiff when she moved.

"Ah...sorry. My mind drifted there for a moment." Placing her fork in her plate, she wiped her hands on her napkin. "I didn't participate in the games, but am looking forward to the dance." She picked up her glass of tea. Before taking a sip, she added. "It really is a shame about the fireworks, though. I can just imagine how spectacular they'd be with these mountains as a backdrop."

At Jake and Ben's arrival, Seth watched with wonder as Lynn transformed from a shy woman to a teasing one.

"My, my, you gentlemen are handsome tonight." Her smile was broad and not in the least uncomfortable.

Ben smiled his thanks. "You too, ma'am." He blushed and stammered. "I mean you look pretty tonight."

"Thank you, Ben. I knew what you meant."

Jake was more elaborate in his response. He reached across the table, took her hand, and placed a quick kiss on it. "Well then, I guess you'll save this old cowboy a dance tonight."

"But of course!"

Seth watched the exchange between Jake and Lynn. For some reason, their good-natured flirting irritated the hell out of him. Oh, hell. He was being unreasonable. Jake made a play for every woman within two hundred miles. But, for Seth, it wasn't in his nature.

Jake sat in the chair beside Maria. "Maria, my love." He put his arm around the handsome woman, hugged her tight and bussed her cheek. "When are you going to marry me?"

Blushing, Maria swatted him with her napkin. "One of these days, Jake, I'm going to say yes and see how fast you can run. I'm just waiting for you to get a little older and slower."

Laughing with good humor, Jake tucked into his

meal.

Lynn leaned across the table to get Ben's attention. "Ben, you'll save us old ladies a dance tonight, won't you? We don't want to be wall flowers."

Flushing with pleasure he nodded and said, "I'd be honored, ma'am." Seth watched as their conversation bantered back and forth. Lynn was comfortable with the other men. Why was she skittish around him? He'd never made women uncomfortable before. Maybe she didn't know him well enough. She'd been around Jake and Ben more. He'd see they got better acquainted by dancing with her several times tonight.

Ben looked up from his meal and reaching around Clara, tapped Jake on the shoulder and pointed in the direction of the dining hall. "Look who's coming."

Lynn watched as Seth and the two women turned in the direction Ben pointed. Unable to resist, she turned too.

A man walked toward them. He was a tall commanding figure, and from a distance, he appeared to wear a uniform. Lynn couldn't see the color of his hair or eyes as he wore a big hat and reflective sunglasses.

Loud enough for the entire county to hear him, Jake hollered, "Hey, who invited the law?"

As the crowd noticed the newcomer, shouts of greeting were added to Jake's remark.

"Who is he?" Lynn asked. The closer he got the more familiar he seemed to Lynn. And, if she wasn't mistaken, he wore a state trooper's uniform. Oh, no, surely not. It couldn't be.

Cowboys slapped him on the back and shook his hand. He gave as good as he got, grinning the entire time, then broke away and strode toward them.

"It's Roark," said Seth. "He's a good friend of Brandon's. Spent a lot of time here when they were kids." Affection laced Seth's comment.

Lynn squirmed in her seat, glancing around to see if she could escape without being noticed.

Seth stood and waited for Roark, clasping him on the shoulders at his arrival. "Glad you could make it, Roark."

He removed his glasses and put them in a top shirt pocket. "Wouldn't miss it for the world. But, I've just got time to eat. I'm on patrol tonight. You know how it is during chili cook-off weekend." He removed his hat and greeted Maria and Clara, shook hands with Ben and Jake, and then turned to Lynn.

"Roark, this is Lynn Devry, our new bakery cook. Wait 'til you taste her bread. It'll melt in your mouth."

Dark blue eyes smiled down at her. Her eyes dropped to the nameplate on his chest. It read Espinoza. *Uh oh, it is him.* What would Seth say when he learned she'd been stopped on the highway by the law? Maybe Roark wouldn't remember.

He extended his hand. "It's nice to meet you, ma'am. I look forward to tasting your famous bread." His smile was polite and friendly and the eye facing away from the others came down in a quick wink.

Her heart jumped into her throat and taking his hand she croaked out, "Thank you." Then added, "It's good to meet you too."

Seth led him away to the serving line.

Maria stacked her paper dishes and stood to leave the table. "Isn't he a fine looking young man? Good boy, too."

"Yes, he is. How'd he get the name Espinoza with those blue eyes?"

"Got those from his mama's Irish side. His dad's grandparents are from Mexico City. His folks own a big ranch in neighboring Pecos County."

For a county this big, it seemed most people knew each other or at least had heard of them. This was a foreign concept for Lynn. Many people lived on the same street in Fort Worth didn't know the names of their neighbors.

She walked with Maria to the trash barrel. It was good to be through eating. Sitting so close to Seth had stirred feelings she didn't want to think about. That after-shave of his was designed to take a woman's breath away and make her all fluttery inside. Plus the shock of seeing Roark and the risk of discovery unnerved her. "See you ladies later. I'm going to walk some of this dinner off."

* * *

As the local band warmed up in the barn, Lynn strolled over to the pasture fence. Seemed she'd developed a fondness for the grassy area and the animals they contained.

She watched a colt frolic about, kicking up his heels, tail flying as its mother stood by, contentedly. He trotted over hoping for a treat. Lynn stroked his head but had nothing for him. He quickly lost interest and went back to trying to impress his mother.

It was a beautiful evening, dusk, with just enough light left to see the horses grazing in the pasture, but not enough to tell if their eyes were open or closed. Hills, cast in deep shadows, were outlined against the darkening sky. One or two stars had appeared waiting to flash and glow.

Lynn took a deep breath of the fresh night air and filed away in her memory the scene before her. Her senses filled with the sights, sounds, and smells around her. The glow of the barn in the deepening gray, laughter drifting on the night breeze, and the aroma of Cookie's barbecue that still hung in the air and mixed with the smells of nature in the desert. This was the most peaceful place on earth. It would be easy to stay here forever.

Now, where had that thought come from, and wouldn't it just tickle Art pink to know the idea had crossed her mind?

Light, laughter, and music drew her toward the barn. The minute she walked through the door, Shorty pulled her onto the floor for a round of Boot Scoot 'n Boogie. Though over seventy, you couldn't call him slow. She had a hard time keeping up with his fast footwork. He had her laughing and gasping for breath when the music ended.

Corby and the other younger children were sitting in chairs around the punch bowl area eating cookies. When Corby saw her, he stuffed the last of a cookie in his mouth and rushed over dusting crumbs off his face as he asked. "Hey, Lynn. You wanna dance?"

"Sure I do. I thought you'd never ask."

Kool-Aid red lips arched into a grin. "Really?"

"You bet."

Corby did more talking than dancing but his footwork indicated he'd learned something at their classes. When their dance was over he headed back for the cookies. She stopped in front of Zane. "May I have this dance, sir?"

Zane didn't act pleased, but stood up and took her hand. He'd learned some manners after all. The song was a fast two-step and what Zane lacked in finesse he made up in speed. He gave Lynn a great aerobic workout. At the sidelines, Zane gave her a wicked smirk and bowed. "Thank you for the dance, ma'am."

Before she could fully catch her breath, Chue stopped in front of her. Face twisted in a grin, he took off his big hat and made a sweeping bow with it. "May I have this dance, ma'am?"

Before Lynn could answer, Chue was swinging her around the room to the refrain of a country waltz. His gimp leg didn't slow him down in the least.

"You thought anymore about getting up on one of them horses?"

Startled, Lynn missed a step but quickly recovered. "Me? I don't think that's going to happen. Remember? I'm afraid of the creatures."

"Better think about it some more and get ready. Not much time left." He led her back to the sidelines. "Remember what I said, gal." He disappeared into the crowd.

What did he mean by that? Not much time left?

Before she'd come up with an answer, Cookie had her stomping and yelling, to the Cotton Eyed Joe. Who would've thought such a big man could move that fast?

Lynn begged out of the next number to rest and cool down. She took a seat on the bales of hay placed on the sidelines and turned her attention to the dancers. Seth was dancing with Julie. He caught her watching, smiled and nodded. As the dance ended, he handed Julie over to Ben and started toward her. Her breath caught at the look of determination on his face. Before he'd taken two steps, Clara snagged him.

At ease on her makeshift seat, Lynn observed the couples as they passed. Her eyes wandered across the room to where Tim stood alone, surveying the couples, Julie in particular. Frowning, his gaze followed her as she two-stepped with Ben. He'd come a long way in the last couple of weeks. There'd been no more complaints about his language or about harassing Julie.

The tortured look on his face tugged at Lynn's heart. It was obvious he was crazy about the girl, but afraid to ask her to dance, in fear of being rejected.

Unable to watch a minute longer, Lynn walked over to stand beside him. Maybe she could ease his fear some.

"Hi, Tim, you enjoying this shindig?"

He smiled in greeting then returned his gaze to Julie and Ben.

"Yea, pretty much."

"Well, how about treating this old lady to a dance?"

Startled, a look of panic crossed his face. He glanced at the others trying to make up his mind. "I'm not very good but…"

"Oh, me neither, but let's give it a whirl."

Lynn put her left hand on his shoulder and grinned up at him. "Let's boogie, cowboy." Laughing they stumbled around the floor. Soon, Tim relaxed, and they were just getting the hang of the steps when the song ended.

Tim started to walk away. Lynn grabbed him and said, "One more round, Tim." We're doing so well, we can't stop now."

When they worked up a steady rhythm, Lynn

asked, "Have you danced with Julie yet?"

His face fell. "No, she wouldn't want to with me."

"It sure wouldn't hurt to ask."

She watched him think about what she'd said. Before he could say no, she continued.

"You know, Tim, women love an apology, especially if it's sincere. Nothing softens the heart faster. But, you better mean every word you say."

With a shy smile, Tim bowed at the waist. "Thank you, Mrs. Devry."

"My pleasure, Tim."

She was dancing with Jake when Tim walked up to Julie. Her friends stopped talking and stood, their attention on him. Lynn held her breath. Tim bent his head, then looked up again and said something while Julie listened intently, her eyes never leaving his face.

Finished, he stood and waited for her to say something. When she didn't, he turned and walked away.

Lynn froze and waited for her to say something. *Oh no, Julie. You've got to do something. Quick, before he gets away.*

Julie shook her head as if to clear it, then rushed after Tim and touched his arm. He turned. She extended her hand and said something to him. Expressions shy, they smiled and walked onto the dance floor.

Lynn breathed a sigh of relief, he heart expanded with the possibility of these two kids becoming friends, something nice evolving from the earlier ugliness. Unaware that she'd stopped moving, she jumped when Jake spoke.

"Lynn, is everything all right?"

She bit her lip to keep the tears at bay. Voice

cracking, she nodded toward Tim and Julie and said, "Everything's just fine."

Noticing her tears, he made a face. "Hey now. None of that." He laughed and Lynn wiped her face as they watched the two young people. "Ah, young love. Ain't it wonderful?"

Lynn sniffed. "Yeah. Wonderful, but painful."

The evening was drawing to an end. Lynn was worn out, her feet hurt, and her hair a mess, but she was floating on a cloud of happiness. She hadn't had this much fun in ages. Actually, since she and her ex-husband, Dan, went out dancing with friends early in their marriage. They'd gone often, and when they returned home, they'd check on Abby, turn the lights down low, and dance to records in the living room.

On Sunday mornings, Abby would climb into bed with them while they read the paper. As Dan read the funnies to Abby, Lynn would watch the expressions transform her face and listen to her giggles. After they dress, Dan would lift Abby onto his shoulders and they'd walk down the street to the donut shop. There had been many such Sunday mornings. What had gone wrong in their marriage?

"How about this next dance, Lynn?"

Jolted from her thoughts, Lynn looked from the hand up to the face of the man. Seth. Her heart did a flip-flop. Why, she had no idea. Okay, she was attracted to him, but the feeling wasn't mutual, and she had no future here. She had a job waiting for her in Fort Worth.

She mentally shook herself. He was no different from the other men she'd dance with that evening, so why not? *And quit being so shy around him. After all, he's just a man, not a movie idol.*

"Yes. I'd like that. I'll try not to step on your toes."
Now why on earth had she said something so stupid?
Oh Lord, he probably thinks I'm an idiot.

He laughed. "You let me worry about my toes."

"Ladies and gentlemen. This is the last dance of the evening, so find your sweetheart or your favorite partner and join us in the *Last Waltz*." The cowboy put his fiddle to his shoulder and started the introductory refrain.

Oh my gosh, she moaned to herself. Why did she have to end up with Seth during this romantic song? She'd feel more comfortable with Jake or any of the other men.

Lynn tried to loosen up and be nonchalant, but held herself rigid and at arm's length as Seth took her in his arms.

"Do I make you nervous, Lynn?"

Stumbling at his question, she recovered then lied. "No, not at all. I'm just not a very good dancer."

"You're doing fine. Relax. Follow me." He pulled her closer. Their bodies were touching, her head against his jaw.

"Now, that's much better. You're a fine dancer. Just enjoy the music." His breath stirred her hair.

Oh my, oh my, oh my, she breathed. This is too nice. Warm and utterly male, his muscles rippled under her hand as they moved to the music. It felt good to be in his arms. Ha! In a man's arms period. She hoped that's why she was enjoying the dance so. *Good grief Lynn, get a grip, you're acting like a silly schoolgirl. This is just a dance.*

She relaxed and gave herself up to the seductive music of the country waltz and the man who led her expertly. They danced well together, as though they'd been doing so for years.

Lynn breathed in his spicy scent. The heat rising from his skin made the combination of cologne, soap, and man intoxicating. Releasing a sigh, she melted against him, feeling his arm tighten around her waist. Was he as attuned to her as she was to him? As if hearing her thoughts, he pulled her even closer. The fit was so right.

If there were other people in the room, Lynn wasn't aware of it. She was locked in a time warp and she and Seth were the only two people alive. An excellent dancer, he led her around the room with ease. She was dancing on air and intoxicated by his nearness, the heat of his hard body, and his scent.

When the music ended, it seemed too soon. They stood, locked in each other's arms for an extra second or two. When Seth drew back, he continued to hold her hand as if reluctant to let her go. Their eyes locked and held. The noise around them intruded, breaking the spell. He gave Lynn a half bow.

"Thank you for the dance." The low timbre of his voice sent a thrill along her nerve endings.

"My pleasure."

He released her hand. "Good night." Then he headed toward the area where the band worked at putting away their instruments.

Lynn watched him walk away, regretting that their dance was over and wishing she didn't care.

* * *

The Worth Museum of Art and History blazed with lights—outside, to emphasize the artistically landscaped gardens and—inside, to reflect the glitter of jewelry and highlight the works of art on display.

Amid the multitude of richly dressed patrons, Abby Devry moved and chatted, a smile on her face. The party was going strong. Waiters kept the champagne flowing and strategically placed buffet tables filled with canapés. Tonight they were displaying paintings of the American Revolutionary War. A soldier or professional war painter had created each authentic piece.

As she circulated, her long, layered dress of purple and azure print chiffon brushed against her legs. She fingered the triple stand of beads at her neck. A gift from her mother, they matched her dress perfectly, and the silver and amethyst earrings in her ears completed her outfit.

The gift was a surprise as her angry mother refused to answer her letters. The month of June had been the longest month of her life. Abby feared she would let her temper ruin the promise of a productive summer.

As the evening wore on, she noticed people staring at her necklace. Some expressed interest in its origin. As she explained that it was a gift from her mother, a tall man, drink in hand, walked up and stood listening. She'd noticed him earlier in the evening as he'd talked with a group of businessmen from Dallas. He was good looking, rugged, and fit. Not pretty like some of the men who frequented the museum.

Oh, my, gosh. He's watching me. She shifted her gaze to the man he talked with. Thank goodness, Mr. White, one of her bosses. She smiled and nodded in greeting. Had he seen her studying him?

"Abby, my dear, where did you say you got your necklace?" She swiveled around at Mrs. White's question.

"My mother sent it to me from West Texas."

"Hmmm. It's lovely, dear." Her lips arched into a smile as the two men joined them. "Hello, John. Did you finally remember you have a wife?"

Mr. White leaned in and kissed his wife's cheek. "How could I forget you, darling?" He turned to Abby. "Abby, I'd like for you to meet Brandon Williams. Brandon, this young lady is one of promising new curators."

Brandon's large hand clasped hers. "Did I hear you say that your mother sent your necklace from West Texas? What part? I grew up out there on a ranch."

"Really? It's a big place. Where about exactly?" Abby studied the man before her. His dark hair was neatly styled but one tendril failed to cooperate and fell onto his forehead. His eyes were blue gray, his smile infectious.

"It's near the small town of Mesa Flats, not far from Big Bend National Park."

She couldn't believe it. "You're kidding? That sounds close to where Mother is staying, a place called Ocotillo Ranch."

"How about that? That's my Dad's ranch. Seth Williams is my Dad. I'm his oldest son, Brandon."

With her hand still clasped in his, he expertly maneuvered her away from the others. Abby didn't mind in the least. She'd like to get to know him better.

"It's a pleasure to meet you, Brandon. I'm Abby Devry."

Before she could respond further, David, her good friend and escort for the evening, walked up.

"Excuse me. Abby, could I talk to you for a minute?"

David put his arm around her shoulder, bent his head close to hers and seemed to be flicking something off her neck as he spoke. She instinctively reached up.

"Hey babe, can you excuse me from taking you home tonight? Something has come up?" He wiggled his eyebrows wickedly.

She patted his cheek. "You run on, lover boy, I'll get a cab, so don't worry about me." He kissed her cheek and hurried back to the brunette.

She turned back to Brandon. He waited with a bemused expression on his face.

"Looks like I've been ditched."

"This must be my lucky day. I'd be happy to drive you home, if you'll allow me."

"Are you sure it won't be too much trouble? I can always get a cab."

"I wouldn't dream of letting you do that. Anyway, I've been trying to think of a good way to ask you, and your friend Romeo came through for me."

"I better let the Smiths know who I'm leaving with."

"Good idea."

She gathered her wrap and met him at the door. "This is very nice of you. I'd love to hear more about your dad's ranch and about the man who made this necklace."

A grin split his face. He looked ready to burst into laughter.

"I can't wait. Shorty will be floored when he learns that you wore one of his creations to this fancy party."

"Really? Why would he be so surprised?"

His answer was a mischievous grin.

Chapter Nine

Seth sat on the side of the bed, elbows on his knees, picture in his hands. Barbara, head thrown back, dark hair shining and brown eyes flashing, laughed for the camera. She was a beautiful woman, even more so now in her forties.

Would this longing ever stop? For years he'd dreamed of her, waking and reaching for her only to find the bed cold and empty. This morning was bad because he'd not dreamed of her in months and thought his torment was over. Something had triggered the dream and it didn't take a rocket scientist to discover what. Lynn, her softness and scent had elicited feelings in him he'd thought only Barbara could produce.

He glanced back at the picture, regret clenching his heart. When Barbara came to the ranch to see the boys or they met in Dallas, she thought nothing of molding her body to his and giving him a passionate kiss. And he never failed to clasp her close and drown in her softness, wanting more than this brief encounter. Things would never be right between them again, yet he continued to torture himself. But that would stop. It only made their circumstances harder and he was a fool for not stopping it long ago. He might not be able to control his heart but he could damn sure control his behavior.

He stuffed the picture in the nightstand drawer where it would stay from now on and dropped his head into his hands. Dammit, why should he feel guilty about being attracted to Lynn? He had no business being attracted to any woman, that's why. Not until he completely evicted a ghost from his heart. Until he'd made a clean break, he'd feel like he was cheating.

* * *

"Good morning, Sam. Isn't it a beautiful morning?" As she patted his head, he thumped the hard packed dirt with his tail. It was Sunday, her day off so she could tie up some loose ends.

As usual, the sky was cloudless, the air so arid it felt brittle. Lynn glanced at the wilting weeds growing near the corral fence posts as she walked toward the corral with a basket on her arm. When the weeds suffered, it was beyond dry.

She longed for that wonderful freshness that rain brings to parched land and the renewal of life. As a child, she'd loved the smell of rain in the air and the sweet aroma of freshly cut grass. It had been years since she'd stopped to enjoy nature's gifts. The next time the clouds opened she'd stop, sit on the porch, and enjoy its fragrance, the sound of it bouncing on the roof, and remember.

Sam's ears flattened in pleasure as she ran her hand down his head.

"Sam, I bet you didn't think this city girl would look forward to a little rain." She glanced up at the sun. The day was beginning to show promise of another boiler. "Make that a lot of rain."

Still early, breakfast wouldn't be served for another hour. She drew the clean fresh air into her lungs as she walked to the corral. Sam trotted between her and each fence post and bush checking for invaders. He found a stick and dropped it at her feet. Tail wagging, tongue lolling, he jumped around her feet. When she threw it, he shot off, leaving a flurry of dirt in his wake. The game continued as she walked.

When she reached the corral, Sam dropped the retrieved stick, sat down and barked.

"You'll have to wait. I have business to attend to. I'll be through in a minute."

Inside the corral, she sat her basket down, then turned and locked the gate. No horses were in the corral this morning, but if Chue found the gate open he'd give her a piece of his mind. No one else was around.

Retrieving the basket, she hummed the refrain of the country waltz she and Seth had danced to last night. Happy, feeling young and carefree, she danced and twirled to the music. "*Dum, da da dum—*"

Sam barked, his excited yips ending in a yowl.

"Is that an ugly comment about my singing, boy?"

Reaching through the two by fours of the gate, she picked up the stick Sam had dropped in the dirt. "Now Sam, this is the last time. I've got work to do. Art needs to receive a surprise package from me."

She tossed the stick as far as her arm would allow. Sam left in a cloud of dust.

Kneeling in the dirt, she took a dustpan from the basket and used it to lift a ripe specimen of horse manure into a plastic bag. Sealing it tightly, she dropped it into the basket with the dustpan. She dusted her hands, then picked up her basket and left the corral.

Seth stood inside the darkness of the barn watching as Lynn danced around the corral. When he saw her pick up the horse manure, his jaw dropped, the bridle he held forgotten. What the hell was the woman up to? Surely this wasn't some new kind of beauty treatment. God, he hoped not. He watched as she closed the corral gate and walked toward the cabins.

Turning his attention back to the bridle, he smiled

and shook his head. The woman was a puzzle. Waltzing in the corral. Was she thinking about their dance together?

"Nah," he muttered. Who knew what was in a woman's mind?

At the memory of Lynn's dance in the corral, he grinned and started whistling the tune of *The Last Waltz*. He stopped abruptly when he saw Chue in the doorway watching, a big grin on his face.

Laughing, Chue walked out of the tack room and yelled, "Hey Seth, let's go have some breakfast."

* * *

When Lynn walked into the dining hall, raucous laughter greeted her. Jared stood at the end of a table entertaining Seth, Jake and the rest of the regular staff who sat drinking coffee. Cookie stood over them with the coffeepot. Laughing, he wiped tears from his face with the tail of his apron.

Chue slapped Seth on the back as he shouted, "I told you that little gal had spunk. Looks like things are gonna liven up around here. Haw, Haw, Haw—" He slapped his good leg.

Jared continued with his story, something about Seth's oldest son at a party. She couldn't quite make out what they were saying, but suddenly they burst out laughing again. Jake choked on a hot mouthful of coffee and spilled half of it down his shirtfront. When he jumped up, he knocked his chair over, adding to the racket. Clara pounded him on the back while Sally mopped at the front of his shirt with paper napkins.

They were so funny Lynn found herself laughing too. She was just about to break in and ask what was so hilarious when Brian's voice broke through the commotion.

"Dad, I just can't believe she'd do something like that. She's so nice and quiet." He looked at the old cowboy. "Shorty, are you sure she knew those beads would crumble and stink like that?"

"Sure she knew, boy! Don't you think I didn't tell her they would? She tole me they were for a gag gift and it didn't matter none."

Brian continued shaking his head. "That poor girl. Don't you know she was mortified?"

"It's them quiet ones you gotta look out for, Brian. They're sneaky," said Chue. "That gal's got sand in her pants. That's a fact. I like women with some grit, keeps a man on his toes."

At Brian's comment about crumbling beads, Lynn froze in her tracks. She was the object of their entertainment. The bottom fell out of her stomach and a blush rushed to the roots of her hair. She felt like the burning bush. How had they found out about her prank? Ducking her head, she eased backwards toward the door.

Jared looked up and saw her. Damn, she'd been caught. Jared punched his dad and nodded in her direction. As Seth's head swiveled, the remaining eight followed to see Lynn nailed to the spot, looking uncertain.

"Um…Good morning. I think I'll take my breakfast to my cabin. I don't feel well."

"Oh no, you don't, woman. Come on over here. You've got some explaining to do," ordered Seth.

"Lynn, you are B-A-D," Jake said, with huge grin on his face. He was certainly enjoying himself. "We didn't know you had it in you."

Lynn made her way to the far end of the table but Seth motioned for Brian to get up and let her sit next to him. She wanted to refuse but Seth appeared adamant. He crooked his finger and pointed to the now vacant chair.

She plunked her tray down on the table and her butt in the chair. And started to eat. Her back was ramrod straight just like her nerves. She tried to act normal. It was difficult, with all eyes on her, waiting.

Let them wait. She blew on her hot coffee and took a sip, then another. When her cup was near empty, they were still waiting.

"What?"

Clara's kind face wrinkled with concern. "How could you do something like that to your own child?"

Without blinking she replied, "Look what she did to me. She'll think real hard, *and* twice, before she tries something like this on me again."

She put her mug down, looked around the table, indignation evident. Seth started laughing and within minutes the rest joined in. Her gaze remained firm as she watched them break down. She tried to stay sober but their hilarity was contagious.

With her napkin she wiped tears from her face. "How did you find out anyway?"

Seth, grinning from ear to ear, unable to speak, pointed to Jared.

"My older brother, Brandon, was at the museum party last night. He offered to take your daughter home. They got caught in a rain shower and by the time they reached her apartment, she was 'smelling like a rose'. During the party the beads had lost a lot of paint and she had a brown ring around her neck. When Brandon told her what she'd been wearing all evening she went ape-shit." He choked and reddened. "Oh, sorry, ma'am." He included the other women in his nod.

"Anyway, she flushed the necklace down the toilet, took a shower, and tried to burn the dress in the fireplace." He added that Brandon had gotten the dress away undamaged and to the cleaners.

"Was she all right when he left?" she asked, growing a little anxious. Her intention hadn't been to scar her daughter for life, just to make a point. The light rain had been an added bonus as it had hurried things along. She'd figured Abby would get home, notice a brown stain on her neck, look at the beads and see that the paint had flaked off enough to show the brown underneath. Knowing Abby's habit of smelling things to determine their composition, Lynn knew she'd detect something stinky was going down.

"He said she screamed for an hour and cried for another. When he left her apartment, she'd fallen asleep on the sofa. He locked up before heading home. He called her this morning and she was better—could even laugh about it some."

What was Abby thinking, letting a man she doesn't know take her home? If that's not bad enough, she lets him stay in the house while she takes a shower and then falls asleep with him still in her apartment. She thought Abby had more sense than that. Of course, she knew Brandon was Seth's son, but still...

Jared must have read the worry on her face because he added. "Oh, one more thing, Brandon said to tell you that the Smiths know him, and that Abby let them know he was taking her home. She didn't just get in the car with a complete stranger."

Lynn breathed a sigh of relief. "Thanks, Jared. I needed to hear that." She turned to Seth. "That was very considerate of Brandon to include that in his tale. You and Barbara did a good job raising them."

He nodded, and a little color rose in his face.

Lynn leaned back in her chair, grinning. She reached for the ceiling, both arms fully extended, jerked them down and shouted, "Yes! I gotcha, Abby. That'll teach you to mess with M-O-M." She chuckled as she took a bite of her cinnamon roll and drank her orange juice.

"Cookie, pass that coffee pot please."

He filled her cup, but didn't leave. "You ever done anything like this before? You know, played a horrible joke on somebody?"

The coffee was hot, so she took small sips. All eyes were on her, waiting for her answer.

She cleared her throat. "Now look, I'm not really mean. I just want people to know they can't treat me wrong more than once."

And that was the truth. After some of the stunts she'd pulled, she'd suffered feelings of remorse, but not enough to apologize. The recipients had deserved punishment.

The room grew quiet as they waited for her to continue.

"All right, all right. Once, when my daughter was a baby, my husband, ex-husband now, bought season tickets to the Dallas Cowboy games."

Jared and Brian whooped and gave each other a high five sign.

Shooting daggers at the two boys, she added. "He was supposed to replace the air conditioner in our home like he'd promised."

"Is that so bad?" asked Brian. "Didn't you like to go to the games?"

Maria was quick to add her opinion. "Of course she did, Brian. But, can you imagine taking care of a small baby in a house without air-conditioning in Fort Worth? It's stifling and the humidity is terrible."

Lynn nodded in agreement. "That's right. And Dan just broke one promise too many. It wasn't the first time."

Seth's brow furrowed. He looked at her, waiting. Lynn could tell he was dying to know what she'd done, but hesitant to ask. She tried to suppress the grin she felt at his discomfort.

"And what did you do, Lynn? Tear up his tickets?" Seth shook his head. "I hope not as that would have been a little too vindictive."

The males in the room added their agreement.

Clara spoke hotly. "You've got to be kidding. You men all stick together. No wonder the world's in such a mess." She gave them all a dirty look then turned to Lynn. "Go on, honey. Tell us what you did."

"Well." She looked around at the waiting faces. They were leaning forward in their chairs in anticipation. "I super glued Dan to a dining room chair." Mouths agape, they jerked back from the table. "Unfortunately, he was wearing shorts and it was the night of the season opener."

"Oh, my God. What did he do?" Jake's face paled.

"Well, he didn't make the game. When it didn't come off with acetone, our friend Art spent hours with a scalpel cutting the vinyl off his hairy legs. Dan was mad for about as long as it took the hair to grow back."

Jake stood, shoving back his chair. "Woman, I can't believe you'd do such a thing."

Clara jumped to her defense. "Jake, don't you fuss at her. The fool man deserved it."

"Man, I'm gonna watch my step around you, lady." Cookie muttered as he walked around filling coffee cups. "Guys, we may have to tiptoe around here from now on. I sure don't want her for an enemy. How about you?"

Mutterings of "No way," and "Hell no," echoed around the table.

As the talk continued, Seth sat and watched the interchange. He studied Lynn. Flushed from the teasing, she looked prettier than he'd ever seen her. Her face was void of makeup except for a touch of lipstick. He looked up to catch Chue watching him. Seth stood, pushing back his chair.

"Better get a move on and get this place cleaned up for worship service. We've just got thirty minutes."

* * *

That evening, Lynn stood at the pasture fence feeding sugar cubes to Beauty. Seth walked up, climbed the fence and sat on the top rail. He reached out to stroke the horse's mane, but she snorted and backed away from him.

"What's wrong with you, girl?" What would she do if Seth reached out to stroke her hair? Probably jump right out of her skin. It'd had been a long time since she'd been touched by a man. There weren't many men she'd even let try. Eyes on Seth's profile, she decided, oh yeah, she'd let this one.

"Chue said she didn't like men. You'd think that being treated well over a period of time would change her behavior."

"None of the wranglers can ride her, except Sally. Somebody, a man, must have hurt her and she's not very forgiving. Kinda like you in that respect."

She bristled. "Are you analyzing me, Doctor?"

"No, ma'am, just making a statement based on observation."

"Humph! Well, in my opinion that makes her a smart horse." She patted the mare's neck. "I'm surprised you've kept her."

"I didn't have the heart to sell her. She's happy here and she's produced some good-looking colts. You'd never believe it she's so ugly."

"She's not ugly! That's just like a man to base his opinion on what a woman looks like."

"Well, she's the ugliest horse I've ever seen, and I've seen my share."

"Don't listen to him, Beauty, he's just teasing."

He snorted. "I'll have you know I don't rate women on their looks. For your information many unattractive women have other attributes that make them beautiful."

She looked down to hide her grin. Hmmm, seems she'd gotten to him with that dig. Snorting, Seth added, "Might have known you'd call her some silly name like Beauty."

"I named her for her inner qualities." She couldn't restrain her giggle. Seth's laughter echoed across the flat land.

As the chuckles faded, they stood quietly, watching the horses. The colts ran, tossed their heads and kicked their heels, showing off for each other.

"Why doesn't Beauty have a colt now?"

"She didn't take to any of the studs this year, wouldn't let one mount her," he said matter-of-factly.

Flushing, Lynn turned her head and muttered under her breath, "That's what I get for asking." *Stuck your foot in that one, Lynn. That's all I need is a lecture on the mating practices of horses.*

"What'd you say?"

"Oh, I said, that's a shame. She's so gentle, I bet she's a good mother."

"She's got lots of breeding years left. Maybe next year."

Yeah, next year—I won't be here to see it. Maybe she was taking this being stubborn business a bit far. Letting her resentment against Art and Abby cloud her thinking.

Seth jumped down from the fence, tipped his hat up and to the back of his head, and stood facing her, his hands in his back pockets.

"I guess this is as good a time as any to bring up the subject."

"What subject?" Probably another assignment. Lord, she hoped it wasn't another long hike. The last one had almost killed her.

"Horseback riding. What do you think about it?"

Puzzled as to why he was asking, she replied, "I think it's great. I love to watch the kids."

"That's good. Actually though, I'm not talking about the kids, I mean how about you riding a horse?"

"Oh no," she said and expelled a weak laugh. "I've done enough around here to get laughed at. You're not putting me up on one of the horses so people can poke fun at me." Shaking her head, she added, "Anyway, I'm afraid of horses. I've already told Chue that."

"Surely you're not afraid of Beauty? She doesn't look like she'd hurt you."

"Well, she's a horse, isn't she? I just told you I'm afraid of horses."

"You're not afraid of Beauty. If you were, you wouldn't stand here at this fence stuffing her with sugar cubes and petting her."

"I just can't do it, Seth. I'm sorry, but I can't." She dropped her head to her arms folded over the rail.

"Why, Lynn? Were you hurt riding at one time?"

Anxiety choked her and unable to speak she shook her head.

She felt his hand on her shoulder and wanted to cry at the tenderness of this gentle man. "Talk to me, Lynn. Tell me what happened to make you so afraid."

She raised her head and stared out into the darkness. Voice hoarse, she began. "When I was ten years old I wanted to take riding lessons with my friend Jonnie Sue. So, my mother and I drove out to watch her one day. Something spooked the horse, and it threw her." If she lived to be a hundred, she'd never forget the scene as her dear friend flew through the air. It happened fast but when the scene replayed in her mind it was in slow motion, the people running, screaming, bending over the girl still and crumpled on the grass. Her mother, voice hysterical, buried Lynn's face against her bosom, saying "Don't look, baby, don't look."

Lynn shivered and wiped at her tears. Seth's hand covered hers, lacing their fingers together. When she looked up his face was filled with compassion and understanding.

Seth handed her a handkerchief and she wiped her

face and nose. "Was your friend hurt?"

"She had a broken collar bone and dislocated shoulder."

He nodded. "Hmm, pretty uncomfortable for a good while there, wasn't she?"

"Yes, she was trussed up like a chicken." Lynn and their friends had felt terrible for her so made sure she had plenty of company, candy, and reading material while recuperating.

"Did they ever find out what spooked her horse?"

She looked up at him. "Yeah, she'd dropped the blanket before putting on the saddle and a missed a goat head when cleaning it. It didn't hurt the horse until she leaned back in the saddle and it made contact."

"So, the accident was her fault?"

Lynn looked at him, shocked he'd say such a thing. "She was ten years old."

He shrugged. "Anyone who's old enough to get on a horse is responsible for the tack that goes on the animal. She was careless."

"That's unfair. She was just a kid." She yanked her hand out of his.

"Look, do you think Corby, who is seven by the way, would put something on his horse that would hurt him or the animal?"

She opened her mouth but he wouldn't let her talk. "No, he wouldn't because he's been taught properly and safety is reinforced every day. We don't let those kids on the horses until we've checked their tack for a full month and know we can trust them.

"Your friend didn't have a very good teacher or one who got careless one day."

What he said made sense but she didn't like it.

"How about your friend? Did she ever get on a horse again?"

She could tell where this questioning was leading. "Yes, about six months later."

"That's what I thought. And I bet you still wanted to take lessons too, didn't you?"

Lynn couldn't look at him. "No, I was too afraid."

He stood, arms folded across his wide chest. "Umm, hmm, I just bet you didn't. I bet the truth is your mother was terrified and wouldn't let you get on a horse if your life depended on it."

"No."

"Lynn, you know what's going on here, don't you? You're mother instilled her fear in you, kept you from doing something you wanted to do."

Her tears were forgotten. She turned on him hands fisted. "That's not true."

He reached for her arm but she jerked away. "I'm not saying your fear's not real, it is. But, it's been reinforced for years by your mother. You need to face that fear, get on a horse, and move past this."

She shook her head. "No, I just can't do it. Please, just drop it."

Losing patience, he yanked his hat off his head and slapped it against his leg. "I guess you just don't have near the spunk the crew thinks you have, Lynn." He threw his hands up. "Just forget I mentioned it. You can ride in the wagon or walk when we're on the trail drive." He shoved his hat back on his head, muttering as he walked away.

"What'd you say?" she yelled, hands fisted on her hips.

He stopped and turned. "I said you're a big

disappointment, Lynn, to me and to the kids. A poor example." With that he stalked off.

"Where do you get off saying that?" She demanded to his retreating back.

A poor example indeed! They didn't look up to her, did they? They knew what it was like to be afraid. Didn't fear make it okay not to try something? For the first time in over a month she felt that uneasiness in her stomach, an ache. Gasping for air, she worked to slow her breathing. *In through the nose...out through the mouth...*

Why should she care if she disappointed Seth? It was none of his business. He didn't have to right to make such demands on her. She shouldn't care what he thought. But she did. Sometime during the past month, she'd begun to. It was because she respected him though, not that attracted kind of caring.

What was that famous saying? "You have nothing to fear but fear itself." Franklin Delano Roosevelt said it in his first inaugural address and she'd heard it often enough. And said it a few times herself when trying to get a student to try something new. Anxiety was just another form of fear, fear of the unknown.

She remembered the young girl Jen on the diving board her first morning on the ranch. Fear...waiting...taking a deep breath...and then taking the plunge—rising from the water with a huge grin of triumph.

She gave the mare a long look. It might not be as quite as scary as she'd imagined to ride Beauty.

"Would you throw me, girl?" She rubbed the coarse hair on Beauty's head. "You wouldn't do that, would you?"

Walking on the trail drive didn't sound like fun. They would be out five days. No way would she walk for five days. Being cooped up in the wagon didn't sound good either.

She could at least try to learn to ride. What's the worst thing that could happen? A couple broken bones, a broken neck, death. But how would she feel if she didn't at least try? Like a failure.

* * *

The next morning at breakfast, Lynn greeted the youngsters and cowboys as she passed out biscuits. She glanced up to see Seth. Most days he was cordial and generous with his smile and greetings. Today he looked disgruntled and preoccupied, no "good morning," no smile, nothing but a curt nod. His gray eyes looked like lightening could strike at any minute.

Mad are you? Well, two can play at that game. She slapped his biscuits on his tray, crumbling one, and returned his curt nod.

When the line trickled to a halt, she walked among the diners to refill juice glasses. Servings were small to prevent waste but refills were encouraged. She stopped at Seth's table to refill his glass.

He waited while she poured and gave her a civil, "thank you."

When she didn't move away, he turned to look at her, eyebrow cocked.

"I guess I'll give it a try," she said. "What time do you want me down there?"

"Excuse me, what did you say?"

"You heard me the first time. Don't ask me to say it again. Once was enough."

"Ten o'clock will be fine. Wear your boots."

"Arrogant man," she muttered as she nodded and turned to leave.

"And Lynn, I'm glad you changed your mind."

Behind the mixing counter, her imagination conjured up a variety of accident scenarios. Oh Lordy, she'd gone and done it now. She'd be in a hospital by suppertime. They'd have to cover her with a tent to keep her from cooking while she lay in the corral, under the blazing sun, in severe pain until a helicopter airlifted her out. Chue would give her a shot of that horse medicine he was so proud of to ease the pain. More likely just to shut her up. She'd seen those needles. They were huge. Her heart started pounding. She focused on the jukebox and did her breathing exercise.

"Lynn, you okay?" Cookie was staring at her.

She grabbed a handful of flour and sprinkled it on the dough before her.

"You're looking kinda pale, about the color of that bread dough."

"Yeah, Cookie, I'm fine. Just woolgathering." Spreading some of the flour on the pastry board, she started working, folding and pressing, the large mound of yeast dough.

Get a grip, girl. You sound like the heroine in a melodrama. And why had she said that about Beauty. She wasn't ugly at all. *Forgive me, Beauty, for the insult.* It's my nerves talking. She lifted the mass of dough and dropped it into a fresh coat of flour. Dust flew up and around her, coating her lightly. She had to do this, not for Art and Abby, but for herself.

* * *

Seth watched Lynn stride down the road. When she

reached the corral, he opened the gate and they walked in together. He had postponed a meeting with the counselors to be here for her first lesson. It was important that this first one be a success. He'd see to it.

"We're going to take this slow and easy. Today, all you'll do is sit in the saddle while we lead Beauty around the corral. That way you can get used to the feel of her under you."

Lynn nodded but as yet hadn't said a word.

"Sally will be here, so don't worry about Beauty's skittishness around me and Chue."

Her fear was palpable, reminding him of Cookie's words this morning. "Boss, after talking to you, I thought she'd fall over in a dead faint."

Sally walked Beauty out of the barn already saddled. Seth gripped Lynn's elbow and steered her over to the horse. Sally handed him the reins and moved to the front of Beauty. He measured her arm length and adjusted the stirrups. The mare looked back and nudged Lynn affectionately. Lynn's lips tweaked at the corners. It wasn't a full out smile, but Seth hoped Beauty's gesture would ease Lynn's fear a fraction. Face pale under her hat; she looked like her knees could give out at any minute.

Chue stepped over and took Sally's position. Beauty raised her head and tried to jerk the reins from his hands, but he held firm and Sally soothed her with her voice.

"Lynn," said Seth. "We're gonna hold her steady while you step in that stirrup with your left foot and raise yourself up into the saddle." As Seth talked, he saw Chue's looks of concern. If Lynn fainted, Chue would be good to have around. He could deal with any type of emergency with animals, the men and the kids, but a woman would be a new experience for him. Like Cookie, Chue had developed a soft spot for Lynn.

"Now, don't pull yourself up by the saddle horn," Seth said. "Use your right foot to spring up. Kinda push yourself off the ground with it. Sally's going to demonstrate for you."

Sally used a saddle attached to a wooden horse made of tree trunks to demonstrate. The kids practiced with it before getting on their horses.

"Don't you have a block or something I can stand on?" Lynn bit her lip and shook her head. "I don't think I can lift myself up that high."

"Yes, you can. You're stronger than when you arrived last mouth. I wouldn't encourage this if I didn't think you were ready." Seth cleared his throat. "If need be, we'll give you a boost on the rear to help you up."

Her expression squelched the laugh that threatened to erupt from Seth's throat.

"I'm joking with you, Lynn." Actually, he would let her stand in his hand and toss her up, but he couldn't resist teasing her. It was effective in taking her mind off her fear. "Okay, let's give it a try."

Determination wrinkled her brow. Seth knew his comment was just what she needed to prod her to action. She'd get in that saddle by herself come hell or high water. No way would she let him give her a boost.

She took a deep breath, placed her left foot in the stirrup, grabbed the saddle horn, and threw herself into the side of the horse. Seth waited until her third unsuccessful try. Beauty whipped her head around to stare at her in reproach and snorted.

Lynn was near tears. "See, I can't do it. I might as

well quit." Pictures of Jonnie Sue lying unmoving in the grass and, her mother's shrieks of terror filled her mind.

Hands out as if warding off a beast, she backed away from the horse. "I'm through. I'll walk on the trail drive."

Seth grabbed her elbow and led her back to Beauty. Arm around her shoulders, he hugged her, alarmed at the trembling of her body. "You can, too, do it. Surely you're not going to give up that easily." He took her left hand and laid it against Beauty's neck. "Look at this girl. She's going to be disappointed if you don't get in this saddle today. You don't want to be the cause of her getting all dressed up and not getting to go for a ride?"

Lynn's lips trembled and she tried to grin but failed. Her distress made him feel guilty for his earlier teasing about giving her a boost on the rear end to get her in the saddle.

"Here, put your left foot in my hand and I'll lift you up." He didn't give her the chance to say no but moved around to her left and lifted her foot. "Grab the pommel." He tossed her up. She landed off balance and struggled to right herself. But, she'd done it. Seth released a sigh of relief.

"Good. Now, put your right foot in the stirrup. Do they feel the right length?"

She shrugged. "I don't know. How are they supposed to feel?"

He noticed her knee was slightly bent; just enough to give her some control but not cramp her legs.

"Just relax now. We're staying inside the corral. Chue will walk Beauty around. I'll walk beside you. Hold on to the saddle horn and sit up tall in the saddle. Beauty will do all of the work.

Then they began. Chue led Beauty at a slow walk. Seth continued to talk, but if Lynn heard what he said, she didn't comment, seemingly oblivious. Face wrinkled in concentration, her eyes flicked back and forth between Beauty's head and the saddle horn.

Seth reached out and touched her leg. "How're you doing?"

She murmured, "Fine," but nothing more. She looked like she could have a heart attack any minute.

"You're doing fine, Lynn. Try to relax. You're stiff as a board. Let your body move with the horse."

Sally caught his eye as she waited by the barn to see if she'd be needed. Beauty hadn't acted up for him or Chue so he gave her a wave to go on. Maybe the horse would tolerate them if they didn't try to ride her. It was interesting how Lynn and the horse had bonded. Both were prickly, had attitudes, and needed a friend. Animals could be a powerful healer for some people. Beauty had sensed Lynn's need and approached her. Lynn knew the mare was in a sense an outcast among the campers. Their friendship had given Lynn and outside interest and if things went like he wanted, it would put Beauty back with the working stock.

When Lynn began to relax and get the feel of the horse's movements, Seth took the reins from Chue and led the horse for a while longer. He smiled to himself. She'd be all right. It would just take time, and patience.

Chue would work with her some this evening. He was a stickler for learning about the tack and how to take care of it and your horse.

Seth stopped in front of the barn.

"I think you've had enough for today." He patted Beauty's neck. "You did just fine, Lynn. Let me help you down."

He took the reins and wrapped them loosely around the pommel.

Her face lit with a smile of relief. "I did, didn't I?"

He took her hand. "Here, hold on to the pommel to steady yourself, then kick both feet free of the stirrups. When you have your balance, throw your right leg over the horse's head. Don't kick her now. Then slide to the ground."

Stiff from tension, she managed, though ungracefully. Her legs were weak when she hit the ground. She wobbled unsteadily.

Seth grasped her hips to brace her. "Careful, now."

Lynn fell against him and grabbed him around the waist. She laid her head against his chest, knocking her hat off in the process, and squeezed him hard. As if of their own volition, his arms closed around her. He stroked her back to ease her trembling. For just a second, he let his head dip and his face touch her hair.

"I did it," she said in astonishment. "It wasn't so bad." With a shaky laugh, she added. "I guess it'll get easier each day."

Lynn released him. Speechless by her display and his response, he dropped his hands and stepped back. She felt damn good in his arms and his heart thundered his appreciation of just how good. In an effort to calm his response, he coughed and cleared his throat.

"Chue will work with you some after supper tonight. He'll want to show you how to saddle up and groom Beauty."

Lynn nodded, smiled and started walking away, her stride unsteady. She turned at the gate, waved, and called, "Thank you."

"My pleasure, ma'am," he said tipping his hat. His pleasure indeed.

* * *

That evening Chue took her into the storage room of the barn and explained the purpose of each piece of tack and how to care for it. Lynn tried to listen but found the talk boring. She didn't need to know all that.

"When can I ride again?"

The second time she interrupted his instructions, Chue growled.

"Pay attention now, gal. You don't ride unless you can take care of your tack. If I tell Seth you don't ride, you don't ride. Period. No questions and no arguments." He scowled at her. "Understand?"

Grudgingly, she nodded in agreement. "Okay. Okay. I'll pay attention, though I don't understand why I have to know all of this."

He sighed and shook his head. "Your horse is your most valuable possession on the range. If anything happens to your horse, you're afoot. Your horse can mean the difference between life and death. So, you take care of your horse before you see to your own needs."

Chue walked her around the room and showed her pieces of tack in need of repair. He looked at her often to make sure she was listening and quizzed her between glowers. His gnarled hands moved over the leather as he showed her places that needed to be softened up.

"This could rub a sore on the horse. No excuse for it happening if you check beforehand. None at all! Do you understand what I'm saying?"

Lynn nodded. He was saying take care of your animals or they won't be able to take care of you.

"Good, I'm glad because if you break one rule, you don't ride for a week." He threw his head back and puffed out his chest. "Don't think trying to sweet talk Seth will get you out of trouble when it comes to your horse."

She blushed to the roots of her hair and sputtered, "Why, I'd never—"

He grinned. "I'm just saying when it comes to these horses, I'm the boss. It's my way or you walk."

* * *

The day before they were to ride fence, as Seth brushed down Chester, he watched Lynn as she groomed Beauty. She used a curry brush and brushed away the dirt that clung to the horse's back. Talking to the mare, she combed her mane and tail and checked for stones in her hooves. He was pleased that she'd learned those lessons well.

Tomorrow, Lynn and Pete would go along to cook lunch. Normally they'd carry a sack lunch but Lynn needed experience cooking over an open fire before the trail drive. Pete would teach her all she needed to know.

But, Chue pulled him aside earlier. "Seth, she does everything I've taught her right except cinch and mount her horse like she's supposed to."

The news didn't sit well with him.

Seth was determined Lynn learn the lessons required to make her a competent horsewoman. He'd have to be the one to teach her.

He returned his gaze to Lynn and the horse. It wouldn't surprise him if Beauty didn't lift her hooves up to be cleaned so Lynn wouldn't have to reach down and pick them up. She'd probably hold her lips back for Lynn to brush her teeth.

He snorted. That dang horse was too cooperative for Lynn to learn the required skills. What would she do if something happened to Beauty and she had to ride another horse? Maybe that's the answer. Yes. That was it—another mount for Lynn.

Chapter Ten

Still dark, the early morning air felt damp and smelled fresh. The night's long needed rain had settled the dust and left puddles around the yard. Seth stood in the barn and scrutinized the group around him. All were in attendance except Lynn.

"You know why I have to do this. If she doesn't learn to saddle up and mount correctly, she'll be dependent on others while out on the range. She won't be able to go with us on the round up. No one," he made eye contact with each of them, "and I mean no one," he stared at Ben, "is to help her."

Seasoned hands, Chue and Jake understood his order, but the younger ones didn't. Mumbling, they filed out of the barn to prepare for the day's work on the range.

Seth watched from one of the stalls as Lynn entered the barn to locate her tack. She hadn't noticed Beauty was missing from the corral. Still watching, he followed to stand at the door. Bent over from the weight of her saddle, she sidestepped puddles of water and dropped it onto a sawhorse. Spotting Chue, she called out.

"Hey, Chue. Where's Beauty?"

Eyes never leaving the bridle in his hands, Chue stopped in front of her. "Rosebud is your mount today." With his head he motioned to the lone horse on the far side of the enclosure.

She glanced over at the mare hugging the corral fence, then back at Chue.

Seth watched the exchange out of the corner of his eye. Damn if she didn't look haughty standing there in her rope-cinched jeans and muddy boots, hat slammed down on that shiny auburn hair. He chuckled. If she didn't get some smaller jeans, she might lose those if a strong wind came up.

He walked outside the corral gate to help Ben load the packhorses. Lord, he hoped she was up to this challenge.

Her brow wrinkled. "How come? Is something wrong with her?"

"Naw, she's fine. The boss wants you to ride another horse, that's all."

She cocked her hip and folded her arms across her breasts. Her chin jutted. "But why? Why can't I ride Beauty if there's nothing wrong with her?"

"Ask the boss," he growled and turned away.

What's going on here? Lynn looked around the yard and located Seth loading supplies, things they'd need for lunch, on a packhorse. Ben helped while Jared and Jake hurried kids along. They grumbled about the early departure, with Tim complaining the loudest.

"It's not even morning yet," he groused.

Several of the younger children ran around, unable to stay still. Tim looked at them with disgust and muttered, "Stupid kids."

Lynn was glad to see Corby with the group. Zane would be going also. A good-looking boy, he had blond hair, blue eyes, and an angelic face. It could look almost demonic though, when abusing others. She worried about that boy.

Corby looked cute with his face still clouded with sleep. He'd combed his brown hair in such a hurry it still stood up in the back. His pony saddled and ready, he jumped from one foot to the other in excitement.

As she walked across the yard to Seth, her boots kept bogging down in the mud. Hard to believe it had rained at last. It must have been a good soaking downpour.

"Seth." Her voice echoed across the yard.

He stopped work and turned to wait for her. Freshly shaven and handsome as usual, he waited with one arm draped over the packhorse's neck and a hand tucked into his back pocket. Even Ben watched her approach, and it appeared Jake and Jared did also. Something wasn't right here.

She stopped in front of him, irritated that his aftershave tickled her nostrils, reminding her of their dance together. On top of that, his smile made her stomach flip.

"Why can't I ride Beauty today? Chue wouldn't tell me anything. Said to ask you." She stood with her hands planted on her hips. "What's going on here?"

"I'm putting you on another horse, Lynn. I need to see if you can follow through on what you've learned." His eyes never left hers as he delivered his reason. "You have to be able to handle any horse I put you on. We can't play nursemaid to you on the range. You've got to be able to take care of yourself."

Lynn stood without speaking. She looked around. All eyes watched her waiting to see what she'd do. Heat suffused her face making her ears burn. She felt like she'd been slapped. Nursemaid indeed, she'd show him and all the others what she could do.

Seth watched her, his face serious, and then turned back to his work. Lifting her chin a trifle, she spun and stalked off. A sweet horse, Rosebud shouldn't be any trouble. *All right, Seth. If this is a test, I'm going to pass it with flying colors.*

Stopping at the sawhorse, she picked up her bridle and walked into the corral. Everyone in the yard watched as she approached the horse. Except Seth, that is. He'd turned his back on her before she could walk away.

Rosebud didn't shy away when she reached out to stroke her neck, slip the bit into her mouth, and put the bridle over her head. Taking hold of the bridle, she walked the horse over to the side of the corral near her tack. When she looked at the others, they immediately went back to what they were doing.

No problem, you arrogant tyrant, I'll show you. She smoothed the blanket over the horse's back, remembering to check for wrinkles. There should have been laughter and talk around her, but the only sounds were the stamping of horses hooves, snorts, and the creak of leather. Even the kids felt the tension in the air. Her back felt like a pincushion with all the eyes trained on it. It took all her strength to toss the saddle onto Rosebud's back, but she managed. She tightened the cinch, noting that rosebud's chest and belly were fatter than Beauty's, and adjusted the stirrups. She led Rosebud out of the corral, her boots sucking at the muck as she walked, and tied on her small bundle of supplies.

"Let's mount up," shouted Seth.

Sam ran around the yard whining.

"Stay, Sam," ordered Seth. The dog immediately laid down and put his nose on his paws with a desolate look on his face.

Lynn grabbed the saddle horn and put her foot into the left stirrup. Rosebud took several side steps making it impossible to get her a firm foothold in the stirrup.

"Whoa, girl," she said and tried again.

The mare moved. Foot caught in the stirrup, she was pulled off her feet. She landed on her butt in the mud.

Guffaws and titters of laughter erupted all around her. Face burning from mortification, tears clouded her vision. Embarrassed beyond words, she wanted to crawl in a hole and hide. Her lips trembled, but she bit the bottom one, hard, to keep from crying. She took deep breaths to control the trembling in her chest.

Walking his horse over, Seth grabbed her reins. She scrambled to her feet as Seth tossed them to her. His gray eyes looked like thunderclouds.

"Remember what Chue tried to teach you, Lynn. If you haven't caught up with us in an hour, we'll know you didn't make it."

He turned his horse and led the group out of the yard.

"I will not cry, I will not cry," she moaned as she watched the group file out of the yard. "I'm going to do this come hell or high water."

She laid her head against Rosebud's neck. She'd come too far to fail now. She'd overcome her fear and learned to ride a horse by God, and she wasn't about to give up.

When Seth tossed her the reins, his gray eyes had mirrored disappointment. For some reason, that look had hurt. Hurt more than the laughter from the others. She hated to admit it, but she wanted him to be proud of her.

What am I not remembering? Something Chue fussed about all the time. The reins, it had to do with the reins. Hold the reins in your left hand while you grip the pommel. She'd finally remembered. Thirty minutes and almost as many tries later, she had mounted the mare and started out of the yard. With a grin of triumph, she prodded Rosebud into a trot.

Lynn hadn't gone far when the saddle shifted. It slid to the side of the mare depositing her in a puddle of mud and water. She landed on her side and rolled, coming to a stop face down in the muck.

* * *

Seth had trouble listening to Tim's chatter as they rode side-by-side. And that bothered him. Tim's behavior continued to improve. He still lost his temper but hadn't been in a fight or instigated any problems among the other teens.

He tried to listen but right now all he could think about was Lynn. If that saddle slipped and she got hurt, he'd never forgive himself. It had taken every ounce of his will power to keep from helping her this morning. God, he hoped she'd make it. For some reason, it mattered. It mattered a great deal.

Glancing at his watch again, Seth twisted in the saddle and scanned the trail behind them. It'd almost been an hour. She wasn't going to make it. Disappointment flooded him.

Ten minutes later, Corby shouted.

"She made it. Lynn made it. Here she comes."

Thank you, God. The tension drained from his body. It took all the self-control he could muster to not turn. She must be okay, or she wouldn't be here. But he needed to see for himself.

Zane's taunting remarks cut through the air.

"Look at Lynn." His laugh was loud and spiteful.

"She's covered in mud. You look like a mud pie, Lynn."

His remarks stopped at the rumble of Ben's voice.

Ben rode with Zane to keep him in line, but it just occurred to Seth that Tim might be more effective in curbing the younger boy's behavior. They shared similar experiences. Divorced parents, abuse by the father, and being raised by a mother who had difficulty dealing with a hurt child turned aggressive.

He cleared his throat. "Tim, I have a job for you that I hope you'll accept."

Tim sat up straighter. "I'd be glad to do anything, Seth. What do you need?"

"Zane's aggressive behavior hasn't improved since he's been here. He needs someone to take him under their wing, give him some extra attention, and show him the proper way to act out his aggressions," explained Seth.

Looking doubtful, Tim said, "I don't know if I'd be any help. Why not Ben or Jared?"

"Because they'll not be able to relate to him as well as you can. You're younger, closer to his age, and have had similar experiences. He's more likely to listen to you."

Seth waited to let Tim think. "Oh, he listens and obeys Ben and the others, but that's because he figures he has to. He probably thinks we'll knock him around. But he'll listen to you because he admires you. He sees you as an older version of himself, the trouble maker or bad boy."

Tim blushed and focused his attention back to the trail.

Seth hadn't intended to embarrass him.

"We all make mistakes, son. Some worse than others, but it's how we correct them that's important. You remember that."

They rode in silence, Tim deep in thought. After some time, he turned to Seth.

"I'll give it a try, Seth. I can't promise anything, but I'll do my best."

"That's all a man can ask, Tim." Seth reached over and clapped him on the back. "You need any help, just let me know."

"Yes, sir. I will." Tim relaxed in the saddle, then turned his horse and rode back to join Ben and Zane.

Tim's hunger for approval tore at Seth's heart. It was important that Tim leave at the end of the summer with a better self-esteem and with a feeling of pride in his accomplishments. Maybe they were on the right path.

Lynn had been a big help. The time she'd spent dancing with him proved he was a likeable person. But his apology to Julie and her acceptance was the most healing for him. A big step for Tim, it took a load off the boy's heart. Tim didn't like his behavior. As a matter of fact, he probably hated it, but he didn't know how to go about changing it.

At the base of the Christmas Mountains, they stopped. "Let's set up camp here." Seth stood for a minute and looked out at the mountains. They towered above them and looked like a line of dinosaurs with humpy backs. It had always been one of his favorite places on the ranch.

He helped the kids tether their horses, loosen their tack, and fold the stirrups up over their saddles. Ben and Jake led the kids out to search for firewood. Lynn and Pete unloaded the packhorses and set out utensils.

Seth stooped to start a fire in the rocked off circle and got his first glimpse of Lynn since she'd joined them.

"Good, Lord. What happened to you?" Her clothes, hair and part of her face were caked with mud and Lord knows what else. She'd probably never forgive him for embarrassing her in front of the others. But, it couldn't be helped. And, she was secure enough now to deal with their laughter and teasing.

She gave him a frosty stare that said, *You laugh at me and you'll die.* "Just exactly what you intended to happen, so don't act surprised."

The glare she shot him was more comical than her appearance. He restrained the laughter that threatened to erupt and shook his head as he looked at her dirty clothes.

"Really, Lynn, I hoped you wouldn't slide off, that maybe Chue and I were wrong about the way you saddled up. It wasn't my intention to humiliate you."

She stood up and searched for a clean spot on her body to dust her hands on, the only place being her butt. "Well, you weren't wrong. It was my own fault. I won't forget again."

He took her arm and studied her closely. "Are you hurt?" He wanted to run his hands over her just to make sure, but he figured she'd probably clout him.

"Nothing but my pride." Then she chuckled. "Actually, the mud was pretty cushy."

"Are you sure? I need to know if you're hurting anywhere."

"I may be sore tomorrow, but I'm fine, Seth."

Seth sighed with relief, grateful that she was all

right. His mind had played out a number of scenarios. What if Rosebud got spooked or came up lame? Lynn didn't have enough experience to handle a situation like that. "I'm glad you're all right and that you made it."

Seth, Jake, and Ben took the kids to ride fence. "Pete, what's riding fence?"

"It means you ride along the fence line looking for breaks. Sometimes the posts need replacing, or maybe the wire's just loose. In that case you might need to hammer in another staple to attach it."

Sounded like hard backbreaking work to Lynn. But, it would be fun for the kids and they'd be back tired and hungry.

Pete tossed Lynn a clean shirt, jeans, and a bar of soap. "Here, take these and go clean up. Can't have you around the food smelling like that."

"Oh Pete, I think I love you."

She started to hug him, but he stepped back and held his hands up to ward her off. "Go on now. You're gonna make the food turn bad just standing near it."

Grabbing a kitchen towel to dry off with she gingerly carried her supplies to the base of the mountain to look for water. She was in luck. From the rain the night before, water trickled down and collected in a rocky area that formed a small pool.

She washed her hair and face as best she could. Without a comb, her fingers would have to do for smoothing her hair. Pete's jeans were more than a mite snug, as was the shirt, but they were clean. Her dirty clothes rolled into a ball, she carried them back to camp.

Lynn and Pete busied themselves preparing lunch. The others wouldn't be back until noon, so they had several hours.

Pete hung the largest of the cast iron Dutch ovens on the tri-pod around the fire and poured in oil to sauté the meat and onions. Then they added the vegetables, tomatoes, water, and seasoning and brought the mixture to a low boil. Covered with the heavy lid, they left the stew to simmer.

Using a pastry board balanced on a flat rock, Lynn rolled out piecrust for apple pie. She was anxious to see how they'd be able to brown the top crust over an open fire. When finished, she set it aside.

It wasn't time to start the biscuits, so she unsaddled Rosebud and wiped at the mud with her dirty shirt. "Hey, Pete. You don't happen to have something I could use to clean Rosebud, do you?"

Pete dug around in his saddlebag and came up with a curry brush. He tossed to Lynn. "Here ya go."

The tall, lanky cowboy seemed to be prepared for anything. The mud was dry, so most of it brushed away. She returned Pete's brush and washed her hands.

Since she'd pre-measured the dry ingredients for the biscuits, including dry milk, all she had to do was cut in the shortening, which she did with her hands, and add water. Before she rolled out the dough, the pie needed to start cooking.

Pete stirred the fire to make it hotter, so she could suspend the pie over its heat. With a small shovel, he arranged hot coals on the lid of the Dutch oven. "Let the lid heat up some before you can put it on." He handed her the metal forked tool used to lift the lid.

"So that's how it browns on both sides."

Pete chuckled. "You got it. Now, let's see what kind of biscuits you can produce out here."

The ovens for the biscuits were heated in the same way but Pete melted fat, and they turned each piece of dough before adding the lids.

By noon, when the others arrived, they were ready to eat.

The stew and biscuits vanished in a hurry. Fresh air and hard work whetted appetites. Lynn surveyed her empty plate. The meal was loaded with fat. At the dining hall, the food was hardy, but Cookie made sure they had fruits and vegetables. How could she eat like this and not gain weight?

"Great meal. You two make a good team." Seth glanced from Pete to Lynn and nodded.

"Pete taught me how to bake over an open fire."

"She's a quick study, Boss. She can cook on the range with me any day." He tried to look serious. "I bet her morning mud bath will be her last, too." He gave Lynn a friendly shove on the arm.

The others hooted with laughter. She tried to keep a straight face, gave up, and joined in. The day had been wonderful. She hadn't felt this happy in a long time. She'd met today's challenge and been successful, figured out what she was doing wrong and rode Rosebud to catch up with the others. What a feeling of freedom, the wind blowing at her body and making the muddy shirt stick to her skin. Ha! She didn't care. It was still great. And being a part of this group. That was the best feeling in the world.

Jake winked at her. "You're a good sport, Lynn. But I have to admit, I'd loved to have seen you when that saddle slipped this morning."

The rest chorused their, "Me too."

Seth, Jake, and Ben helped clean the empty ovens

with salt and aluminum foil brought along for that purpose.

As they worked, Seth mentioned Rosebud. "Chue would be proud of the way you cleaned her up out here." He was damn pleased himself.

Surprised at his comment, Lynn said. "I couldn't let her suffer because I'd been stupid, could I?"

"No, but you'd be surprised how some people would've thought only about themselves, not about the horse."

She nodded and went back to scrubbing. "I found a small basin of water up near the rocks. We could take these up there to wash them."

"It'll be easier to clean them back at the ranch. Let's load 'em up."

They doused the fire, collected the trash, and wiped clean as many remains of their visit as possible. As they rode out, Lynn brought up the tail end. Seth fell back to ride beside her. She felt more at ease with him than she had before as they talked about the upcoming roundup that would take them out for five days. She looked forward to it, as Cookie would go with them. They'd prepare three meals a day with supplies from the chuck wagon.

"How do you like Rosebud?" Seth asked, breaking into her thoughts.

"She's fine. Not as good as Beauty, but she'll do."

"Glad to hear it. On the trail drive, each person takes two mounts. Not that you'll need them since you'll stay in camp, but that's the way it's always been done."

It was late afternoon when they arrived at the ranch.

As Lynn left the barn, Seth waved. "See you at dinner." She smiled and waved back.

He turned back to Corby and Zane to check their progress.

"Hurry it up, you two. Aren't you ready for a shower?"

Corby looked at him with sorrowful eyes. "Ah, Seth. Do we have to take a shower?"

"You sure do." He ruffled each boy's hair. "You stink."

Seth was pleased with Zane's behavior. Though he'd been reprimanded several times, it was an improvement overall. He was wary of Tim's attention, but as the day wore on, he'd relaxed and responded to the older boy's encouragement.

He marveled at Lynn's ability to adapt to the ranch activities and work. It was as though she'd been born to it. Except for the riding, of course. But, she'd met that challenge head-on and succeeded. He chuckled at the memory of her covered with mud. She no longer resembled the haughty woman who'd arrived in late May. He liked this one a lot better. Maybe he liked her too much.

* * *

In the dining hall that evening, Lynn suffered under Seth and Jake's teasing about her morning mud bath. Brian and Jared hadn't heard the story, so Jake entertained them with the account. She took their ribbing in stride.

"You know, some women pay good money for a mud bath. I got mine free."

Jake nudged Seth. "Maybe you should add *mud bath* to that tab you're keeping on Lynn. Let's see, there's the door, wonder how much those spas charge for a—"

Brian patted his pocket and interrupted. "Almost forgot, Dad. This letter came for you this morning."

"Thanks, son." He took the letter, turned it over, and examined the return address before tearing it open. As he read, the joking was forgotten. Damn. Disappointment engulfed him. He refolded the sheets of paper and put them back in the envelope, then turned to Lynn.

She returned his stare, concern etched in her wrinkled brow.

Well, this was what she'd been wanting since the day she arrived. He couldn't control the icy tone of his voice. His anger wasn't called for, but he couldn't seem to keep it from lacing his words. "It seems, Mrs. Devry we have a replacement for you. You can leave us at last." He stood, and stuffed the note in his shirt pocket.

"As a matter of fact, you can leave as soon as you're packed."

He turned to Brian. "Be ready at eight in the morning to take Mrs. Devry into town." He stood shoving his chair under the table. He stared at Lynn, trying hard to control the anger he knew his eyes reflected. Her hazel eyes never left his face, a stunned expression on hers. Was she shocked at his announcement, or his anger? The deed was done, so it didn't matter anymore. Their new bread cook would leave Odessa in the morning.

He waited for some kind of response from her. Anything, "hooray" or "at last!" Or, "I really don't want to go, Seth." But didn't get one. All eyes were on them. No one spoke. They just looked from one of them to the other. He spun on his heel and stalked out of the dining hall.

* * *

Sprinkled with stars, the sky was pitch black, the full moon hidden behind a cloud filled with rain. Chances were slim that its moisture would reach the ground in this part of Texas, but maybe somewhere in Mexico. The earth beneath the dry, packed top layer was still moist from the previous night's rain. It was quiet. The only sounds were the haunting tones of nature in the desert—the soft hum of cicadas, the rustle of ground squirrels searching for food, the occasional hoot of an owl, the sharp cry of a rabbit as the owl's talons dug into its flesh. A horse snorted and stamped its hoof. She could hear the whoosh of a horse's tail as it swished through the air. A whiff of creosote reached her and blended with the smell of earth and manure. Lynn leaned against the fence rail and gazed at the dark shapes before her.

It was two o'clock in the morning, and she couldn't sleep. She'd left the dining hall and packed, feeling neither excitement nor relief. When the shock of being ordered to leave wore off, she'd spent five minutes rejoicing and dancing around the room.

Then reality hit. No longer would she rise at four a.m. for her shift in the dining hall. Duck wouldn't be harassing her about her laps, and she'd miss giving him a hard time. No more hen sessions with Maria and Clara or long hikes with the kids. She should be jumping with joy.

But, she wasn't. It galled her to admit it, but she liked her job and didn't mind the time she spent with the kids. She'd miss them and the camaraderie of the ranch staff. The ranch and its inhabitants had been good for her. Her toned and slimmer body testified to that.

Of more importance was her feeling of empowerment. The pride she felt in her stronger body and abilities. She'd overcome her fear and learned to saddle and ride a horse, by God. The fun-filled weeks she'd spent without depression, anxiety attacks, or migraines were a testament to the benefits of hard work and exercise. Well, she'd come close to having an anxiety attack a time or two, but she hadn't.

Leaving Sam would break her heart. She loved that dog. Never before had she become this attached to an animal. And Beauty… She'd regret not being able to ride her every day. Every day? More like, ever again.

The thought of not seeing Seth again caused an ache deep inside and she stifled the urge to cry. She had replayed last night's scene in the cafeteria over and over again. Why had he been so angry? He'd never given her reason to believe their relationship could be anything but friendship. Yet she knew he was proud of her progress, and he liked her. And, she liked him, respected and admired him.

After her initial joy at going home, she'd turned morose, and ways to tell Seth she wanted to stay ran through her mind. Three times she'd made the decision to leave, only to change her mind again. Maybe by eight in the morning she'd know what she wanted to do.

Did she have a choice? Would Seth let her stay if she asked?

A large shadow made its way toward the fence. Beauty, tossed her head as she offered a soft nicker in greeting. Lynn chuckled when the horse nuzzled her shirt pocket looking for a treat.

"Sorry, girl, I don't have anything tonight."

A lump formed in her throat as she stroked Beauty's head. "How am I going to be able to leave you, girl?" Her voice cracked as she laid her head against the horse's neck.

"You've become such a good friend, you and Sam. I've never had friends like you before, and it's been so...healing." *And, I've never had a friend like Seth before, either.* Oh, that wasn't true. She had Art, but her feelings for Seth were different. They were emotions she had no business having.

* * *

Seth had tried to sleep, but tossed and turned and cursed. His bed was a disaster, the sheets strewn all over the floor. He checked the time on his watch. Damn, it was almost one a.m. His stomach growled reminding him of his dramatic departure from the dining hall and his uneaten tray of food.

Remembering his out-of-character behavior, he cursed again and pounded his pillow into a submissive lump. Odds-on he'd given the staff enough gossip fodder to entertain them for the remainder of the summer. He slung his pillow against the wall. It landed with a plop.

"Might as well get up," he muttered. He sat on the side of the bed. Elbows on his knees, he dropped his head in his hands and moaned. *What the hell is wrong with me?* Stepping into jeans and then his boots without taking the time to put on socks, he drew on a shirt, leaving the buttons undone. He headed for the door, zipping his jeans as he headed out.

Sam, always ready for a stroll, was at his heels. He eased the French door shut to not wake the boys. That's all he needed, questions on why he couldn't sleep.

They walked toward the corrals. The moon slipped in and out of scattered clouds leaving enough light to maneuver by. Ahead, across from the cabins, dim outdoor lights glowed from the dining hall porch. On occasion, a couple of older kids tried to raid the refrigerator. Not that the light deterred them much, but it made identifying the culprits easier. His stomach rumbled again. If he thought he could eat, he might try it himself.

As they reached the cabins, he stopped in front of Lynn's. Behind the curtains, a faint glow squeezed through to torment him. He should walk on, but waited, hoping to see movement behind the curtains. There was none. She'd probably fallen asleep with the light on. He kicked a rock and moved on. One thing was for certain, she wasn't having difficulty leaving, or she'd have come to see him, ask him if she could stay. Or told him she planned to stay whether he liked it or not. Why the hell was he having such a difficult time letting her go?

Sam saw her first. Seth stepped into the shadows of the barn. She stood on a rail of the pasture fence with her face against Beauty's neck. Though dark, he could see she wore those baggy jeans. Her hair glowed in the filtered moonlight.

What was she doing out here? He heard her voice. His throat tightened. She was saying good-bye to Beauty. He shook his head. She was good with animals. They responded to her voice and touch. Beauty trusted her and now showed signs of beginning to trust him and Chue.

With Sam, it was love at first sight. In fact, some days he felt Sam cared more for her than him. He stayed at her heels all day long. But, he always showed up at dinnertime and slept in Seth's room. Sam wanted to run to her now. His body quivered with excitement. Seth stilled him with his hand. "Quiet, Sam. Stay."

He observed from the shadows, an ache in his chest adding to his frustration. The woman had been as irritating as a grass burr when she arrived. Now she was like a balm. He liked having her around, seeing her with the kids and hearing her laugh. But she was returning to Fort Worth. She'd be missed. Dammit, he'd miss her. That's what galled him.

At the sound of her teary laugh, Sam whined quietly. Seth let him go.

The horse whinnied and butted her in the chest. At the sound of Sam's "woof," she jerked around. He bounded up and wiggled with happiness. She dropped to her knees and hugged him, giving his ears a good scratch.

Seth remained in the shadows. Watching. He could hear her voice, but not the words. It was evident she wasn't happy. Why the hell not? He'd like to know. Wasn't this what she'd been wanting from the minute she arrived? He damn well hoped she felt half as bad as he did. He was miserable and sure as hell didn't know why. Ah, hell, he did too, and his need for her company scared him to death.

Her body tensed. She must have realized Sam wouldn't be out alone. She stood. Her eyes searched the shadows of the barn.

He waited for her to locate him. She froze, like a doe caught in a spotlight.

Stepping from the shadows, hands in his back pockets, he stood. And waited. Their eyes locked and held for an eternity. He had nothing to say to her, but he'd listen to anything she had to say. And he sure as hell wouldn't beg her to stay.

Sam bumped against Lynn's leg, breaking her trance. She started walking toward him.

Seth waited, body taut and alert. The short distance seemed immense. Unable to remain rooted in place, he moved, shortening the distance between them. They stopped a yard from each other.

Her eyes traveled his face. He didn't try to hide his anger. Like a tight rubber band, he was ready to snap. He stood rigid, hands fisted at his side and looked at her. She twisted her hands and took a step back. His heart lurched. Surely she didn't fear him. He struggled to relax his features, but he wouldn't make this easy for her. He waited.

Though dark, he could see her eyes were swollen from crying. Why? She'd gotten what she wanted, the opportunity to get away from the ranch. Her replacement was on his way.

She started to speak but her voice cracked. Her features contorted. Tears glistened in the moonlight as they ran down her cheeks. The discomfort in his chest deepened. He wanted to massage the muscles around his heart. It took every ounce of his will power to remain still.

She tried again, but only managed, "I don...want..."

He shook his head not understanding.

She covered her face with her hands and cursed in frustration. The next thing he knew, she'd knocked him off balance. When he righted himself, her arms were locked around his neck.

He clasped her close and breathed in her clean scent. His heart thundered. *What the hell am I doing?* Bending his head to hers, his breath rustled the hair over her ear.

"What are you trying to say, Lynn?" His voice, hoarse with emotion, sounded foreign to his ears.

She shuddered, drew in a deep breath and cried, "I don't...want...to leave, Seth. Please. Let me stay."

She trembled, head tucked under his chin, waiting for his reply. Her grip on his neck was like a vise.

Seth exhaled, aware of the intense relief that swept through him. He should let go of her, step back, and distance himself. But that pang around his heart wouldn't let him. He pulled her closer with one arm, the other slid down her back to mold her body to fit his own, hip to hip, heart to heart. The nagging ache diminished. This woman felt so right in his arms—like a missing part of him had been found.

"Thank God, Lynn. I don't want you to go."

He stroked her hair, intrigued by its texture. It was silky with a will of its own. He captured a tendril, rubbed it between his fingers before it escaped to rejoin the auburn masses. Turning his face, he enjoyed its feel against his skin, his scratchy jaw a strong contrast to the smoothness of hers. He'd only meant to touch her hair and savor her fragrance once more before releasing her. Unable to resist, his lips stroked her skin.

Lynn sighed in relief at his words. She could stay. When she'd thrown herself in his arms, she hadn't intended to initiate this embrace. But she wasn't about to turn it down. It felt right to be in Seth's embrace, and she couldn't move if her life depended on it. She froze when his hand moved in her hair, eliciting sensations she'd not imagined or at most, had forgotten. Who knew having her hair touched could be so sensual? When his lips touched her cheek, goose bumps rose on her flesh. She shivered and lifted her face in anticipation.

Their eyes met and held, surprised and searching. His head descended and, his lips placed a gentle kiss on hers. So soft, it was more a whisper than a kiss, like the brush of a butterfly's wing. He teased each corner of her mouth, her bottom lip and moved on to her neck. With a moan of frustration, she grabbed his face with both hands.

"Are you going to kiss me or not?"

Voice thick with desire, he chuckled. "Greedy, are we?"

She flushed at her boldness and raised her chin.

Seth cupped her jaw and looked into her eyes. "Oh yeah. I'm going to kiss you all right."

His head dipped, his tongue traced the outline of her mouth, his teeth nipped at her lower lip. He took his time and she was ready to scream with frustration.

Just when she was ready to shove him away his mouth seized hers. This time Seth didn't tease. His hand captured her head and turned it up to his liking. Then his mouth played upon hers like a bow on a finely tuned violin. Her knees sagged. Lordy, this man knew his kissing.

Too soon the kiss ended. He released her and stepped back, hands at her elbows, an odd expression on his face.

Oh, no. I hope he doesn't think I'm chasing him. She hadn't planned the kiss. Of course, she had thrown herself into his embrace. But his arms had enfolded her, and his lips had traveled from her cheek and hair to her lips.

Sam jumped and planted his forepaws in the middle of Seth's back. He stumbled forward, taking Lynn with him. He righted them before they fell.

They broke apart laughing. Seth put his arm around Lynn's shoulders and led her in the direction of the cabins. With her arm around his waist, their hips bumped as they walked. Lynn relished the physical closeness, and he seemed as reluctant to break the contact as she did.

Chapter Eleven

Lynn woke to the sound of activity on the roadway outside. The familiar sounds of kids laughing and talking soothed her as much this morning as they annoyed her that first day. She'd come a long way from the grumpy woman who'd arrived at the ranch. What would Abby and Art think if they could see her now?

Stretching, a smile on her face, she replayed in her mind last night's kiss. It was by far the best kiss she'd had in ages. After the divorce, she'd dated, but there'd been no emotional link when they kissed, just the mechanics. There'd definitely been an emotional link between her and Seth last night. The barest touch of his lips…

She glanced at the clock. Eight o'clock! She shot to a sitting position. What was she doing sleeping this late?

Thank goodness it was Sunday. Yawning, she bounded out of bed, grabbed clothes from her suitcase, and headed for the bathroom. She'd have to hurry as Cookie stopped serving at nine o'clock. Bible study started at nine thirty on the dot.

In the dining hall, when she sat down between Jake and Sally, Jake slung his arm around her shoulders and squeezed.

"Glad you decided to stay, Lynn. It might have been boring around here without you." He winked.

A chorus of voices echoed his sentiments.

Lynn felt her throat tighten. These people cared about her. They'd become friends in a short period of time.

"You gotten revenge on anyone lately we don't

know about?" Jake asked.

"Don't worry, Jake." She arched one eyebrow. "You'll be one of the first to know if I do." She unwound her cinnamon roll, broke off a piece and popped it into her mouth.

"Don't know if I like the sound of that," muttered Jake. "Do I have a need to worry?"

"Only you can know that." As she looked at Jake, she noticed Seth at the counter filling his tray. She turned back to Jake and prodded him with her finger. "Feeling guilty about anything?"

He shrugged his big shoulders. Everyone at the table waited for his answer. "Not anything I know about."

Everyone looked at him, waiting, as if he'd confess to murder at any minute now. Chue's stare didn't waver.

Jake glared at Chue. "I did not lock you in the tack room yesterday, old man. It must've been one of the kids."

Chue snorted. "Well, when you catch those rascals, thank them for me. Best nap I've had in weeks."

Laughter erupted up and down the table. Jake blushed but didn't say a thing.

Seth joined them with a smile and a good morning. He grabbed a chair from another table then nudged Jake so he'd move down to make room beside Lynn. Jake grumbled and looked at him in question but moved.

Their eyes met for a brief moment. They nodded, but didn't speak. Lynn relaxed, disappointed yet relieved. Last night's experience was too new, and she didn't know how to interpret their kiss, or if their relationship would grow. Until she knew the boundaries, she didn't want her feelings exposed. And maybe not even then. Loving someone involved risks; it required trusting another person, and giving up long harbored fears. One opened themselves up to be hurt again. At least she felt comfortable around him and for now that would be enough.

Cookie looked at Seth. His brow wrinkled with concern. "You're mighty late this morning, Boss. It's odd for you to be the last at the table. Not sick are you?"

Seth glanced at Lynn then returned his attention to his plate. "Nope, feel fine. Guess I just needed the extra sleep."

Lynn figured they probably wondered what had transpired between them. When had they talked and she'd decided to stay? Just the fact that the issue wasn't out in the open embarrassed her. Lynn tried to remain calm, hoping they knew nothing more than what Brian told them earlier, that she'd be staying. Evidently Seth had left a note for the boys before going back to bed.

Thankfully, Clara and Pete started a discussion, more like an argument, on how to make hot water cornbread, both insisting their mother's recipe was the best.

Lynn was relieved they'd changed the subject. She'd worried that seeing Seth this morning would be awkward, but it wasn't. The only hint he'd given that their relationship might be different was making Jake move over. It didn't mean their relationship would deepen and grow. They'd shared a kiss. Okay, a darn passionate one. It had curled her toes as none other had, but that didn't mean happily ever after. And from what she's been told, he still cared for his wife. That alone gave her reason to be careful.

"By the way, Lynn." He drained his coffee cup. "What did you do with all that horse manure you collected in the corral the morning after the dance?"

She took another bite of her cinnamon roll, and licked the sugar from her fingers.

"Well, I needed to teach Art a lesson, so—" Taking a drink of her juice, she continued. "He loves plants. So I mixed the manure with muddy clay and a little grass and shaped the concoction into a pot."

Noticing the look of distaste on their faces, she quickly added. "Oh, I had on rubber gloves at the time."

"Whew," and "Thank goodness," rumbled up and down the table.

"Well, that's a relief," added Cookie, shaking his head.

"Anyway, then I left it out on the back porch to bake in the hot sun for several days. It's on its way to Fort Worth right now. I called one the nurses at Art's office and asked her to pick up a plant and some Spanish moss to keep the plant moist and have it waiting for Art when he gets back from Europe. And, to let him know that I'd sent the gift."

To their repulsed expressions, she replied. "Look, in all honesty, it's quite attractive. Not to brag, but I'm rather artistic and good at modeling with clay. It looks as good as something you'd buy."

She swatted at a fly that had decided it liked her perfume. "The only problem is that it'll smell every time the plant gets watered. And thinking I've forgiven him, Art will be so grateful for the gift, he won't dare throw it out."

Finishing off her coffee, she looked around the

table as everyone stared at her without speaking. "What's wrong? It's not like you guys aren't always playing jokes on each other."

Mutters of "yeah, we do," and "remember that time," echoed around the table.

"Yeah, but that was downright mean," Jake muttered.

Seth added, "Some of yours have gone a bit far, too, Jake. You don't have any room to talk."

"Art deserved it," said Lynn. Yeah, Lynn thought, Art deserved it but the revenge wasn't as sweet as it would have been a month ago. Things were different now. She'd changed. Oh, she was still mad, but for the first time, she could admit Abby and Art had been on the right track. This place was good for her, as were the people.

Cookie pushed his chair back. "Let's get a move on. It's almost nine thirty and the kids will be piling in here for Bible study."

Lynn helped clear the table. "Hey, guys, are we going riding after services?"

"You bet," said Ben. "The kids would riot if we didn't."

At the corral, activity grew hectic, as kids got ready for their morning ride. Lynn saddled Beauty. Rosebud nickered from the pasture, so Lynn walked over to greet the mare with a sugar cube.

Though hot, a slight breeze cooled her skin as perspiration evaporated. Once upon a time she'd have been mortified to admit that she could sweat. All southern women knew they didn't sweat—they glowed. Now, she appreciated its purpose as the wind across the moisture cooled her skin.

She rode in front of the group, as far ahead as she could. Usually she rode at the rear. Today she wanted to enjoy the landscape without the distracting chatter of the kids. Seth might not like it, but if not, he'd let her know. She needed to think about Seth's kisses and her response, her forward behavior. Whoa, mama, there was definitely heat between them. Added proof was her boldness the night before. It was shocking in a sense, but if a side effect of being healthier and happier, she kinda liked it.

The grin she'd been wearing slipped. Where could her attraction go? Lynn didn't think Seth the type to lead a woman on, but he still cared for his wife. And what about her? Was she strong enough to try love again? Possibly. Would she be able to move on with her life if it didn't work out? There lay the clincher, right now she didn't know. So, to protect herself, she'd be careful, go slow.

She sighed and leaned forward in the saddle to stroke Beauty's neck, then straightened. "Isn't this a heck of a note, girl? Me going gaga over a man's kisses at my age." Of course, she wasn't dead yet, but she never dreamed she'd be facing these issues of sexuality at this point in her life.

Since it had rained recently, the sage happened to be in bloom, its purple flowers casting their color across the barren ground. The amethyst haze was broken in places by large rocks, cactus, and buffalo grass. In sporadic spots, tall yucca plants, some young and healthy, others dry, bent, and dying, protruded above the scrub brush. A few mesquite trees, bowed and undersized, competed for height with the yuccas.

Ocotillo plants grew with abandon among the

cactus, sage and buffalo grass. They loved the rocky terrain and remained healthy throughout the severest of droughts. Their stalks, bare of leaves last week, were covered with small green leaves. She felt much like the dry looking plant. She'd shed a layer of discontent, and new interests, pleasures and accomplishments emerged from beneath. The analogy, though odd, waxed true. She wasn't the same woman who'd faced Seth in his study two months before.

The terrain changed quickly, this area thick with juniper. The rocks were one feature that didn't change. These boulders had been moved and some formed by glaciers thousands of years ago. Those strewn about had fallen and rolled down to their present resting place.

Beauty started climbing and Lynn leaned forward in the saddle. She'd not been this far up the trail before. At a level area, she pulled Beauty up and stopped to wait.

Turning in the saddle, she looked to see the ranch far below them. They'd been moving up hill most of the way but she'd not realized it.

She saw Seth and, the others far behind, riding to meet her and waved. How would he act toward her while they were alone? Her stomach trembled and her palms were sweaty. Would he regret last night? Or, would he kiss her again? God, she hoped so.

He pulled his horse, Chester, to a stop beside her.

"I decided I better not go further by myself."

"Smart move." He removed his hat, pulled a handkerchief from his back pocket, and with it wiped the moisture from his brow. He motioned, "Follow me."

They rode single file for a while until they came to a clearing, and then pulled up to wait for the others. Foliage was greener here as a small basin caught rainwater as it poured off the rock mountainside. *It must be beautiful in the spring when the wildflowers were in bloom.*

Tying their horses' reins to a bush, they found a place to sit. A large rock provided enough space for them both. Lynn inhaled the fresh air and caught a scent of something strong and sweet, somewhat irritating to her nostrils. Her nose twitched. She held her breath and resisted the urge to sneeze.

"What is that smell?"

Sniffing the air, Seth replied, "That's the creosote bush. The smell is much stronger just after a rain."

"It's awful." She rubbed her nose.

"The animals won't eat it so it must taste similar to how it smells. I've read that the Native Americans used it for medicinal purposes, as an antiseptic. Guess if you're out on the trail and get into a bind it would be worth a try."

They sat, enjoying the quiet. It felt nice not having to keep a conversation going. He used a stick to draw designs in the dirt. Lynn sneaked sideways glances. She'd never been this close to him and noticed little things she'd not seen before. He had a scar above his right eyebrow and another above his upper lip. Had he been a fighter in his youth? It was hard for her to imagine, but she'd seen his eyes change color just like the sky on a stormy day. He definitely had a temper. This morning they were a clear gray with sunlight dancing behind the clouds.

She liked how he looked. His face was strong and

chiseled, his forehead broad, his chin firm. Lines deepened around his mouth and eyes when he smiled or scowled. He probably had to shave twice a day as stubble already appeared on his jaw. But without a doubt, his kisses were worth a little razor burn. She couldn't help but wonder. Did his wife leave him or did he leave her?

Noticing her appraisal, Seth looked at her and asked, "What?"

Shaking her head, she said, "It's really none of my business. I don't want to pry."

"I'll let you know if you're prying, go ahead and ask."

She gathered her courage and searched for the right words. "Okay, I've been wondering what happened to break up your marriage."

He spent several moments in thought. "My ex-wife, Barbara grew up in the city. Our marriage was great as long as we lived in the city." He studied her face as he talked. "Which we did for many years. I had a booming practice in Dallas, made big bucks, but wasn't happy." For a minute he remained quiet. His eyes searched the landscape. "I talked her into moving out here to the ranch and she couldn't stand it. She felt isolated here, had nothing to do. Before the year ended, she'd moved back to Dallas."

Staring out at the horses, his shoulders sagged and he added, "I packed up and followed her and the boys, but we were never quite as happy. I missed this too much." He threw his arms wide and made a sweeping gesture. "I couldn't breathe in the city anymore." She laid her hand on his arm. He added, "As much as we loved each other, it just wasn't enough."

Sighing, he continued. "When the boys were old enough to decide for themselves, they wanted to live here on the ranch." He shook his head. "God, it was a bad time, broke her heart and tore the boys up too. In time we all adjusted. She came to visit them often and when possible, I took them to see her. Now that they're older, they visit her on their own."

"Does she ever visit them here, now?"

"Oh yes, she'll probably be here for the dance at the end of camp."

He reached for her hand, placed it on his knee, and covered it with his. "What about you, Lynn? What happened to your marriage?"

Smiling wryly, she replied. "Same old story. Depressed woman thinks only of herself and her problems, and neglects her man. He leaves and marries a younger woman, has another family. A very common scenario.

He scowled. "I don't believe that."

She shrugged. "Oh, I don't know, in all honesty, I felt I couldn't live up to his expectations and felt threatened. We did a lot of formal entertaining because of Dan's job and I just didn't enjoy it and that affected the relationship. I wasn't interested in the country club scene and to scratch his way to the top professionally, he needed a wife who was. He was also somewhat self-centered."

Seth's eyes were sympathetic. "And your self-esteem suffered as a result."

"Yes, and I wasn't strong enough. " She glanced at the large hand covering hers. Turning hers palm up, she laced her fingers with his. When his folded over hers in comfort, her heart thudded with contentment.

"Remember the season tickets to the Cowboy games? If I'd had a stronger personality perhaps we'd still be together."

They sat listening to the quiet sounds of life in the desert, the occasional rustle of a small creature, a wisp of wind lifting the dirt.

Brow furrowed, lips tight, he asked quietly. "Do you still love him?"

It felt good telling Seth about Dan. She smiled. "No. Even before the divorce, I knew our love for each other was gone."

"Were you devastated?"

Lynn thought a moment. Was she? At that time, her anger at him and at the life in general meshed so it became hard to distinguish between the two. "Yes. But, I knew it was for the best and in time I got over it. Now five years later, Dan and I can actually be civil to each other when the occasion arises." Not that they saw each other that often. He seemed happy with his new family but the last time she'd seen him, for just a moment she'd seen regret in his eyes. Maybe the society life he'd so wanted wasn't all he'd thought it would be.

Lynn studied Seth's face as he looked out on the land—his land—land passed down for generations. With his craggy features, he appeared as much a part of it as the rocks, cactus and prairie grass.

He released her hand and leaned back against the rock, propped on his elbows. She crossed her feet at the ankles and swung them up and down. "What about you, Seth?"

"Are you asking if I still love Barbara?"

She nodded. The gossip around here said that he did.

"Yes, I do. She's the mother of my sons." Lynn couldn't argue with that and respected him for it. He sat up and looked into her eyes. "Until recently I believed I was still in love with her."

Lynn remained quiet, enjoying what he'd just admitted. A shout from below drew their attention to the line of riders approach at a relaxing pace, voices drifting toward them on the breeze. They sat quietly and watched the horses nibble at the small patches of grass. Buzzards circled some unfortunate creature on the dessert floor to the east.

Seth stood, walked to his horse and withdrew a pair of binoculars from the saddlebag. At the edge of the basin, he put them to his eyes and scanned the ground below the birds.

He turned back and smiled. "Just a coyote with his lunch. The buzzards are hoping he'll leave some scraps. We don't have any calves out here but you never know when one might get loose and lost." He returned to Chester.

Lynn studied him as he re-packed the binoculars. He moved with a loose-jointed fluid grace, relaxed and sure. His long legs encased in worn denim were straight, not at all bowlegged, as she'd pictured cowboys. She knew that was a myth, as some bowlegged people had never seen a horse, much less ridden one.

The view of the basin below drew her to the cliff's edge and Seth joined her. Its vastness amazed her. A longing seized her heart. If only this summer didn't have to end. It did, however, and in another month she'd return to Fort Worth and her job. She'd be changed, of course, but would she be as content?

Would it last? She looked at Seth with a shaky smile, her eyes misting, and her voice cracking. "You know, I've been happier here than I've been in a long time. Sometimes that happiness scares me."

Her eyes beseeched him, "What if it's not real, not lasting?" She wiped at the tears on her cheeks.

He put his arm around her and pulled her to his side. "You have to have faith in yourself, Lynn. You're much healthier now, physically and emotionally. Give yourself time—time to adjust to a different way of living, of doing things. It'll take practice and determination. You can't go home and fall into old habits." He turned her to face him and chucked her under the chin.

"You want to stay in shape for next summer, don't you?"

Lynn's lips trembled but she smiled at him. "You mean you'd want me back?"

Yes, that Seth knew for a fact. "Of course. Things wouldn't be the same around here without you."

Tenderness for this woman overwhelmed him. Her self-confidence was vital if they were to build a relationship together. Where had that thought come from?

Hell, he'd seen it coming. The hug in the corral had opened the door to his heart—their kisses last night locked her in. Lynn enjoyed the ranch and took pleasure in the wonders around her. Could she be happy so far from the city? Better yet, would she commit to an old cowboy and live in the dessert amidst a herd of cattle and rough cowhands?

The first of the campers rode into the clearing. Lynn left his side and moved to greet the kids as they dismounted to stretch their legs. Seth watched as she and Corby chatted. Even Zane had something to say to her today and as he watched she ruffled his hair. Yes, she was good for the kids, and for him, too. He enjoyed her company, she made him laugh, and she made him long for something more in his life.

When had he started thinking about Lynn in that light? Maybe from the start he'd felt something, but ignored it. The afternoon she'd ridden Beauty, she'd glowed with the pleasure of accomplishment. She'd thrown her arms around his waist and hugged him hard. That hug had made his day.

They both needed time. Time together and apart to see if their relationship had promise. She had commitments in Fort Worth and his were here on the ranch. Never again would he move to the city. Love, though a powerful emotion, wouldn't be strong enough to hold them together.

If he and Lynn were to have a chance together, she needed to know how he felt. It was selfish to ask her to do all the giving but he'd never survive in the city. He'd wither and die. He belonged here with the kids during the summer and the cattle in the winter. Would she consider sharing that life? A teaching job in West Texas wouldn't be a problem. Good teachers were at a premium. And he had no doubt she was one of the best.

She had to trust him and the relationship they could build together. They had to be equally committed before she could make such a major change in her life. Her first marriage had made her insecure. He wanted a wife confident enough to take a broom to his hide if he deserved it.

Lord, here I'm thinking about marriage and we've

just shared one evening together. He couldn't deny his attraction to her. The kisses they'd shared last night had been hot and his body was ripe for more. Tormented, he'd tossed until the wee hours of the morning. No wonder he'd slept late. He wouldn't rush her. There was too much at stake and too little time. The summer would be over in a month.

* * *

Maria called to Seth from the kitchen as he came in the front door.

"Seth, Barbara's in the living room."

Barbara here, now? What could she want? Just what he needed to destroy his hopeful outlook and allow past insecurities to resurface. His heart skipped a beat and then resumed its normal rhythm.

He walked past the living room. "Be out in a minute, Barbara." Barbara didn't like the smell of horses on his clothes. So, when she came, he usually took a shower, shaved and put on clean clothes. Damned if he would this time. It just made more work for Maria.

Seth stood in the doorway and watched her, taking note of the sheen of her dark hair, now cut just above her shoulders, shorter than he'd ever seen her wear it. The style suited her. Memories of her dark hair against the sheets, a fine sheen of sweat covering her beautiful body flashed in his mind. As did images of her big with child, carrying their boys. His heart had once wrenched with regret for what they'd once had, but did no longer. Had he really loved Barbara the past seven years, or was it just habit?

Her shoes discarded on the floor, legs tucked under the skirt of her red dress, she lounged on the sofa.

Makeup perfect, not a hair out of place, she was absorbed in the glossy fashion magazine in her lap. One she'd obviously brought with her because their reading material had never run along the same lines.

He strode into the room. "Barbara, have you seen the boys, yet?"

She unfolded her legs and walked barefoot toward him. "Seth, darling. You know I haven't. They've been with you all morning."

Mischievous smile on her face, she put her arms around his neck. His arms instinctively circled her waist. He breathed in the heavy scent she'd used for years.

"Have you missed me?"

Had he? Not as much as he had in the past, which surprised him.

"That's a stupid question."

She had the grace to blush. He'd been missing her for the past seven years. Had he finally let her go?

She pulled his head down for a kiss. Unable to resist, he obliged her and sealed his mouth to hers. Her lips opened and his tongue slipped inside to mate with hers. His body responded but his heart didn't. The kiss left him cold and empty.

His thoughts flashed to another woman, another kiss, and a light perfume that drifted softly as she moved. Taking Barbara's shoulders, he gently pushed her back and held her at arm's length.

"This serves no purpose, Barbara. Remember, we divorced seven years ago. You chose the city over me."

She walked to the sofa and slipped on her shoes. "Actually, you chose this ranch over me."

His body stiffened, then relaxed. "Yes, you're

right. I did. This is old territory and we don't need to travel it again. It won't change anything." They'd both suffered, together and apart. She'd stayed one year, then took the boys and moved back to the city. Life hellish without them, he'd worked from dawn to dusk clearing brush, pushing his body to its limit. At night he drank until he fell into bed exhausted enough to sleep. Shuddering, he pushed the memories aside.

Seth glanced at the liquor cabinet, locked tight while the kids were on the ranch. Damn, he could use a couple fingers of Scotch. He sighed in resignation. Rules were to be kept, not broken. "Would you something to drink, tea or a coke?"

Barbara shook her head and sat down on the sofa, an angry flush on her face. "We cover the same ground every time I visit," she said.

He looked out the window toward the row of cabins.

"You're right, we do. And every time we see each other you throw yourself at me as if we'd never divorced, rubbing salt in an old wound." He tossed down the scotch, sat the glass on the cabinet and turned to face her. "I want it to stop, Barbara."

"Seth, I—"

Hand up, he said. "I don't want to hear it. You've strung me along for years, and fool that I am, I hoped we'd eventually get back together. I'm as much to blame as you are. I didn't discourage you." Hell, he'd been a willing participant.

For the first time in years, he felt a load lift from his heart. "We both know that's not going to happen. And frankly, it's no longer what I want."

Barbara froze, shock transforming her features. For

a minute he felt guilty, but...

"You're welcome here anytime you want to see the boys. But, you'll eat in the dining hall with the rest of us." He started for the door then stopped and turned back. "And, I think, from now on it's best if you stay in one of the guest cabins. One of the boys will help you get settled." It should have been that way from the day of the divorce.

All those years he'd wasted, they'd both wasted, trying to keep the past alive. He felt like a fool. He, of all people, should know it's the future that's important, not the past.

* * *

Lynn wiped down the stainless steel counter, rinsed the rags and hung them to dry. Since serving time had been over for an hour, when the door opened she didn't look up until Cookie spoke.

"Barbara." He bustled over to greet the woman, took her hand and patted it several times. "It's good to see you."

So, thought Lynn. This is Seth's ex.

Barbara gripped the hand that patted hers. "It's good to see you too, Cookie."

The kids working looked at the newcomer with curiosity. Lynn had to admit she looked too. The woman was beautiful. No wonder Seth still loved her.

"Lynn, come on over here."

She joined Cookie at the counter.

"Barbara, this is Lynn Devry, our baker for the summer. Lynn, this is Seth's wi—uh, ex-wife."

She turned to Lynn, her dark brown eyes alert, sizing her up. "Hello, Lynn. I hope you're enjoying your summer." Her smile aloof, she extended her hand.

Lynn took it and nodded. "Yes, I am. More than I expected, actually." Barbara was a contradiction. Dressed like a glamour queen in her designer jeans and boots, she appeared reserved, but Cookie seemed to like her so she must have some redeeming qualities.

Lynn couldn't help but be jealous of the woman's beauty and perfect body—the one that Seth longed for and dreamed about. *That's not fair, Lynn.* Barbara wasn't just a body and Lynn knew sex wasn't the only reason Seth loved her. She was a person, with wants, needs, and a personality. And, she had Seth's love.

Barbara nodded and studied her a minute more. Lynn grew uncomfortable under her scrutiny.

Cookie cleared his throat. "Ah, Barbara, you remember Clara and Pete, don't you?"

She laughed, tossing her dark hair. "Of course, I do. Hello, Pete, Clara."

Pete said, "Howdy, ma'am." Clara glanced her way and snorted, then turned back to rolling out piecrust.

Barbara flushed at Clara's rudeness but didn't comment. "Cookie, I don't suppose you have anything left from breakfast? I overslept this morning."

From Clara's direction, Lynn heard, "Don't you always?" Cookie looked uncomfortable but Barbara ignored the remark.

Ah, now she understood why Clara disliked Barbara.

Embarrassed, Lynn offered. "We've got a couple of biscuits left. I'd planned to give them to Sam but he won't mind if you have them."

"Good, good, Lynn. You get 'em and I'll pour Barbara a cup of coffee." Cookie led Barbara to a table. "Have a seat and we'll have you fixed up in just a minute." He moved back around the counter and Lynn heard him fussing at Clara.

Lynn put the biscuits on a plate and left them for Cookie to serve. Anxious to get away from this woman, she tossed her dirty apron in the laundry bin and made for the door.

* * *

Clara sat on the sofa in Lynn's cabin, a scowl on her face.

"I don't understand how you could be nice to that woman, Lynn. She's nothing but poison. Coming here and throwing herself at Seth the way she does." She snorted. "It's just not decent."

"Oh, Clara, she's not that bad." Why did Clara dislike Barbara? She looked at Maria for clues, but she appeared to be counting the ice cubes in her glass of tea.

"You tell her, Maria." Clara's eyebrows almost reached her hairline as she nodded and cocked an eye at Lynn. "Go on, tell her."

Maria remained fixated on her glass of tea. Now she was drawing swirls in the condensation.

"Looks like she's not going to tell you, so I will." Clara took a drink of her tea and pursed her lips. "Every time that woman comes, to see the *boys*, she throws herself at Seth."

"Seth put Barbara in one of the guest cabins last night." Maria's comment dropped out of nowhere.

"Really?" Clara leaned forward ready to hear more. Lynn sat back and watched the exchange between the two women.

"Yeah, I think he must have told Barbara he was tired of her coming out here and being all lovey-dovey.

She's been stringing him along ever since their divorce."

"Hot, damn!" Clara slapped her leg and chortled. "It's about time that boy woke up and got over that woman."

"Yeah, it is," said Maria. "You should see the way she acts around him, Lynn. Throws her arms around his neck and kisses him. Not a little peck, mind you. I'm talking about a real clincher."

Maria got that distant look again.

"But it's not all Barbara's fault," Clara added. "Seth could have put a stop to it long ago. He should've put her in a guest cabin right after they separated."

Maria held her hands up. "Let me finish. I've been in that household for thirty years. Barbara is a good woman, maybe a little inconsiderate and spoiled, but she was a good wife and mother. She still loves him, but not enough to give up her life in Dallas."

Lynn felt sorry for the woman. It must be hard to have to choose between the man you love and a profession you love. "Maybe Barbara doesn't feel alive without her job. Some women aren't happy if they're not working at something they love."

Maria shook her head. "There's no reason why she couldn't have worked on her novels from here. Seth had a fax machine set up, wireless Internet installed, the whole nine yards. Anything she couldn't take care of at the house, she could tie up with a couple of trips a month to Dallas."

"Maria, how long have you known the Williams family?"

"Seth's parents hired me a couple of years before Seth and Barbara married. My husband Juan was alive then, God rest his soul." Maria's expression grew solemn. "Seth and Barbara were happy in the early years of their marriage, when the boys were being born and little. Of course they were living in Dallas at the time. They used to come in once a month. Little by little, Seth seemed to show his discontent. He and the boys would saddle horses and camp out all weekend. Barbara never wanted to go with them. Spent most of her time at her laptop."

Clara snorted with disgust. "I just can't imagine giving up a good looking man like Seth. Even if he was butt ugly, he's sexy as hell. Bet he's great in the sack."

"Clara!" screeched Lynn and Maria in unison.

The older woman looked at them and shrugged. With a nod to Lynn, "Well, I bet he is and if I were a younger woman, I'd find out just how good!"

Clara burst out laughing, and when they got over their shock, Lynn and Maria joined her.

Lynn felt sorry for Seth and Barbara. Both were victims. Well, she didn't come out here to find romance and a man. Yet she cared deeply for Seth. But no way would she take the back seat to another woman. His body's response to their kisses had been genuine. She knew Seth cared for and respected her, but how much? For her it would have to be all or nothing, and the decision had to be his.

* * *

Lynn fell in behind Jared in the serving line for supper. "Mom, have you met Lynn?"

"Hello, Lynn. It's good to see you again." She put her arm around Jared's waist and hugged, then released him. "Lynn and I met this morning, son. She saved me from starvation."

"Is that so? Late for breakfast again, huh?" Jared looked down at his mother, and shook his head.

So, being late wasn't a one-time occurrence for Barbara. She could see how this would irritate Seth. And tick Clara off if it fell to her to find the woman something to eat. At one time, Lynn had been the same way.

"Guilty as charged." She threw up her hands. "I know, Jared. Don't give me your father's lecture. And, by the way, Lynn, your biscuits were delicious." The line moved ahead so Barbara moved on.

Jared loaded his tray with hefty servings of meatloaf, mashed potatoes, and green beans. Barbara's tray was almost empty. She had a small serving of meatloaf, salad, and no dessert. In her designer jeans and spandex top, her figure was model-thin and didn't have a roll or lump anywhere. Lynn couldn't help being envious. Her servings weren't large, but she'd taken some of everything, including dessert.

"Actually, Lynn, Mom works late hours and sleeps late in the morning. She's a writer."

"Really, what do you write?"

"Romantic suspense under the pen name of Brandy Williams."

Lynn's heart skipped a beat. *Oh, my, God. She's famous.* Lynn had read all of her books. "I love your books. I think I've read them all."

Barbara beamed. "Great. I'm pleased to hear that."

Oh, God. Her stomach churned anxiety. As if being beautiful and sexy wasn't enough, she was also a famous writer. Lynn was way out of her league here.

All three approached the table where Seth sat with Brian and Jake. Seth patted the chair beside him. "Here you go, Lynn. Have a seat over here."

Lynn paused, surprised and confused by his invitation. She felt awkward as if being played against his ex. Maybe this was his way of reinforcing the break he'd made with Barbara yesterday and to confirm his statement, "I'm no longer in love with her," on the mountain.

Lynn put her tray on the table and slid into the chair beside Seth. Seth had better not be using her to make Barbara jealous. Barbara sat across from Seth with her sons on either side. The woman's lips trembled and she hadn't looked up yet. Lynn's heart sank.

For several minutes they ate in quiet. Seth looked uncomfortable the concerned glances being exchanged by his sons. The tension was more than Lynn could bear, she asked. "Barbara, how long have you been writing novels?"

"For fifteen years." Barbara tucked a stray tendril of hair behind her ear. "It took five years of trying before I got published."

"I guess it's pretty time consuming," said Lynn.

"Yes, it is. Do you have children, Lynn?"

"Yes, one daughter. Abby's a junior curator at a museum in Fort Worth. As a matter of fact, she met your son, Brandon, at a—"

Before she could continue, Jared interrupted. "Mom, you're not going to believe this but Lynn sent her daughter one of Shorty's necklaces to wear to the party. But, she told him not to seal the beads with polyurethane." He started laughing and was joined by Brian and Jake.

Seth watched the discussion in silence.

Barbara's nose wrinkled in distaste. "Whatever

for?"

Jared laughed so hard he had difficulty talking. "It…was…a gag gift because—"

Seth interrupted. "I don't think we need to rehash that right now." He brushed a fly away from his plate. With the door opening and closing so often, it grew hard to keep the pests out. "Barbara, what are your plans for tomorrow?"

"I'll be leaving right after breakfast."

Seth nodded and tried to keep his eyes off Lynn as she gathered her trash and prepared to leave, her food half eaten. He admired the fact that Lynn made an effort to make Barbara feel more at ease. And he appreciated her efforts. It wasn't his intention to hurt Barbara and discourage her from returning. He'd discussed his decision with Jared and Brian that afternoon, and though saddened, they understood.

"Good to meet you, Barbara."

"You too, Lynn."

Seth's gaze followed her as she deposited her tray for washing and left the dining hall. Feeling Barbara's eyes on him, he picked up his cup of coffee.

"She's a very nice woman."

Seth nodded. "Yes, she is."

"Is she married?"

"Divorced. Her ex-husband has remarried and now has a three- year- old son." Seth stood and pushed in his chair. "Which one of you boys is going to drive your mother into Mesa Flats in the morning?"

Jared lifted his hand. "I will, Dad. I need to drive into Alpine. You need anything?"

Seth rubbed his chin. "Let me think about it and let you know in the morning." He nodded to Barbara. "See you in the morning at breakfast, Barbara."

* * *

Seth stood in his office and watched through the French doors as Jared helped his mother from the Suburban. The morning sun beat down on the blooming prickly pear that lined the circular drive. A few hummingbirds dove in for a taste of nectar.

When he heard the click of her heels on the Saltillo floor, he walked to meet her in the hall.

They stood for several seconds. Her lips trembled and Seth reached out and pulled her into his arms. He felt her silent sobs against his chest.

"Hush, sweetheart. We'll be all right."

She clutched at his waist and struggled to speak. "I still love you, Seth."

He leaned down and put his cheek on the top of her head.

"I love you too, Barbara. You're the mother of our sons and for that you'll always be in my heart. But, I'm no longer in love with you."

She shuddered. He patted her back. "Shhhhh, don't cry now." He wanted to cry with her, for the past and for what could have been. They had wonderful memories of their years together. Hopefully they'd forget the pain of the last few years of their marriage. "You know in your heart you're not in love with me either."

She pulled back and started to speak. Placing his finger on her lips, he shook his head.

"No, you're not, Barbara. If you were, we'd never have been apart these seven years." He cupped her cheek. "We had some wonderful years, produced three fine young men, but we've grown apart. We can't go back, only forward. You know I'm right, don't you?"

Biting her lip, she nodded.

He walked her to the Suburban and opened the door. She turned. He smiled, then leaned down and placed a light kiss on her lips.

"Goodbye, Barbara."

Tears glittered in her eyes and she tried to speak, but couldn't and shook her head. She mouthed, "Goodbye, Seth."

Chapter Twelve

"Lynn, get on that dang horse so we can pull out." Cookie snorted in disgust. "You've checked the supplies fourteen times. At this rate it'll be noon before we head out."

Cookie sat atop the chuck wagon barking orders and looking much like the old cook on the television show *Wagon Train.*

Corby rode up beside her. "Yeah, Lynn. Come on. Time's a wastin'."

Sam barked in agreement. He sat on the wagon seat beside Cookie, looking around proud as a peacock.

The kids had pleaded with Seth for a week to let Sam come along. When he explained about the dangers of the terrain, the horse crippler cactus and thorns, they talked Shorty into making leather boots to protect his tender paws. The first time he wore them he'd tried to chew them off. Seth told him, "no," and he'd howled his displeasure. When he walked, he shook each foot trying to dislodge the boot. Corby and Zane fell over laughing.

The sun had just peeked from behind the mountains, the sky pink, when they were ready to leave the yard. The air, still cool, smelled fresh from the early morning dew.

"All right, all ready. I'm coming." Lynn left the wagon and walked over to Beauty and mounted up.

Excitement vibrated in the air.

Seth shouted, "Move out."

Their group consisted of ten people. Corby and Zane were the youngest of the kids while Tim, Jason, and Julie were the oldest. Julie would lend a hand with the cooking and clean up when not helping with the calves. She and Cookie would also help if needed.

They would travel to the north of the ranch and set up camp. Calves would be brought from the surrounding area where they'd be vaccinated, wormed and castrated before turning them loose. Then they would move on to another location. Thinking about what the poor little calves had to go through gave Lynn the willies. Lynn felt better about wielding a syringe than a branding iron. Or that gruesome looking device used for castration. But she wouldn't miss the trail drive for the world. She was as excited about the experience as the kids were.

Of course, this exercise was for the kids to get a taste of outdoor life and the way it used to be. Seth held a real roundup in the fall. It might take the wranglers two or three days on the trail to gather a herd and bring them to the ranch. A large corral and barn several hundred yards from where their horses were kept was equipped to treat the cattle. Then the cowboys would head out for another herd. Lynn didn't know how many acres Seth owned but many of these big West Texas ranches had between 60,000 and 100,000 acres. That was a lot of ground to cover.

By the time they reached their campsite at noon, Lynn's butt was dead. On unsteady legs she walked to remove the kinks. She'd be sore the next day. Thank goodness she'd be able to forgo riding until time to move again. Glancing at the girls, she noticed Julie and Sally looked as though the long ride was a walk in the park. She was the only one who could barely walk.

Seth chuckled at her wobbly gait. "You'll get used to it."

Lynn nodded and gave him a weak smile. "Lord, I hope so."

"Lunch will be ready in fifteen minutes, Boss." At the sound of Cookie's voice, Seth turned back to unloading supplies.

"Okay, we'll be ready when you are."

Lunch was a thrown together affair, but good and filling—ham sandwiches on homemade bread, an apple and Clara's raisin oatmeal cookies. Seth tossed the remains of his cup of coffee into the fire and carried his plate and cup to the end of the wagon. The kids watched and mimicked his actions.

He nodded approval. "Good, that's the way we do it every meal. Now, Corby and Zane, this afternoon you two will stay and help Cookie and Lynn."

"Oh, man, do we—"

Seth raised his hand and Zane shut his mouth. "You'll get your turn. The rest of you, mount up." The kid was learning.

As they rode out, Cookie led the two boys to the end of the cook wagon and gave them each a wooden box to stand on. Grumbling but obedient, Corby and Zane washed and dried dishes. By the time they were finished, they were laughing and both a little wet. They each grabbed a stick and sat down with Lynn at the campfire. A game of tic-tac-toe kept them occupied.

Lynn looked around at their surroundings. Their camp was located near a manmade tank surrounded by a fence. Dirt built up to formed a berm that gradually sloped down to the water.

"Cookie, why the fence?"

He poked the boys. "Listen up, you two, you're about to learn something." He'd brought along a folding stool. She wondered how it held up under the weight of his large body. He stirred the coals.

"Sometimes you want the cattle to move to another area to graze. If you lock the gate so they can't get to the water, they'll seek water elsewhere." Zane and Corby listened, and then turned to study the fence with interest. "Saves having to drive them from one place to another."

Lynn had been wondering how they'd keep the calves together once they got them here.

Cookie gave each boy a pat on the back. "Y'all go on and play now, but be careful."

They took off without a backwards glance.

"Look at Sam. He's in hog heaven," said Cookie with a laugh. Sam was around the tank, checking each fence post and marking it before moving to the next one.

Corby and Zane chased each other around the tank, whooping and yelling. They appeared to be getting along. They stopped and started skipping rocks across the water.

Lost in a daze enjoying the sunshine and quiet, Sam's excited barking drew Lynn's attention to the tank just in time to see Zane push Corby down the incline toward the water. She heard his cry, "He...el...p!" as he left her line of vision.

"I'm coming." Lynn took off at a run. Cookie, moving as fast as a large man could, was on her heels.

By the time Lynn got through the gate, Corby was going under again, his arms flailed, churning the water. She lunged into the shoulder height water, and made a grab for Corby catching him by his shirtfront. He clutched at her frantically.

"I've got you now, Corby. You're just fine," she said as she plowed through the water to the bank. Cookie reached down, took her hand, and pulled them out and to the top of the berm. They were soaked to the bone.

Zane stood to the side laughing. "You look like a couple drowned rats. Especially you, Corby, with your hair hanging down in your face."

When Lynn sat Corby on the ground, he flew at Zane with fists and feet flying, screaming, "You pushed me. You bully, you pushed me."

Trying to fend off Corby's blows, Zane continued to laugh, repeating, "I did not. You big baby, you fell over your own two feet. You're just a clumsy baby." Angry now, Zane started swinging back.

Corby continued to kick and punch as Lynn grabbed him from behind and pulled him away from Zane.

Cookie seized Zane by the collar, shook him to get his attention, and hustled him toward the wagon.

A resisting Zane was half walked, half shoved back to camp. Cookie stood him against a wagon wheel. His face, red from exertion, eyebrows drawn in a scowl, looked fierce enough to scare the toughest of kids, but it didn't faze Zane.

"If you think we're going to put up with this crap for five days, son, you're wrong," Cookie said. "Seth may not believe in blistering your butt, but I'll do it in a heartbeat." He shook Zane's shoulder as he continued, "You understand me, boy?"

Zane sobered and nodded.

"Sit down there and don't move a muscle until I have time to deal with you."

He whistled for Sam. "Sit, Sam. Guard. If he even twitches, bite him."

Sam sat down on his haunches and drilled Zane with an unblinking stare. Not a muscle in his body moved.

Cookie and Lynn knew Sam wouldn't bite anyone unless it was a life or death situation, and certainly not one of the kids. But Zane didn't.

Cookie, huffing and puffing, stalked back toward Lynn and Corby. "Is the boy all right?"

"He's fine, Cookie, just scared and mad."

She led Corby to the wagon. "Let's get you into some dry clothes before you catch a cold."

Corby rummaged through his bedroll, found a change of clothes and took them behind a bush to change.

Lynn pointed to a stunted mesquite. "Hang your wet ones on that bush. Be sure all the water is out of your boots, and bring them over here by the fire."

Walking over to Zane she ordered, "Give me your boots."

Glaring at her he challenged, "I ain't gonna do it." As if to emphasize his "no," he crossed his legs and sat Indian style.

At the tone of Zane's voice, a low rumble started in Sam's throat. Zane jerked to attention.

She put her hand on Sam's head. "Easy, Sam. Give me your boots, Zane. You're not going to need them for a while and Corby does. You'll get them back when his are dry enough to wear."

Glancing at Sam to see if it was all right to move, Zane reached down and pulled off his boots.

Corby, a short distance away, watched the scene.

Most kids would've taken pleasure in Zane's predicament, but Corby looked uncertain, cautious.

Lynn took the boots and handed them to Corby. Cookie helped him arrange his wet pair so they'd dry but not burn.

Now that the crisis was somewhat over, the wetness of her clothes became an issue.

"Cookie, I'm going to change." Thank goodness she'd brought tennis shoes or she'd be going barefoot.

She emerged from the wagon, wet clothes slung over her arm. When they were rung out and arranged on the now sagging mesquite bush, she joined Cookie at the fire.

"Why don't you take Corby for a walk, Cookie, while I have a talk with Zane? Take Sam with you."

She waited until they were out of sight before she approached Zane.

His first response was to try to get up and ignore her. She put a hand on his shoulder and shook a finger in his face.

"Don't think for a minute that I won't paddle your butt. People around here have tried to talk and reason with you, but if the only thing you will respect is physical punishment, I can oblige you."

His face puckered up and Lynn felt guilty. After all, he was just a boy. A horrible one most of the time, but was his behavior his fault? Was this child mentally ill or just need some structure in his life? Well, that was Seth's department.

"Why do you feel the need to be mean to others, Zane? Especially Corby."

She let him think on her question.

"He could be a really good friend if you'd let him."

She sat down cross-legged and faced him. He wouldn't look at her, just sat with his chin down, mouth clamped shut.

"You know, Zane, what really scares me? What might've happened if Cookie and I hadn't been close? Corby could have drowned. You'd remember the horror for the rest of your life."

His head came up. "Corby knows how to swim. He was just being a baby," he said, his smirk slipping as he spoke.

"Yes, he does, when he's wearing a swimming suit. But jeans and boots weigh more, and he was scared and panicked. Even adults can drown in situations like that, when their clothes weigh them down."

His eyes grew big as if he hadn't thought of that possibility. Zane's chin dropped another two inches. It'd be on his chest soon. Lynn felt her heart constrict as a tear rolled down one of his cheeks.

"Now, I know you act tough, but you have a good heart." She reached over and tapped him on the chest. "I can tell by the way you treat your pony that you're not all mean."

"I didn't mean to hurt him. We was just playing."

Lynn's voice broke and tears of sympathy pooled in her eyes. She struggled for composure.

"Your pony loves you. I've noticed his ears perk up when he hears your voice."

An expression of hope crossed Zane's face making her heart wrench. Lord, this little boy needed love and acceptance in the worst way. Or so she supposed. This too was Seth's department and she'd seen crocodile tears drop from Abby's eyes enough to suspect Zane's might be also.

"I've also seen you sneak glances at Sam. You'd like to be his friend too. Isn't that right?"

His body shook with sobs as he nodded and said, "But…he…don't like me."

"He would if you were nice to him. You haven't given him a chance to get to know you. Would you want to be friends with someone who aggravated you all the time?"

His shook his head.

"Zane, I know you're upset so I'm going to leave you alone to think about what we've talked about. I imagine Seth will want to have a long talk with you tonight.

"You know he'd never hurt you. Nor would Cookie or I. We spoke out of turn when we threatened to paddle you. What you did upset us, causing words to come out of our mouths which we later regretted."

She lifted his chin a fraction. "Do you understand what I'm saying?"

He sniffled and his head bobbed up and down.

"To make sure you understand I need you to explain it back to me."

Blue eyes, still moist with tears, looked at her. "You and Cookie said you'd spank me 'cause you were upset. You wouldn't really do it."

He said the words but his wrinkled brow showed doubt.

"That's right." She chuckled. "If we did, Seth might spank us. Can you see Cookie getting a paddling?"

A smile split his face. With a choked laugh, he looked to see if she was teasing.

"You're a very special young man, Zane, and

someday you'll be a grown man and might have a special little boy of your own. I know you can be the type of person that little boy will be proud of, but you have to start now, practicing for that time."

Lynn hoped her words would help Zane but he was a tough little customer. God she hoped Seth could help him. It'd been a shame for such a precious child to continue down a destructive path. If she helped make a positive change, every sore muscle she'd experienced would be worth it.

At the beginning of the summer, she'd been ready for a break from kids, but being with kids in this environment was different. Here they learned by doing, experiencing. Maybe Abby and Art had been right to trick her into this summer job. The thought made her feel somewhat guilty about the necklace.

It wasn't long before Cookie and Corby returned from their walk. Cookie put a brisket to cooking on a grate over the fire. He gave Zane the job of brushing it with sauce and making sure it didn't burn. Zane was quiet as he worked, but not sullen.

* * *

Dusk had fallen, and all Lynn could see was two silhouettes, Seth and Zane, as they sat on the berm of the tank.

As their talk progressed, Zane inched closer and closer to Seth until their two shapes merged into one. She imagined Seth had his arm around Zane, giving him a gentle hug has they talked.

Lynn's heart twisted with grief for the small boy who'd suffered so much hurt in his short lifetime. And with wonder for the man who had so much compassion and love for children. His ability to communicate with them was to be admired. For the first time, she considered how painful it must be to get attached to these needy kids, and then watch them leave every year.

When the dishes were washed and put away, Lynn sat with the others and gazed into the flames of the cook fire. There was something about a fire. It represented home and hearth—comfort. And love. It had been a long time since she'd sat around a campfire and relaxed. Probably not since her last summer at Girl Scout Camp. At home, on lonely winter nights, she could curl up on the sofa and stare into the flames of her fireplace and remember.

As Cookie, Ben and Sally talked and drank coffee the kids got their bedrolls and prepared for bed.

Lynn held a tin pitcher filled with water. "Okay, guys. Get your cups and toothbrushes over here and brush your teeth."

Ben hooted. "Brush their teeth? We don't brush our teeth out here." He looked around at the others for support.

Lynn motioned to the kids, "Come on. I know you have your tooth brushes because I told you to pack them."

Giving Ben a knowing glance, she pursued the issue. "Anyway, clean teeth make a man much more kissable."

Smiling, she watched Ben's face flush. He was sweet on Sally and lately she'd been returning his interest.

When he thought she wasn't looking, Ben talked Tim out of some toothpaste and brushed his teeth vigorously with a frayed twig.

With Corby's help, Lynn found Zane's bedroll and

got it spread out near his. She bent over to tuck Corby in. Before she could tell him goodnight he asked, "Why don't Zane like me, Lynn?"

She sat on the end of his bedroll. Sam padded up and lay down with his head across her knee. Deep in thought, she scratched Sam's coat as she searched for the right words.

Her eyes wandered to the silhouette on the bank of the tank, barely distinguishable in the fading light.

"I don't know, Corby. But we can see he hasn't learned how to be nice."

She took the hand that lay atop the cover and patted it with her other one. "So, that's what you and I can do for Zane, be nice to him and teach him how to be kind."

Standing, she bent down and ruffled his hair. "I think one of these days you and Zane will be the very best of friends. And, I think that Sam will be one of his friends too, just like he's mine and yours."

It was pitch dark when Seth carried Zane, fast asleep, to his bedroll, removed his boots and tucked him in for the night. He snapped his fingers and Sam trotted to him and settled in between Zane and Corby.

Seth poured a cup of coffee, walked over and sat down by Lynn on the dead tree trunk they were using for a bench. He looked drawn and tired.

"How'd it go?"

"The boy's had a rough time. Evidently his father was cruel and constantly mistreated him, emotionally and physically. His father's way of playing was aggravating him until he struck back, which made the old man mad so he'd spank him. That would tear down any child's self-esteem."

"You don't think there is anything psychologically wrong with him, do you?"

He shook his head. "No, the psychiatrist he's been seeing ruled out dissociative mental disorder which is characterized by an inability to react properly in normal situations. If Zane had been diagnosed with a mental disorder, he wouldn't be one of our campers.

Seth tossed the dregs of his coffee into the fire. It hissed and shot sparks, then calmed.

"I just think he has to relearn how to relate to others. We got a lot out in the open tonight. He cried for a long time and wore himself out. Sam will watch over him tonight and let us know if either boy needs us."

"I'm curious. Why didn't you go ahead and get a medical degree so you could prescribe medication?"

He shrugged. "I like behavioral management and other cognitive therapy techniques. While I believe a medication is definitely needed in some cases, it can be an overused tool."

"I can understand that." She knew people, who'd see a psychiatrist for fifteen minutes, walk out with three prescriptions and not have to return for a month. A scary thought in her opinion.

Seth took Lynn's hand and twined their fingers together. His gaze moved from the fire to her. "How're you holding up? Some of that soreness easing out of your muscles?" He grinned. "If not, I've got some of Chue's horse salve. Smells terrible but sure helps the pain."

"I think I'll pass for now."

"Okay, but you may feel different tomorrow after sleeping on the ground tonight."

"I'll keep that in mind."

He pulled on her hand. "Scoot over here closer so we can talk."

Her heart lurched in happiness and she moved over. "What do you want to talk about?"

"You and me. Us."

"Is there going to be an 'us'?"

His eyes met hers. He cleared his throat. "I hope so. Though from the first day we met, when you pissed me off with your uppity demeanor, I was attracted to you. Over the weeks, I've come to admire and respect you. My feelings have grown. I've tried to deny them, but after our kisses at the corral, I can't any longer."

Lynn choked out a laugh. "Uppity behavior?"

"Yes, don't you remember? You wadded up your schedule and hit me in the chest with it."

"If I thought I could have stuffed them down your throat, I'd have tried." But he'd been mad because of the paper ball she'd launched, and she felt their discussion had gone far enough. It had been childish on her part, but she'd been upset at the time. And from the look on his face she knew it was time to get the hell out of Dodge.

Seth put his arm around her shoulder and pulled her closer. "What about you, Lynn? Do you care for me at all?" He kissed her hair and she leaned into his embrace.

"My feelings for you are strong, too, Seth. I've never met a man I could respect and admire as much as I do you." She added. "I've been attracted to you from that first day, too. I tried to deny it, but our kiss the other night broke through my defenses." Falling in love hadn't been in the picture for her, this summer or ever again. It wasn't something she'd thought about or wanted, at least consciously. Her idea for this summer had been to work six hours a day, maybe exercise and tone up, and then relax. But instead, she'd immersed herself in work and activities and received a valuable unexpected gift. With no time to focus on her own problems, she'd found happiness.

His hand was in her hair, turning her face up to his. She watched his lips descend and cover hers in a short, but firm kiss. He drew back and with his thumb traced the outline of her jaw. "I wasted a lot of years thinking I still loved Barbara. I want to see if this attraction between us can grow into something permanent."

She dropped her head to his shoulder. "I want that too." He smelled of horse and sweat and Seth, the combination not unpleasing.

Seth caressed her arm, his fingers slipping just under the sleeve of her shirt. "You've never told me much about your depression. I'd like to know if you want to tell me."

Did she want to? It was only fair that he know. "I guess my depression struck before Dan filed for divorce. Climbing the corporate ladder was so important to him that Abby and I took a back seat to his job."

"Unfortunately that happens to a lot with couples."

"Yeah, I guess if I'd wanted to too, we might have survived." But she hadn't and he found fault with her for it. "I couldn't do things to please him anymore. Why didn't I go buy some stylish clothes, or have lunch at the country club with the other wives?" She curled her lip in disgust. "The women were snooty and made me feel inadequate. It wasn't education, as I had more than they did, it was style and glamour. They wore designer clothes, had sculpted bodies to match their fake tans and fingernails." She'd felt gauche and countrified. "So, I stopped going with him, made excuses. This caused more arguments." With a sigh, she shrugged. "After the divorce, I let all those things worry me, blamed myself for being a failure as a corporate lawyer's wife, and tried to become more like the woman he'd tried to mold me into for several years. That's when the anxiety attacks began."

"What have you learned about yourself since then?"

She thought for a while. "For one thing, I am who I am and can't be anyone else. It's a shame I didn't know Dan wanted recognition so badly and that he didn't know I wanted a quiet life. We both failed at knowing the others goals."

"Perhaps. But then, how many people know that when they marry? Dan could have compromised when he moved up. Yes, some entertaining and hob-knobbing is necessary, but maybe he went to the extreme."

Yes, thought Lynn, he did. "He was unbendable and controlling." And she was the one to break under his rigidness.

Seth kissed her forehead. "I'm glad you told me."

"Me too." She tipped her head up and kissed his jaw. They sat for a while watching the flames flicker as the wood burned down.

Seth rose and put a couple more small logs on the fire. Lynn watched his reflection in the firelight, the graceful yet fluid movements as he went about the task.

When he rejoined her on their makeshift seat, she couldn't resist saying. "I have to tell you, Seth, what attracted me most about you that day was your good-looking butt." He froze, reddened, and then hugged her tightly as his body shook with silent laughter.

He had difficulty speaking. "Well, I'm extremely flattered. I don't think I've ever been given that compliment before."

"Maybe no one's had the opportunity. But, women think about those things, you know, just like men do." She tapped him on the chest. "And, don't think a woman doesn't know when a man's admiring a part of her anatomy." She arched an eyebrow.

He grinned. "Guilty as charged." His eyes dropped to her chest. "They are a beautiful pair."

* * *

Lynn was jolted awake by the soft nudge of Cookie's boot.

"Get up, lazy bones. The sun's almost up and we've got a hungry crew to feed."

Pushing herself to a sitting position, she shook each boot before putting it on. She'd seen enough westerns to know scorpions and spiders liked dark places. Standing up was painful, but she managed to get from her knees to an upright position.

"Oh…oh…oh…."

Cookie shot her a sympathetic look. "It won't be as bad tomorrow. Or, it could be worse."

"That's an encouraging thought." If it got worse, she was in big trouble. A body could handle just so much. How did Cookie manage sleeping on the hard ground? He was older than her, but then he had more padding.

Cookie had coffee boiled and bacon frying by the time Lynn had her sleeping bag rolled up and stored in the wagon. She stretched and twisted to work the kinks out of her body as she walked to the fire. She poured herself a cup of coffee.

She took a deep breath of the fresh unpolluted air, her thoughts floating back to Seth's words and his tender kiss. And the look on his face when she'd said he had a good looking butt. She didn't know what was wrong with her, but, she'd been saying and doing things she wouldn't have dreamed of ten years ago.

She looked to where he slept, as did Ben and the boys. "Everyone's still asleep, Cookie. You sure we have to start breakfast this early?"

Before the words were out of her mouth, Seth, Ben, and Sally started to stir. Seth stretched and rolled to a sitting position and scratched his head. He sat for a minute and then pulled on his boots, yawning as he did so.

"That answer your question, gal? Better get at them biscuits."

By the time she had the biscuits baking in the Dutch ovens, the first shimmer of sunlight peeked over the mountains to the east. It cast a pink glow behind Seth and Ben as they stood, coffee cups in hand, at the fence around the tank. She refilled her cup and sat down to watch the sun rise.

Lynn felt Seth's eyes on her and looked up. She wanted to believe he no longer loved Barbara, but he'd made an about face so fast, she wasn't completely convinced. But, Seth was a grown man, a man grounded in reality. It could happen. Maybe he'd been ignoring the truth for a long time.

When Seth and Ben returned to the fire, Cookie nodded to Seth. "It's time."

Sam still lay between the two boys. Awake, his

head rested on his paws.

Seth whistled softly and patted his leg. "Come, Sam."

Sam rose to his feet and stretched, kicking out each back leg. He shook himself and walked to Seth.

"Wake the kids, Sam. Go get 'em, boy!"

Body shaking with excitement, Sam loped to the first of his victims, Corby and Zane. He tickled ears and noses with his wet tongue and nose.

The two young boys jumped up, shrieking. The older boys weren't as excited. Jason's head peeked out. "Get away from here, Sam, it's still dark out."

Tim and Jason tried to hide their heads, but when Sam started nipping anything that protruded, they jumped up and started running. It didn't take the older boys long to get ready but Ben spent fifteen minutes getting Corby and Zane out of the bushes, washed, and to the campfire to eat.

Corby and Zane perched on a rock with their breakfast. Sam sat in front of Corby and watched him as he ate. Corby broke off a piece of bacon and offered it to Sam. He swallowed it whole and nudged Corby's knee for more.

A few minutes later, Zane broke off a piece of his bacon and held it down for Sam, but Sam's attention was on Corby.

Watching, Lynn said, "Call him over, Zane. He doesn't see it."

Voice soft and cracking, Zane called, "Here, Sam."

Sam looked at the offered bacon, then back at Zane as if trying to make up his mind. He walked over and took the bacon, watching Zane the whole time.

"Remember, it's going to take a while for him to

trust you. Be patient." Zane needed Sam's affection as he did hers. Guilt assailed her for her negative thoughts about the boy when she'd arrived. She'd been thinking only of herself, not seeing Zane's behavior as a cry for attention.

* * *

The day flew by with no serious problems. Calves got loose and had to be chased. Scrapes and bruises needed disinfectant and bandages. By early afternoon, Lynn was so tired she ached. She remembered one of her mother's favorite expressions. "If you see something dragging along behind me, pick it up, it's just my butt. That's how tired I am." Sore muscles and thoughts of Seth the night before had interfered with her sleep. She dreamed they were living in the old west and Indians had captured her. Seth had ridden to her rescue. Riding in front of him, with his arms around her, his hands… Whoa, it had been hot. Plus, the ground wasn't the most comfortable of beds. Needless to say, she tossed the rest of the night.

By the time they had everything cleaned, packed, and ready to move the next morning, Lynn thought she couldn't take another step. Breaking camp proved to be a chore. But, she felt so sticky she wouldn't be able to sleep unless she washed her hair. Gathering a towel and shampoo she started for the tank.

Seth stopped her as she was leaving camp. "You're not going to try to bathe in that tank, are you?"

She shook her head no. "I just want to wash my hair."

Seth fished a bucket out of the wagon. "Here. Use this to rinse with. Be careful though, there could be water moccasins in that tank."

She looked from him to the bucket, then again.

"Are you teasing me?"

"Come on, I'll go with you. And no, I'm not teasing. There could be snakes."

Lynn hurried to keep up with his long strides. He slowed his steps.

"Do you know how to tell a poisonous water snake from a non-poisonous water snake?"

She shook her head. "No, I don't remember covering that in biology or life science."

"Non-poisonous snakes swim with their faces in the water, like this." He held his hand out straight, "But poisonous snakes, like the moccasin, swim with their heads above the water like this." His wrist was bent up at an angle.

"Where'd you learn that?" The man was a walking encyclopedia.

"From a park ranger at Balmorhea. As a kid I took a guided nature tour around the lake. Never forgot most of what I learned."

Lynn knelt while Seth, towel over his shoulder, poured water over her head, soaking her upper body in the process. She didn't care—she'd be clean.

Seth stepped behind her. "Lean over and keep your head down." He poured shampoo on her hair and bending, worked it into lather. His large hands massaged her scalp.

Lynn was afraid she'd melt and slide into the water. Having Seth wash her hair was romantic and erotic. Each stroke of his strong hands heightened her imagination as to what they'd feel like touching her elsewhere. Desire curled in her body. She wondered if the sensuous ritual at all affected Seth. Just when she was ready to moan, he stepped back and poured water over her head. He lathered and rinsed again. Putty in his hands, Lynn wanted to cry when the shampoo was over.

"Thank you."

Seth handed her a towel. "You're welcome."

She wrapped the towel around her head turban style. When she tried to stand, she lost her balance and started to topple headfirst into the tank. Seth jumped up and grabbed her jeans from behind, but slipped on the wet bank. They both went down on their butts, Lynn landing in his lap.

Laughing like fools, they tried again to get up. Lynn turned to face him and gain purchase with her knees and the toe of her boot. She went down again, this time with her face landing in his crotch. All she could manage to get out amid his rumbling laughter and her shrill giggles was "Oops!"

Reaching down, Seth grabbed her and pulled her towards him. Her hands were on his shoulders and his moved to her waist. His thumbs stroked up and down.

Her eyes were level with his. If he'd lean forward just a smidgen, their lips would touch. And she wanted that touch.

His eyes never left hers. Could he read her thoughts? Could he see how much she desired the touch of his mouth, his hands?

Her tongue darted out to moisten her lips. She couldn't help it—they were dry. His eyes moved from hers to her mouth. She groaned. "Are you ever going to kiss me again, Seth?"

He pulled her forward and rubbed his cheek against hers, breath warm on her ear. Her gasp caught in her throat. "I don't know—this is rather nice. Looking at you, feeling your soft skin against my face, inhaling your scent." He nuzzled the soft spot under her ear. "Umm, heavenly." He drew back and studied her, a grin tweaking his lips. "I'm afraid of what might happen if I kiss you. If I remember correctly, you're a greedy woman."

Heat rose in her face and she pulled back. Thank goodness it was dark.

"Don't be embarrassed. I'm teasing you."

He tugged her closer and turned her so that she sat across his legs. His large hand captured her face, then moved to the towel twisted in her hair and pulled, exposing her neck. His kiss started at the pulse point of her throat, his lips gauging the rapid beat of her heart. She shivered as his tongue forged a path up her neck to nuzzle the sensitive spot below her ear then moved around to capture her mouth. This time there was no teasing, just possession and hunger. Seth leaned back and rolled, flattening her beneath him. She sighed with pleasure as his lips moved around to her other ear.

Lynn reached up to draw Seth's mouth to hers and Sam's long tongue swiped them both across the face.

She screeched and Seth bellowed. The towel she'd wrapped around her head came loose. It was like a red flag to a bull. Sam grabbed it and took off at a run.

Seth muttered, "Damn, dog." He laughed and using his fingers like a comb, raked her hair back from her face and kissed her again. So slow and tender it was almost painful. When he drew back, he traced the shape of her face with his finger. "Nothing like untimely interruptions."

Lynn reached up and touched his lips. "Yeah, and I have a feeling Cookie sent him on a mission. We better get back."

"Yeah." He helped her to her feet and grabbed the bucket.

It was quiet when they returned to the campsite. Everyone had turned in except Cookie. He sat on a rock whittling on a piece of wood.

"Got so quiet out there I thought you two had fallen asleep."

Taking the towel from Sam, Seth asked, "Is that why you sent Sam to check on us?"

"It was Sam or the kids. They wanted to join y'all when all that laughing started." Cookie struggled to keep a straight face.

"Wouldn't want any of them poisonous water moccasins to sneak up on you while you were unawares." His chuckle told them he was enjoying their discomfort.

Blushing to the roots of her auburn hair, Lynn retorted, "We were just talking, Cookie."

"Uh-huh. Yep. That's what I figured."

"Weren't we, Seth?" She said catching the grin playing on Seth's lips.

Seth cleared his throat. "Yep, talking. Lips flapping. Tongues wagging. Talking." Then he threw Lynn a wicked grin. "Yep, best talk I've had in a long while."

Chapter Thirteen

They rode out early and by mid-morning reached their new camp spot located on higher ground by a natural spring. The water looked cool, fresh and inviting as the sun glinted off its smooth surface. Tall cliffs of rock enclosed it on three sides. The ground in front was rocky with small salt cedars and scraggly mesquite forming a shield. Though diminutive, they did provide some shade from the sun.

Corby and Zane jumped off their ponies and made a dash for the water. Ben grabbed them by their belts and pulled them back. "Whoa, guys. Work first. Then we'll swim."

Nodding with reluctance, the boys walked back to their ponies.

Lynn and Cookie started lunch while the men and Sally took the kids out to round up a few calves.

At the ranch, the kids had been taught how to handle a rope, and what to do with a calf if they were lucky enough to catch one. Today they'd practice with the real thing.

Just after noon the guys came in herding several young calves. Bawling mama cows trailed along behind.

Corby galloped up waving his hat in the air and shouting.

"Lynn! Lynn! I got one. I got one."

"Come back here, Corby, and give us a hand," Seth shouted, trying to stifle a grin.

"Yes sir, Seth." Pulling his pony to a halt, he turned it around and headed back to join the others.

Lynn inspected their haul. "How about you, Zane?

Did you get one too?"

Face sullen, he nodded. "Yeah, but Seth did most of it for me."

Lynn clapped him on his thin shoulders. "But that's great, Zane. Now you know how. Next time you can do it all by yourself. You've still got tomorrow."

He thought for a minute and then smiled. "Yeah. I do, don't I? Yippee!"

He threw his hat into the air. A slight breeze caught it and he danced around trying to catch it before it hit the ground.

Cookie walked over and tossed the boys a bar of soap. Zane was fastest and caught it before it landed in the dust. "You guys go wash up for grub."

With fewer calves today, they were finished by late afternoon. Cookie announced they'd have calf fries for supper.

"All right," piped Ben smacking his lips. The others voiced their appreciation.

Lynn wrinkled her nose in distaste. "Thanks, but I believe I'll pass." Just the thought of eating testicles gave her the shivers.

"Me, too." Corby said. He looked like he was going to be sick.

"Yuck. That's gross," Zane added.

The kids swam the remainder of the afternoon. It was probably the best bath they'd had all summer. Lynn couldn't wait until tonight when the women had a turn. A thorough bath would feel wonderful after several days of sponge baths.

Lynn, along with Julie, Corby, and Zane managed to fill up on leftovers from the cooler while the others feasted on calf fries for supper. The "chickens" received good-natured teasing but stood by their decision. Corby and Zane showed their disgust by having a hacking and heaving contest. Their efforts caused Ben to look a little green.

After supper the kids practiced roping. Mouths twisted in concentration, Corby and Zane tossed their ropes time and time again. Corby was more skilled and Zane was resentful. Zane lost his temper and shoved Corby. Corby shoved back, and it turned into a scuffle.

Seth isolated both boys to give them time to settle down and think about their behavior. Before rejoining the group, Zane had to apologize. "I'm sorry, Corby, I guess I was jealous. I just wish I was good at roping."

The boys shook hands. "Well, gee whiz, Zane, you're better at riding than me. Wish I could ride as good as you."

Zane shuffled his feet in the dirt. Lynn watched him weigh Corby's words. Finally, he smiled and gave Corby a friendly punch on the arm. Of course he was punched back.

Lynn's heart swelled. Zane was learning. At that moment, she knew in her heart that he'd be okay. He would make it. He'd have friends that cared about him. And Corby's self-esteem had improved enough to take up for himself, not let Zane run over him. Again she marveled at the wonders Seth worked with these kids.

When time to turn in, Seth sent the two young boys over to Ben. "He's going to show you guys how to use a twig for toothbrushes just in case you ever forget to bring one along." Laughing, Seth clapped Ben on the back and winked at Sally. Sally giggled as a flush spread from his neck up to his ears. Sheepish expression on his face, he helped Zane and Corby find a suitable stick and fray the ends. A few minutes later they were all three working vigorously to clean their teeth.

Seth, Lynn, and Cookie sat around the campfire drinking coffee. Ben and Sally had wandered off to sit by the water. A beautiful night, the humming of cicadas blended nicely with the crackling of the fire. In the distance, lightening flashed across the sky.

Cookie stood up and stretched. "Looks like they might be getting some rain over in Mexico, Seth. You reckon it'll blow on over here?"

Seth watched the light show in the distance. "I doubt it. Let's hope not. That would be an experience to remember for the kids, wouldn't it?"

Cookie chuckled. "Yeah, it would. For Lynn, too." He scratched his generous belly and yawned. "Well, good-night. I'm turning in."

Lynn refilled Seth's cup and then her own. Seth watched as she dumped the coffee grounds and rinsed the pot with water from the water barrel so it would be ready for Cookie in the morning.

Seth moved to the other side of the fire and sat down beside Lynn, on the rock Cookie had vacated. He'd been curious about something since the beginning of summer. He might as well ask.

"Lynn, how well do you know Art?"

"Gee, Art's one of my best friends. I've known him and Loretta a long time, probably close to twenty years."

She smiled at the memory. "We met in the early '80's on the dance floor at the Ridge Wood Country Club in Fort Worth." Her face lit with humor. "It was after the disco craze but it didn't matter to us. We both loved to disco."

He laughed. "Don't feel alone, Barbara did, too. At her insistence we made it to a disco club or two. I never mastered the art of the dance style, though."

Hell, he'd hated it. Country western was his kind of music and the two-step his style of dance.

"Ah, I don't believe it. I bet you could put John Travolta to shame. Did you wear platform shoes with your bell bottom polyester casual suit?"

"God, those clothes were awful," Seth said with a shudder. "Go on with your story."

He wondered how she looked at that age. What would she have been, twenty or so? No, she'd have been a teenager at the height of the craze. By twenty, she was married with a baby.

"I twisted my ankle and made a spectacle of myself on the dance floor. Art checked to see if it was broken. Dan and I spent the next two hours visiting with him and Loretta. We've been friends ever since."

Finishing her coffee, she walked to the water barrel and rinsed her cup. Tonight she wore a snug fitting t-shirt, not one of those baggy things she'd worn when she arrived. As she walked toward him, the movement caused her breasts to undulate beneath the shirt. They were beautiful. She was beautiful. His body leaped in response, and he almost groaned out loud. God, he wanted—

"One weekend Abby got sick and it was go to the emergency room or call Art. He came right over. She had the measles but you know how it is when your kids are sick and so little."

Seth nodded. Yes, he knew the agony a parent endures when a child is ill or hurt, regardless of their age.

She leaned forward, elbows on her knees, and her chin propped on her hands. "What about you. How do you know the Wayne's?"

He cleared his throat and forced himself to keep his mind on the discussion. "I've never met Loretta, though I've talked to her on the phone. And you know Art, he talks about her all the time."

"Yeah. Boy, aren't they a love match to admire?"

"Yes, they are." He sat quietly for a minute, thinking. With a stick, he drew circles in the dirt. "I met Art in college, a couple years before he started medical school. He was older, and at the time, I wasn't the best of students. For some reason he took me under his wing and tutored me." He tossed the stick into the fire, sending sparks dancing in the low flame. "Oh, I was smart enough, but undisciplined when it came to school. I wanted to be on the ranch, working cattle. He got me interested in psychology. From then on, I was hooked."

"Art has a way of bringing out the best in people, doesn't he? Have you kept in touch all these years?"

"You bet. Though there've been years when we didn't see or talk to each other. I owe my son's life to Art."

"What happened? Which son?"

He tossed the dregs of his coffee onto the dirt. "My oldest son, Brandon. Six years ago while a sophomore in college, he was in a car accident on the freeway near downtown Dallas. He was taken to Parkland Hospital." He'd been damn near crazy himself with worry. "Barbara and I both were hours from Dallas, so I called Art. He supervised Brandon's care and stayed with him until we got there."

She reached for his hand and squeezed. "Was he in critical condition?"

"No, but I was scared to death. The hospital uses a lot of interns in the emergency room and all I could think about was what if those kids didn't know enough or did something wrong."

Her hand, once soft, was rough from work. Seth wished he could stroke the callus spots away. He kissed the palm delighting in Lynn's shiver of response. "Are you cold?"

"A little"

He put his arm around her. "Scoot closer to me." When she did, he wrapped his other arm around her to warm her arm. His arm grazed her breasts and he froze. He kept his arm there against her softness, and felt her nipples tighten. It was all he could do to keep from groaning. When she didn't try to move, he ran his hand up and down her arm, stroking her breasts with his forearm as he did so.

Before this woman came into his life, all he could think about was having a successful summer camp with as few problems as possible. At first, Lynn had been like a grass burr, irritating him at every opportunity. Now she was a bother in an entirely different way, one he couldn't wait to satisfy.

When Seth's arm brushed against Lynn's breast, a zing of intense pleasure shot through her. She choked back the gasp of pleasure his touch elicited. Her nipples hardened, her brain told them not to but her body wasn't listening, just reacting. She leaned closer. As if that wasn't enough, as his hand slid up and down, warming her arm, his forearm brushed them making her body ache. He had to know what he was doing to her. She hoped he was enjoying it as much as she was, and aching as much too.

* * *

Lynn sat on a rock beside the pool and watched the moonlight throw shadows across the smooth surface. Occasionally a ripple, where a bug landed or a fish nabbed a tasty morsel, would gently radiate out from the spot of impact. Sam nudged her wanting attention. She put her arm around him and patted his side.

"Wouldn't it be nice to have a cabin right here, Sam? You could see this view from your back porch every day. On hot days you could take a dip in the water and shake it all over everybody when you got out."

She laughed as Sam cocked his head to listen. Sighing, she turned her thoughts to the few remaining days she had at the ranch. Saturday night they'd have a dance with some of the parents in attendance. It would be an exciting event, one that under normal circumstances, she'd look forward to.

But, she couldn't this dance. It was the last event of the summer, and time to go home to her little house in Fort Worth and her job. She didn't want to go, to leave what she'd found here. She'd changed, tossed aside old habits, and somehow she would remain changed. Not for Abby and not for Art, but for herself. There was no doubt in her mind about that. But Fort Worth and her job would never be the same. It would be better because she was healthier and happier, and because her experiences with these kids had enriched her life. As a result, she'd be a better mother, friend, and teacher. Could she be content to go back to the city and continue to teach? Or would she wake every morning longing for the wide-open spaces and the touch of a man who had enough love to share with hundreds of kids. She blinked back a tear. Leaving was going to break her heart.

Sam jumped off the rock and went to Seth. No one could sneak up on that dog.

Seth squatted to scratch his ears. "Sam, go to camp and watch the boys. And stay."

Lynn watched Sam bound off without a fuss. What a shame kids couldn't be trained to behave like that. Seth sat down beside Lynn, put his arm around her shoulder and pulled her closer to his side. She slipped her arms around his waist.

"Where's Cookie? Aren't you afraid he'll send the posse out to check on us?"

Chuckling, he nuzzled her neck. "I made sure he was snoring before I left camp. We're the only ones still up." He wiggled his eyebrows, making her laugh.

"What are you doing out here by yourself?" Seth moved his hand up and down her arm, caressing, enjoying its soft texture and remembering the sensations from the night before.

It took her a long time to answer. She smiled through a shimmer of tears, then turned her attention back to the water. "Just thinking, storing up memories to take home with me."

He tilted her chin, and with his fingers, wiped the moisture away. "What's this?" His mouth softly grazed hers. "Why the tears?"

Her voice was thick. "For all I'll be leaving when I go home next week, and what I'll miss."

His heart skipped a beat. Was it possible she might want to stay? Did she believe what he'd said, that he no longer loved Barbara?

"What is it you'll miss, Lynn?"

"I'll miss everyone here. The people I've worked with and Corby. It's going to be hard to see him leave. Zane, too, I've grown attached to him the last couple days."

Tugging a lock of her hair, he growled, "Come on. You're stalling. What else are you going to miss?"

"There's Beauty and Sam. And I do kinda like Rosebud after getting to know her. And my cabin, my homey little place. The pasture, the purple sage, the cactus, the—"

He kissed her to stop the endless list of West Texas flora and fauna.

"I would love to see the ocotillo in bloom. I've heard there's not a sight in the world like it—a sea of red." With an expression of innocence, she fluttered her eyes at him. *Innocent my ass, she's baiting me.* "Of course, you could send me some pictures."

"You're playing for time again, Lynn."

She put her hands on each side of his head and pulled his face closer to hers. "I'm going to miss you, Seth Williams, your company and laughter, your voice, your taste and smell. Are you satisfied?"

She drew him closer and kissed him, opening her mouth under his, giving as well as taking. And take he did. But, he gave too. He poured years of loneliness and need into the embrace. He drew her nearer, the softness of her body against his, making him throb with need.

He broke the kiss, cupped her face and gazed into her eyes. She was beautiful. Her eyes sparkled, reflecting the moonlight. His chest felt like it would explode. If only he could see inside her soul, know her heart and mind. He loved this woman and wanted her to love him too. Was it too soon to tell her how he felt? Probably. Was he kidding himself thinking he knew his heart after loving Barbara for so many years? Maybe. But, he didn't care.

His desire for Lynn seared his soul, as well as his body, making his heart ache with a longing he'd never felt before. He'd loved Barbara, loved her deeply, but not with the intensity he felt for Lynn. Maybe, in early manhood, he didn't have the capacity and depth of emotion he did today.

"Yeah, I'm satisfied. Relieved, because I'm going to miss you too." His hand traced her face and neck, memorizing her features. She shivered at his touch. He pulled her onto his lap and buried his face in her hair, enjoying its silky texture, her tantalizing smell. Okay, so there was also the smell of prairie dust and a little sweat. To him it was the sexiest scent in the world.

They sat for a long time locked in each other's arms, enjoying the quiet and the closeness, chatting about everything, and nothing.

How would he manage a year without her? Next summer was too far away. He could visit her in Fort Worth. Would she truly miss him? Or had this just been a summer romance to her, no commitments, and no strings? No. She wasn't the type.

He propped his chin on her head and cleared his throat. "Lynn, you don't have to go."

She leaned away from him to look into his eyes. "What? You'd let me stay and work for you? But the kids will be gone next week."

"No, I don't mean to work. Stay with me, Lynn." His hand cupped her chin as he watched her reaction. A variety of expressions crossed her face, joy, confusion and questions.

"Do you think you might love me, Lynn?" Unable to resist the column of her neck exposed by the moonlight, his lips found that spot just under her ear. He nuzzled and nibbled. "Because I think I love you. I know I want you so badly, I'm afraid to get too close to you around the kids for fear I'll embarrass us both."

She drew back, both hands on his chest.

Fear clutched his heart. *Oh, God. She doesn't love me.*

"You think you love me?" Her chin trembled as she bit her lower lip. She wrapped her arms around his neck and squeezed, almost choking him.

Fearing the worst, he held her close just the same. "I know we've only known each other a short time. But, I don't want you to leave without knowing how I feel."

"Oh, Seth. Yes, it's been too fast, but I think I love you too. I never dreamed you might care as much for me."

Relief and joy overwhelmed him. "What do you think all this kissing has been about, woman? I don't toy with a person's affections. You better not be, either."

He slid off the rock down to the partially grass covered bank and used the boulder as a backrest. He drew Lynn down beside him and cradled her in his arms, her head on his shoulder, her arm across his chest. The reflection of the moonlight on the water cast a glow across Lynn's body, emphasizing her breasts. He reached out and with a finger drew imaginary circles around the fullness. She gasped and arched against his hand. With his thumb, he teased the nipple to a hard peak, then leaned down and drew it into his mouth. She bucked and yelled, "Se——," before he captured the sound with his mouth. Oh, Lord, she was going to be a screamer. He looked at the stars. *Thank you, God.* He held her close and cursed himself for starting something they couldn't finish.

If three teenagers and two little boys weren't asleep just a short distance away, he'd be tempted to strip Lynn of her clothes and love her for the remainder of the night. He could see her nude body washed in moonlight, gleaming breasts and thighs waiting for his touch. He shuddered. *Man, stop torturing yourself.*

But, those children were his responsibility and they had to come first. He'd worked long and hard to make this camp a success and too much was at stake. His behavior and reputation had to be impeccable.

"I want us to get married, Lynn. But I can't ask you to give up your life in Fort Worth. I know I can't live in the city. My life and work are here. That's unfair, I know. But I want to be honest with you." She tried to talk, but he put his finger to her lips.

"But I'm sure now. I don't want to wait any longer because I know—"

"What, Lynn? Tell me what you need in life to make you happy. Think hard and be honest." He prayed it was something he could give her.

She was quiet for so long he feared he didn't have anything to offer her. "First, and foremost, I need to know that you're truly over Barbara, that I'm not a substitute, second best."

His body tensed. How could she think something like that?

Her hand stroked his cheek. "Don't be mad, Seth. I

want to be honest."

He relaxed. If their situations were reversed, he'd feel the same way. He turned his head and kissed her palm.

"Lynn, I swear I'll find a way to prove it to you." And he would if it took his last breath.

Voice choked with emotion, he asked. "What else do you need, Lynn? There has to be more."

"I need work because too much free time isn't good for me."

He nodded, fully understanding her reasoning.

She pushed up to look at him. "See, I've learned something this summer. No, not learned, accepted it, internalized it, and I have a plan of action."

"And that is?" Her answer was important for both of them.

"I need to always have a summer job, not have long periods of time with nothing to do." She put her head back on his shoulder, rubbing her cheek against his chest. "I love you, Seth. But, if things don't work out between us, I can handle it. Oh, I'll be hurt, and I'll cry and rant, but I'll be strong enough to go on and will be a stronger person for having had this summer experience and for having loved you."

His chest swelled with joy for her and his throat tightened, delaying a response. All he could do was hold her and kiss the top of her head. He cleared his throat. "You need to finish telling me what you need."

"Teaching is important to me and I'd like to get in a few more years so I can draw retirement. It doesn't have to be in Fort Worth, or any big city." She was quiet for a second and then added. "It could even be in the boon docks."

A laugh burst from his mouth. Man, she was fun. If her blunt sense of humor remained intact, life with her would never be dull.

"Is that all? What about shopping malls, the theater, cable television and nice restaurants?" Those things probably never entered her mind, because she was as different from Barbara as night from day. They'd been important to Barbara's happiness and she felt so isolated out here. And because of that, he'd had to ask.

"If I had a handsome man to keep me entertained in other ways, I wouldn't miss those things." She tapped him on the chest. "Of course, that man would have to be you."

He swallowed. "I bet that man could take you to the city on occasion to indulge in those other things. He might even buy a small house in the boon docks so his wife wouldn't have to do all the driving back and forth to her teaching job."

She gave him a look that said, "So?"

"I love you, Lynn. I want you to be my wife and partner, to——."

She tried to interrupt but he placed his fingers over her lips.

"No, don't answer right away. I want you to really think about what you'd be giving up. I want you to know, beyond a shadow of doubt, that you're the woman of my heart, not Barbara. Plus it will give us time to get to know each other."

She dropped her head to his chest and he stroked her back.

"I don't want your decision now. You need to go home, think things through so when you give me your answer, you'll know exactly what you're giving up. I want there to be no doubts when we spring it on our kids and the staff."

"You're a hard man, Seth Williams, but a wise one."

He didn't know how wise he was, but had proof of how hard.

Chapter Fourteen

"Did too!" Corby shouted.

"Did not!" Zane yelled and gave Corby another playful shove.

Lynn watched as she kneaded biscuit dough and laughed at their antics. Cookie was bent over a big skillet at the fire, frying bacon, but keeping an eye on the pair.

Right now the shoving was playful, but it could turn ugly. Seth located a Frisbee in the cook wagon. Lynn watched as he took turns with Corby and Zane tossing it for Sam to catch. Sally and Ben had their heads together talking in quiet tones while the older kids played cards.

It was a glorious day. Excitement oozed from her pores, and she couldn't seem to concentrate or stand still. She wanted to be out there tossing that Frisbee, and playing with Seth and the boys.

Kneading and rolling out biscuit dough usually relaxed her, but this morning, it was too staid an activity for the exhilaration she felt. Keyed up inside she needed some way to release her pent-up energy. It would have been nice if they'd thought to bring a softball and a bat. She'd been a darn good pitcher in her younger days. Looking down, she squeezed the massive lump of dough until it bulged between her fingers. She shifted the mass from one hand to the other, and then molded it into the shape of a ball. She tossed it up and caught it. It landed with a "splat."

She glanced over to see what Cookie was doing. Busy frying bacon, he wasn't paying attention to her or the kids. Should she or shouldn't she? She didn't know

Seth very well and didn't have a clue as to how he'd react. But, she couldn't resist and would soon find out.

Grinning, she stepped away from the drop down table at the end of the cook wagon. Taking her stance, she wound up and let the dough fly through the air. Those years on the high school softball team paid off. Her throw was right on target.

Smack. The wad hit Seth in the middle of his back. It clung for a second before it slid and fell to the ground with a splat.

His shoulders stiffened. He stood stock still for several seconds, then whirled around and stared at the wad of dough at his feet. A murderous glint in his eyes, he turned to Lynn. The grin on his face didn't fool her for one minute. Those eyes of his were accurate barometers. They read trouble.

"Oops," she squeaked. Maybe she'd made a mistake.

Talk stopped, gazes bounced back and forth between them as if watching a tennis match. Lynn backed up. Her grin vanished, replaced with apprehension. In a flash, Seth started running toward her yelling.

"Come on, you guys, let's get her!"

Both boys whooped and yelled as they took off after Seth, a barking Sam leading the way.

Lynn ran, shrieking at the top of her lungs.

"Wait. Wait!"

Seth was on her before she'd gone ten feet past the cook wagon. He grabbed the rope holding up her baggy jeans and jerked her back. His arms locked around her like a vise.

"I'm sorry, I'm sorry. Please Seth, I give...up."

She was laughing so hard she couldn't talk.

Before the words were out of her mouth, Seth twirled her around and lifted her over his shoulder. With a "whoosh" all the air left her lungs.

"You got her," the boys shouted with triumph.

"Dunk her in the pond, Seth. Yeah, that'll get her back. Dunk her!"

She shook her head. "On no, that's not a good idea, guys."

With long strides, Seth walked to the pond, boys and dog jumped around him in excitement. "Yeah, a cold bath will do her good."

"Please Seth, I don't have any clean clothes," she wailed and began to squirm in earnest. "Pleeeeease! I was just playing."

"You should've thought about that before you started slinging biscuit dough. You wanna play, you gotta pay. Right, guys?"

"Right, Seth. Lynn, you wanna play you gotta pay," echoed the two traitors.

"Corby, Zane, you each grab a boot and pull it off. We don't want to ruin her boots." They obliged with enthusiasm.

Seth turned Lynn, cradled her in his arms and walked out as far as he could without getting water in his boots.

She grabbed him around the neck and squeezed. If she was going in, he was too.

Seth's voice against her ear was a whisper. "Darlin', if you take me in with you, I promise I'll find a delicious way to retaliate." He blew in her ear making her start.

She gave him her sexiest grin. "I can't wait to find

out how, sugar." At last she'd left him speechless.

"Hey, what are you doing, Seth? Are you kissing Lynn?"

Lynn wasn't sure which boy asked the question, but Seth's body went rigid and Lynn, unable to help herself, started laughing.

"Guys, she's got me in a death lock. If she doesn't turn loose of my neck, I'll end up in the water with her."

He gave them a serious look. "Reckon we should negotiate. I want a pecan pie all to myself. What do you guys want?"

Corby and Zane put their heads together and talked in low tones. Lynn relaxed her grip on Seth's neck. "You're a sweet man, you know it? A pecan pie, huh?"

"My favorite."

"Lynn, me and Corby want—"

With a mighty swing, Seth tossed her into the middle of the pond. She went under with a big splash that sent her tormentors stepping backwards.

Her rump hit bottom. She surfaced and wiped the hair and water out of her eyes. The entire group stood laughing and clapping at her expense.

"You cheated, Seth. We had a deal!"

"We hadn't shaken on it yet. It wasn't final."

Corby tugged on Seth's shirt. "Does this mean we don't get our fudge brownies?"

Seth ruffled Corby's hair. "Nah, I bet if we beg long enough she'll fix some."

"Might as well enjoy it now that I'm wet." Lynn splashed, and bounced up and down in the water, unaware that her wet t-shirt clung to her breast and the bouncing set them in motion. "Anyone want to join me?

Sam! Come on, Sam."

Sam made a lunge for the water, but Seth caught his collar.

Seth was tongue tied, unable to draw his eyes away from Lynn's breasts as they jiggled in that wet shirt. He looked around, and expelled a breath of relieve to see that Sally and Ben had ushered the kids back to camp. Why was Cookie still standing there?

Cookie cleared his throat, a weird expression on his face. "Is everybody finished with their frolicking?"

Seth snorted. Damned if Cookie wasn't about to crack up at his discomfort.

Cookie glared at Lynn. "Gal, get out of that water and make another batch of biscuits. At this rate it will be noon before we break camp." He turned to join the others.

"Okay, Cookie, I'm coming." Lynn started sloshing out of the water, a grin on her face.

Seth watched, his eyes dropping from her face to her breasts. He knew instantly when she realized how exposed she was. Her arms flew up to cover herself and her face reddened.

He coughed back a laugh. "I'll get you a dry shirt."

Corby's voice carried from camp. "But, what about our brownies and Seth's pie?"

* * *

It was late afternoon when they rode into the yard at the ranch. They were a tired, scruffy bunch. Lynn knew she looked terrible in the clothes that had dried on her body. She was still in shock over Seth tossing her in the pond. Corby and Zane would get their brownies, but the vote on the pecan pie was still out. Boy, a long, hot shower would be heavenly. As would clean, wrinkle-free clothes.

As they neared the corrals, Lynn saw a young man bearing a strong resemblance to Seth. He stood at the fence talking to a lanky young blonde woman in cut-offs and sneakers. She had great legs. The two made a nice looking couple. A horse stood at the fence and kept butting the young man's shoulder. He stroked its forehead as he talked. The young woman put her hand out to touch the horse then jerked it back.

She acts just like I used to.

Seth rode up beside her. He nodded in the direction of the couple, a happy grin on his face. "That's my oldest son, Brandon." Pride reverberated in his voice. "Don't know the girl. He hasn't brought many home with him."

"He's a fine looking young man, Seth. You have every right to be swollen with pride over your three boys." She reached over and touched his arm.

He inhaled making his chest expand. She giggled.

"Yeah, I guess I am pretty proud, and puffed up too. Just a little." The grin he gave her wasn't in the least bit humble.

"Just a little, huh?" If Brandon was anything like Jared and Brian, Seth had every right to be proud.

The couple turned around and Brandon raised his hand in greeting. "Hey, Dad!"

Seth returned his wave. "Hey, son."

The girl studied them a minute and then turned back to Brandon, her head tilted in question. In that short period of time, Lynn had gotten a good look at her face. A face she knew well—Abby, her daughter.

"What on earth is Abby doing here?" Lord, she hoped nothing was wrong.

Seth leaned forward in the saddle. "You mean that's your daughter?" He watched her. Lynn knew he was gauging her reaction to this turn of events. "She's a beauty, Lynn."

"Yeah, she is, isn't she?" Evidently, Abby and Brandon had become friends.

Abby Devry watched the two people in front who both rode their horses with ease. Or so it appeared to her. Her mother probably wasn't that good on a horse, yet, so the woman couldn't be her. She recognized Brandon's father right away. Mr. Williams was handsome for an older man. His graying hair gave him a distinguished air and his body was lean and fit. Who was the woman beside him, and where was her mom? Probably bringing up the tail end. The fact that her mother had actually learned to ride was a wondrous feat in itself.

Mr. Williams was off his horse, hugging and pounding Brandon on the back. It was nice to see their open affection.

"It's good to see you, Brandon. We've missed you around here."

"Missed you too, Dad." Brandon returned his father's hug. He took her hand and pulled her over. "Dad, I want you to meet Abby Devry. Abby, this is my dad, Seth Williams."

"Very happy to meet you, Mr. Williams." Abby extended her hand and Seth's swallowed hers in a firm grasp.

"I'm happy to meet you, too, Abby. And please, call me Seth." He turned back to the woman on the horse. "Lynn, come down and meet my son Brandon and greet your daughter."

Abby turned to the woman sliding off the horse. Like a sleepwalker, she ambled toward the lady. This couldn't be her mother. This lady was slender and the baggy jeans that hung on her frame were tied with a rope. Her clothes were dirty and wrinkled, and the hair under her hat hung almost to her shoulders. If it was her mom, she'd lost a lot of weight and in dire need of a makeover.

"Mom, is that you?"

Her mother pushed her hat off and let it fall to her back.

Oh, my goodness! Stunned, Abby clapped her hands over her mouth. She was beautiful. Her tanned face was rosy with health and happiness. Those hazel eyes sparkled with humor as she watched Abby take inventory.

"You look fantastic, Mom." She propped her hands on her hips. "Though it wouldn't hurt to try smaller jeans and get a haircut." She threw her arms around her mother and they hugged and rocked for several seconds.

"Nag, nag, nag! That's all I ever hear from you." The teasing in her voice was music to Abby's ears. "It's good to see you, Abby. But what are you doing here?"

"What do you think? I came to check up on you. See how you're doing. And you look great." Her mother's change was worth all the anxious weeks she'd spent wondering if they'd done the right thing. "I can't wait until Uncle Art sees you. He's going to flip. I told him our plan would work."

Her mother gave her a stern look. "Don't push your luck, young lady. You're not completely forgiven, nor is Art."

"But Mom, Uncle Art's worried himself sick about you. Though he did feel better when he got back and saw the plant and the beautiful pot you made for him. Is that pot going to explode or something when he least expects it?"

"Who knows, Abby? Only time will tell. Not me."

"Come on, Mom, I want you to get acquainted with Brandon." Arms around each other, they walked to where the men had carefully watched their exchange.

Brandon asked. "Is it safe to be close to you two?" His father laughed and clapped him on the shoulder.

Lynn started to shake Brandon's hand, but hugged him instead. "Hello, Brandon, I'm Lynn and you're safe, everything is fine."

Abby followed her mother to the barn to unsaddle and bed Beauty down for the night. Brandon had offered to do it, but her mom refused. What a surprise. As was the ease and ability with which she groomed the horse. It was an ugly creature, but she didn't dare voice her opinion. Her mother seemed fond of the animal. As if Beauty could sense her disdain, the horse looked her straight in the eye, curled back her lips and blew air out making them flutter, which resulted in a disgusting noise.

Before they left the barn, her mother's horse was fed and comfortable, and the tack cleaned and put away. They stepped out of the darkened interior into the blazing heat. Abby wished she'd thought to wear a hat.

"You do that very well, Mom."

"I've learned a few things while I've been here."

"I can see that." Abby felt an overwhelming surge of love for her mother. She looked so good and happy. Her eyes sparkled as she talked and her skin glowed.

Locking an arm around her mom's waist, they continued to walk, bumping hips and laughing as they did so.

"How's your baby brother?"

Abby couldn't restrain her grin. He was the cutest little bugger. "He's great. You should see him mimic the way Daddy walks. Keeps me and Lorraine in stitches." Abby loved her dad and stepmother. She was worried about them. "They're in counseling."

Her mother stopped walking. "Dan and Lorraine?" She shook her head. "I'm sorry to hear that."

"Yeah, me too." They resumed walking. "Hopefully it will work. I think Daddy's really trying." If he wasn't he sure put on a good front.

When they reached the cabin steps, Abby couldn't wait any longer. "He asked me to give you a message."

Surprised, her mother stood waiting for her to continue, a puzzled expression on her face.

Abby cleared her throat. "He said to tell you he now realizes how unfair he was to you, and he's sorry." She wasn't sure what her parents' problems had been. Neither ever elaborated on why they were divorcing. They'd just told her they weren't happy together. But Abby had her own ideas. She'd watched her mother try to please him and attend parties when she'd rather have been doing something with just the three of them. He wanted the social whirl, she didn't, and they argued about it constantly.

Tears gathered in Lynn's eyes and Abby thought her heart would break at the pain she saw there. "Mom, you don't still love him, do you?"

"No sugar, I don't." She smiled through her tears. "Tell him I appreciate the apology and that I hope he and Lorraine can work things out." She swung the door open. "Let's get in out of the heat."

Relief flowed through Abby in a wave. She so wanted her mother to be happy. Smiling, she stepped into the coolness on the clay tile floor.

Inside Lynn's cabin, Abby looked around with appreciation. "This is great, Mom. I love it." She plopped down on the sofa.

"Yeah, it is, isn't it?" Lynn pulled off her boots, grabbed clean underwear and headed for the bathroom. Stopping in mid-stride, she turned. "Where's your stuff? Aren't you going to stay with me?"

"No. Brandon put my bags in one of the guest rooms at the ranch house." Actually, Abby hadn't been sure of how she'd be received, and grateful her mother was over her mad spell. *I still can't believe it!* Her mother looked great, healthy and happy.

A minute later, her head appeared around the bathroom door. "Anything going on between you and Brandon?"

"Not yet. I'm interested and he seems to be, but we're not rushing into anything. For now, we're just friends."

Interesting question, actually. She'd noticed a couple of intimate glances pass between her mother and Seth. Hmm... Wouldn't that be nice? Seth was a nice man with lots to offer a woman. Not money and material things, though he might have those too, but from Brandon's description of his childhood and the care he gave his summer charges, he had a large capacity for love. Her mother needed the love of a good man. And Seth wasn't just a good man—he was a hunk.

Abby could hear the sound of the shower running.

She stretched out on the sofa and flipped through a paperback novel. When her mother came out of the bathroom tying the sash on her robe, she couldn't resist asking. "What about you, Mom? Anything going on between you and Seth?"

She ran a comb through her hair removing the tangles. "Oh, we've been having an illicit love affair for about a month now."

Abby bolted up off the couch. "Mother! You're teasing me, aren't you?" Her mother flashed a smile and then she started tossing clothes around. No way would her mother have an affair. She didn't think. If she did, she sure as heck wouldn't broadcast it, especially to her.

"What on earth am I going to put on?" Lynn rejected everything she picked up.

"Try on those size ten jeans, Mom. You should be able to wear them now." Why wasn't she wearing them already rather than those baggy things she tied on with a rope?

"I don't know. The last time I tried them, they were too tight. I should have ordered some 12's from Maria's catalogue."

Her mother's head disappeared in the closet, her rear end bobbing as she looked through clothes in a basket. She pulled out a pair of jeans that didn't look too wrinkled. Abby shook her head. They were borderline. Maybe when they were on the wrinkles would relax. When her mother zipped them up and turned toward her, Abby nodded her approval.

"Hey, they fit perfect." Her mother looked pretty darn good for an older woman.

Not convinced, Lynn turned this way and that in

front of the full-length mirror. "Don't you think they're a little too tight?"

"Nope. They'll give some as you wear them. In an hour they'll be comfortable."

When Lynn and Abby walked into the dining hall, Seth blinked at the snug fitting jeans hugging Lynn's curves. His eyes followed her as she filled her tray. Lord, she had a good- looking ass. He'd never actually gotten a good view of her tush as it'd had been hidden underneath those baggy jeans. Hopefully those damn things were in the trash.

Seth noticed a rustle of interest ran through the male population when they spotted Abby. Thank God she'd changed out of those shorts or there would've been a stampede. Brandon went to greet Abby and escorted her to a seat beside him. From the good-natured grumbling, the men had gotten Brandon's message. They were a good bunch of men and thankfully treated all women with respect.

Their lack of interest in Lynn was a puzzle. They liked her, loved her baking, and teased her on occasion. But none had shown an interest in her outside the dining hall. True, at first she'd been unapproachable, but when she started hanging around at the barn and corral, she was relaxed and fun to be around. Did they believe he'd already staked a claim? If so, they knew him better than he knew himself.

Seth eyes went back to Lynn, entranced by the graceful sway of her hips as she walked toward him. When she reached the table, he stood, took her tray and sat it on the table. He put his arm around her shoulders to give her a hug. Her face was tilted up to his. He leaned down to give her a light kiss when a discreet,

"Harrumph," from Cookie stopped him.

Remembering where he was, Seth moved back and they sat down. Lynn's face reddened but the twitch of her lips indicated she wasn't upset. He cast furtive glances around in hopes no one had seen his slip, but from the smiles and looks being passed between the wranglers and crew, he knew few had missed the exchange. He felt his face heat. Dammit, Chue was actually chortling. When Brandon and Abby caught his eye, they both grinned. Brandon had the gall to raise his thumb in the air. Shit.

He wasn't ashamed of his feelings. Lord, he was proud that'd he'd found Lynn. But, this wasn't the place or time to reveal them. Not in front of the camp kids. If it had just been the staff, it wouldn't have mattered.

* * *

Abby had spent the night at the main ranch house but brought her things down to her cabin to dress for the dance. "For the umpteenth time, Abby, nothing is settled between us. When, and if it is, you'll be one of the first to know." She turned to Abby and gave her long braid a tug. "Now, give it a rest. Okay?"

Abby didn't know what to believe. She knew bugging her mother wouldn't help. Darn it, she hated being in the dark. Was her mother capable of an illicit love affair? Nah, she didn't think so. She'd been teasing. But the look in Seth's eyes when he bent to kiss her mother in the dining hall last night hadn't been the least bit teasing—it was *hot*!

Just in case something serious was brewing, Abby loaned her mother the dress she'd planned to wear to the dance tonight. If her mother wanted him, and it looked like she did, Abby was not above stacking the deck. She wanted to seal that good-looking man's fate. She really liked the man and wouldn't mind in the least having him for a stepfather.

Abby watched her mother as she studied her reflection in the mirror, turning from one side to the other. Abby had talked her into letting her trim her hair. After shampooing and hot curling, her mother's shiny auburn hair fell in a soft pageboy just below her chin.

Abby held the dress to help her mother slip in without messing up her hair. She zipped it up and stood back to look at her mother.

Made of faded blue denim, the color enhanced her auburn hair and peachy skin. It dipped low in the front, was sleeveless, and fell in soft tiers from the waist. The bodice hugged her mother's curves, showing just enough cleavage to be sexy but not enough to look brazen.

"I can't wear this, Abby. It's too low cut." She pulled at the bodice, trying to raise it an inch or two.

"Leave it alone, Mother. It's perfect."

"I don't know. I feel naked."

Abby fastened the western belt trimmed in silver low on her mother's waist. It matched her boots and complemented her silver earrings and bracelet.

"You look beautiful, Mom. With your tan, the blush and lipstick are just enough."

"You look great yourself." Lynn pulled Abby around in front of her so she could see both their reflections in the mirror. She tugged the neckline of Abby's top a little higher to cover the small amount of cleavage showing. "Though I think maybe you look too sexy in that outfit."

In black jeans, black boots, and Lynn's red silk t-shirt, Abby's skin looked like alabaster. The silver heart she wore suspended on a black ribbon with silver earrings added to its luster. Her hair was pulled back into a French braid and tied with a black ribbon.

Abby adjusted the *décolletage* of her top. "Mom, you've got to remember I'm not a teenager anymore. I'm a grown woman. You can't keep me in ruffles and Mary Jane shoes forever, you know."

"I know, but it's hard." Lynn glanced down at her own slightly exposed bosom. "Are you sure this isn't too low?"

Before Abby could answer, there was a knock on the door.

"Mom, can you get that? I need to put on just a little more makeup." She dashed into the bathroom and shut the door.

Lynn opened the door to the two men. Smiling, they stepped inside.

She felt Seth's eyes caress her as they traveled from her head to her toes, then back up to her low cut neckline. He winked and mouthed "Wow."

Heat rose to her face. *Wow yourself, Mister.* Dressed in his freshly starched Levis, Lynn would have to be blind to not notice how they hugged his long muscled legs and everything else. His white dress shirt complemented his tanned face and the white of his teeth as he smiled. His gray eyes sparkled with mischief. Lynn swallowed the lump in her throat. This man was beautiful.

"You want to sit down? Brandon, Abby will be out in just a minute."

Seth took Lynn's elbow and led her out on the

porch.

"You look wonderful," he said as his eyes moved over her. "Nice dress. And I like how it shows so much of this soft skin." He ran his palms up and down her bare arms, then ran a finger across her collarbone. "Silk. Your skin feels like silk." His fingers trailed back and forth across the low cut neckline.

She shivered, aching for his touch. Just the thought of his hands on her bare flesh made her gasp. "You better stop that. Remember, you're sending me home in two days."

"Don't I know it?" He dropped his arms as Brandon and Abby joined them on the porch.

The barn had been cleaned in readiness for the dance. Coal oil lamps hung from hooks on supporting timbers. The glow from the few windows and the barn door was inviting as they walked down the road to the barn.

Inside, the light cast a soft glow across the large area. When they entered, the band had already started their first number.

Seth held out his hand. "May I have this dance?"

"You may."

She stepped into his arms. They hadn't completed a turn around the floor, when Jake tapped Seth on the shoulder. "I'm cutting in, Boss."

Before Seth could claim her, Cookie grabbed her hand and led her back to the dance floor. "You going to be back next summer?" He watched her face for her answer.

"You bet, Cookie. Wouldn't miss it for the world."

He gave her a gentle hug. "Good, this place needs you. Seth needs you."

Before she could reply he was gone and Pete took his place. She enjoyed dance after dance, but was grateful when she found herself alone on the sidelines. It gave her time to catch her breath and look for Seth. She turned toward the bandstand, her eyes floating over couple after couple. Not spotting him, she turned back. Tim stood beside her.

"May I have this dance, Lynn?" Lynn's heart jumped. This young man had come a long way in just a few months. He was no longer sullen and she felt honored that he'd gathered the courage to ask her for a dance.

"I'd be honored, Tim." His dancing skills had improved since their last dance together. And, he wasn't as shy and hesitant. "Have you had a chance to dance with Julie this evening?"

He flushed and his head bobbed up and down. "Yes, ma'am, we've danced several times. We're going to write each other during the school year."

"Oh, that's wonderful, Tim."

At the end of the dance, he walked her back to the sidelines as he'd been taught. When he didn't leave her side, she asked, "You want to dance again?" He shook his head and cleared his throat.

"Ma'am, I want to thank you for all you've done for me this summer."

"Oh, Tim. You're welcome." She hugged him tight. When he submitted to her embrace and clasped her back, her throat tightened. "And I want to thank you. You weren't the only one who needed to make some changes and adjustments."

He flushed with pleasure. "Really?"

"Yes, really. Now you go find Julie and dance with

her again."

She needed something to drink. Corby and Zane stood by the refreshment table, stuffing their mouths with cookies and wiping crumbs on their jeans. Spotting her coming their way, they gave her open mouth smiles and waved.

"Have you young men danced with your mothers this evening?"

They looked at each other before shaking their heads.

"Well then, don't wait another minute. Show them what you've learned. That's a two-step the band's playing. That should be an easy one to start with."

Looking like they were escorting the Queen of England, they led their mothers onto the dance floor. Both women smiled proudly as their boys counted off the beat. Their mothers, trying hard not to laugh or cry, looked down at their sons with joy and hope etched on their features.

"Save one for me later," she called. She moved closer to the refreshment table.

Seth joined her and picked up two glasses of lemonade. "Let's get some fresh air." At the corral, they leaned against the fence and sipped their drinks. The music was a nice accompaniment to the night sounds, the swish of a horse's tail, the stamping of its hoof, and the hum of cicadas

"Umm. This is delicious. But it would be just perfect if it had just a touch of peppermint."

"Would you be referring to that secret ingredient you put in your iced tea?" Seth quipped.

Lynn blanched. "What do you know about my secret ingredient?" She looked at him in accusation.

"You've known about it all along, haven't you?" Glass clutched in her right hand, she folded her arms across her chest and tried to look stern. "How'd you find out? And how come you never said anything?"

He finished off his lemonade and set the empty cup atop a fence post. Reaching out, he slid his arms around her unyielding body and put his ice-cold lips on the skin just under her ear and nibbled causing her to shiver.

"Because, sweet lady, I smelled it on your breath the evening I asked you about the etiquette classes." His lips continued their tickling journey causing her to giggle. "When I saw what a good mood you three ladies were in after your little socials, I put two and two together and twisted Maria's arm until she confessed."

Lynn stiffened.

"A figure of speech, I assure you. Anyway, she said your stash was depleted so I figured no harm done."

She punched him playfully in the gut. "You scoundrel. That's not fair. You should have told me you knew." He laughed and side stepped as she lunged for him.

When Sally started singing with her husky voice, he took her glass and sat it in his on the fence post. He placed her arms around his neck, and with his around her waist pulled her close. His lips brushed the skin at her temple as he sang the words to the love song. He moved his hands up to her rib cage and stroked the sides of her breasts.

Lynn couldn't hold back her moan of pleasure. His thumbs moved to her nipples and stroked. The sensation was so intense she jerked in his arms and trembled.

Voice thick with passion, he asked, "Do you like that, Lynn, me touching your breasts?"

"Oh, yes, Seth."

His hands moved to her bottom, pulled her against his arousal, and held her still a moment before moving his arms back to her waist.

She felt him shudder.

"Soon, love. We'll have all the time in the world to touch and taste." He gripped her tighter and dropped his head to nuzzle her neck.

"Seth."

"Mmm?"

"Do you believe in premarital sex?"

He froze. Then laughter rumbled from his chest and echoed around her. She giggled at his response. He whooped louder and squeezed, lifting her feet off the ground.

"Shhhh, Seth. Stop it. It wasn't *that* funny and people are going to hear you."

"Oh God, Lynn. You're good for me."

"We better get back inside. Your guests will be missing you." And, be speculating about what we're doing out here, especially after that loud outburst. She wished it had been a heck of a lot more. But, Seth was very discreet when it came to the camp kids. She respected that and felt the same way, but it sure didn't keep her from wanting.

He nodded between chuckles then sobered. "Yeah, you're right. But, I know as soon as we get in there, someone will be cut in and take you out of my arms." He leaned down and gave her a soft kiss. "Oh well, duty calls."

The rest of the evening went by in a whirl. Lynn

caught glimpses of Seth as she danced by in someone else's arms. She'd just sat down on a hay bale when Roark joined her with two glasses of lemonade.

"May I join you, ma'am?"

"If one of those glasses is for me, you surely may."

They sat quietly for a few minutes while they drank and watched the dancers.

"Roark, thank you for not ratting on me at the barbecue."

"You're welcome. But, actually, I don't blab about work." He took her hand. "Come on, let's dance." They dropped their glasses in the trash and stepped on to the floor.

He was a good dancer, one of those men who could expertly lead a woman on the dance floor, even if she had two left feet.

"Have you met my daughter?"

"Is she that pretty blonde with Brandon and Barbara?"

Ah, Barbara was here. Seth hadn't mentioned she'd be back so soon. She probably came whenever she wanted, had an open invitation. Of course she would. Her sons were here. Jealousy gripped her.

"Yes, that's her." Her voice sounded weak. She hoped he didn't notice.

"I've not had the pleasure. Would you introduce us?"

Hand at her back, he maneuvered her toward the bandstand where Abby stood with Barbara and Brandon.

Before they got far, Seth appeared at her side and Lynn sighed with relief. He slapped Roark on the back.

"Hey, Roark, I'm cutting in."

Roark grinned. "You mean I have to turn her over to you, old man."

Seth snorted. "Who're you calling old, pup?"

She laughed. "You two stop it. Seth, I want Roark to meet Abby."

As they approached the group, Brandon stood with his back to them with his arm around his mother's shoulders. Abby watched their approach, her face pinched with concern.

Barbara turned, her pretty red mouth smiled, and she called out, "Seth, darling!"

Seth froze in his tracks and stared in surprise, and then he looked down at Lynn, squeezed her waist and winked. She sighed with relief. Pulling Lynn along with him, Seth walked to the woman, dropped Lynn's arm and opened his arms. "Hello, Barbara. What a surprise to see you again so soon."

Without even a cursory glance toward Lynn, Barbara stepped into Seth's arms, placed hers around his neck and tilted her face up for his kiss. Seth avoided her lips, gave her a friendly hug, then released her and stepped back.

He turned to Lynn and put his arm around her shoulders. "Barbara, you remember Lynn."

Barbara smiled and nodded, but the smile didn't quite reach her eyes. "Good to see you again, Lynn."

"You too, Barbara."

"And, I'm sure you remember, Roark."

"Of course I do." She hugged him and patted his cheek. "You've grown up, just like my boys."

He laughed. "We tend to do that, especially when you're not looking."

Brandon and Roark were shaking hands, and

joking around.

"Brandon, please introduce Abby to Roark. I'd like for them to meet."

"Ladies and gentlemen, this is the last song of the evening. You know the routine, find him or her and get ready for *The Last Waltz*.

Brandon joined Seth and Lynn as they walked to the middle of the dance floor. Barbara stood visiting with Roark and Abby.

"Lynn, may I have this dance?"

Lynn was shocked that he'd ask her and not be dancing with Abby. She looked at Seth.

He clasped Brandon's shoulder. "Son, Lynn is my partner for this number."

He looked from his father to Lynn. "But you always dance this one with Mom."

"Not anymore, Brandon. Things change."

"Oh, okay Dad." He clasped his father's arm and smiled.

"Why don't you dance this one with your mother and get Roark to partner Abby."

"Sure thing, Dad."

The music started and Seth pulled her into his arms. She melted against him, conscious only of the feel of his body against hers, his wonderful smell, and the rapid beating of their hearts.

Seth had given her all the proof she needed.

Chapter Fifteen

Abby knew her face was dark and stormy, but couldn't help it. "Mother, if you laugh I'll never forgive you."

Gone was her long beautiful braid and in its place was an exaggerated upswept do. It was so stiff from hairspray, a typhoon wouldn't muss it. She had on enough makeup for two women, and if the daggers she'd thrown Brandon with her eyes were real he'd be dead by now. Why had she agreed to accompany Brandon when he stopped by to visit his mother before breakfast? Barbara had been getting dressed and talked Abby into letting her fix her hair. One thing led to another and now she looked like a rodeo clown.

Her mother coughed to cover up her snickers, while Seth, sitting beside her, shook with unrestrained mirth.

Brandon looked dutifully contrite. His shoulders dropped.

"Abby, I'm sorry. She'll be leaving here in a little while and you can wash that crap off your face and braid your hair." Brandon explained to Lynn. "Mom loves to do hair and makeup and since she first met Abby, she's been itching to get her hands on her hair."

"I don't understand." Lynn said. "Barbara doesn't wear that much makeup and her hairstyle is modest. Why would she fix Abby up to look like a lady of the evening?"

Brandon blushed and started to defend his mother when Seth cut in.

"Abby, Lynn, don't take this wrong. Barbara wears a lot of makeup but with her coloring, it's more natural.

Obviously on Abby, it's not appropriate. And Barbara has always wanted to wear elaborate hairdos but never felt comfortable with one." He waved at Abby's hair. "This was just a chance for her to try some of her fantasies."

With a hearty guffaw, he reached across the table and clasped Brandon on the shoulder. "Just be glad you weren't born a girl, son. Look what you'd have been exposed to."

Even Abby couldn't keep a straight face after that remark. She joined their raucous laughter.

Lynn swiped at her tears of hilarity. "Maybe we should get the camera and take a picture for posterity." Abby didn't find the remark amusing.

After breakfast, activity in front of her cabin escalated as counselors helped campers carry luggage from the bunkhouses to the dining hall to wait for their rides. Since the dining hall would be the official sendoff site, Seth remained close by to supervise and arrange transportation for those who needed it. Brian, Jared, and Brandon stayed busy ferrying parents and kids in to Mesa Flats to meet their rides or pick up their vehicles.

By noon, several vehicles loaded with kids were ready to pull away. Lynn stood with Cookie, Pete, and Clara as the staff, even the wranglers, lined the road to wave as carloads drove by. Seth was their last stop. Lynn turned from the departing campers to see Tim standing before Seth. He pulled the boy in for a tight hug, and then held him at arm's length. "Bye, Tim. I'm real proud of you." He clapped him on the back. "Let me hear from you on occasion." Tim, doing his best not to cry, gave Seth a distorted smile and nodded. He looked at Lynn and waved.

Hand clasped over her mouth to keep from crying, Lynn waved. She braced herself to say goodbye to Corby and Zane. They were waiting with their mothers for one of the Suburbans to return. She joined them, leaned down, and gave them each a hug.

"I think I may want a picture or two of you guys on occasion to see how you're growing. How about that?"

"Okay, we'll send you one of our school pictures, won't we, Zane?" He looked at his friend for affirmation.

"Yeah, though they'll probably look dorky. Mine always do."

Zane's mother ruffled his hair. "They do not. I love them and have saved every one for your baby book."

"Yikes! For your baby book, Zane!" At his comment, Corby ran with Zane chasing on his heels.

Both mothers laughed and assured Lynn she'd receive pictures and letters on the boys' progress. They glowed with joy at the change in their sons.

Corby and Zane returned, arms slung over the other's shoulder. They were a delight to watch. She hoped their friendship would grow and be one of those that lasted a lifetime. Everyone needed a friend like that.

Seth hugged Julie and then held the door for her while she climbed in the Suburban. Waving as they drove off, he turned and walked toward them.

"Okay, you two little cowpokes. You and your Moms will ride in the next vehicle that stops here."

"Ah, Seth, can't we stay another day?" asked Corby. "My Mom wants to ride a horse."

"Is that right?" He looked at Corby's mother who was shaking her head and laughed. "Maybe next summer."

Zane's eyes were round as saucers. "You mean we can come back next summer?"

"I think we can arrange that. Would you like to come back?"

Both boys threw themselves at him, yelling. He put an arm around each of their shoulders. "You bet. Oh, man, do you mean it?"

"Sure do. As long as it's all right with your mothers. And of course, you've got to work hard in school and mind at home."

"Yippee!"

"All right!"

Squatting, Seth pulled both boys around and between his legs. As he held them close, his heart lurched with pain. Their earthy, little boy smell reminded him of his own sons. Arms twined about his neck, they each planted a shy kiss on his cheek, and then hugged him as tightly as they could.

"Thank you, Seth," said Corby. "I'm going to miss you."

"Me too, Seth, I'm going to miss you too," added Zane in a small voice.

Voice gruff, Seth said. "I'm going to miss you guys, too." A returning Suburban made a U-turn in the road and stopped. He stood. "Okay, guys, here's your ride. Get the door for your mother's."

* * *

Dinner that night was a festive affair. Wranglers and the full time staff gathered to say good-bye to the college students and summer crew. But saying goodbye was difficult.

Cookie clasped her in a tight hug. "You be sure

you come back next summer, Lynn." He sniffed. "Don't know how we'll make it through the winter without you."

Fighting back tears, she kissed Cookie on the cheek. "You've been a good friend, Cookie. Thank you for everything."

Clara and Maria promised to write. When Pete clasped her in a quick hug, and said, "We're gonna miss you, gal," she lost the battle and tears rolled down her face.

Her tears turned to laughter when Shorty presented her with one of his deer dropping necklaces. He put it around her neck with a flourish. She kissed him on the cheek, then looked down at the beads and fingered them gingerly.

"Don't you worry none, gal. I sealed them real good."

The roomful full of people laughed and clapped their hands, then looked at Abby. Abby blushed scarlet while shooting daggers at Lynn. Lynn shook her head and pointed at Brandon. When Abby lit into Brandon, the laughter increased in volume.

Seth suspected everyone thought he and Lynn were having a relationship, but Seth hadn't revealed the particulars. Curious glances were cast their way, but the subject wasn't mentioned.

When the party was over, Chue met them on the porch. Agitated, he took off his hat and slapped his knee with it several times. He looked around to make sure they were alone.

Seth waited for him to speak then finally asked. "What is it, Chue? Is something wrong?"

"Wrong? Damn sure is. Anybody with two eyes in

their head can see you two are stuck on each other." He glared at Lynn, "But you're leaving," and shook his fist at Seth, "And you're letting her go." He looked from one to the other. "I sure as hell wish I knew what the devil was going on."

Slapping his hat back on his head, he turned and walked off muttering something about them being, "Loco."

They watched him walk toward the corral. Lynn felt sorry for him. "Bless his heart. He wants to see us happy."

"He will. But, just not as soon as he'd like." Seth draped his arm over her shoulder. "Never thought of Chue as a romantic."

They stopped at the door of her cabin.

"You want to come in for a while?"

She leaned against the door. Seth, arm propped against the wall, leaned in and cupped her cheek. "You think that's wise?"

"Probably not. But, come on in for a while, anyway."

Seth followed Lynn inside. They sat on her sofa. Lynn, with her feet drawn up under her, faced Seth, arm across his shoulder. His hand brushed back and forth over her knee. She twined her fingers in his hair.

"What have you told your sons about us?"

"As little as possible. But they're not blind and know something is brewing. Especially after the dance last night." As the music ended, he'd held her a second longer, and in front of their kids and all his guests, leaned down and placed a soft kiss on her lips. "I love you, Lynn. No one but you." His fingers had trailed down her cheek. "Do you believe me?" Choked with emotion, she couldn't speak but nodded. As people gathered around to say goodbye, Seth kept her at his side, his arm around her waist.

"Come here, let me hold you." He drew her on to his lap and when he leaned against the arm of the sofa they were almost reclining.

Arms around her, he stroked her hair. She sighed with pleasure. His fingers moved to undo the buttons of her white blouse. He ran his knuckles across the flesh above her bra, then dipped just under the edge and continued stroking.

Lynn couldn't breathe. *I've died and gone to heaven.* It had been so long since she'd been touched intimately, too long.

Seth said. "You know that dance is pretty much considered a public declaration around here."

"Huh…um hum…yeah…that's…what I figured."

He kissed her ear. His hand slipped inside her bra and closed over her breast. She gasped. When he thumbed her nipple, she arched into his hand. Oh, God, he was going to be a good lover. If she was this turned on by him touching her breasts, what would happen if he touched her… No, she better not think about that. But she couldn't help it, as her body wouldn't let her stop imagining. It hummed with a mind of its own.

His voice raspy, he asked, "What about you? What have you told Abby?"

"I keep telling her…oh, Seth that feels so good…that nothing is final." He knew just how to touch her. "That's she'd be…the first…to know."

With a groan, he nipped her ear, then removed his hand from inside her blouse, but continued to stroke her breast through the fabric.

"Actually, I've been telling her we've been having an illicit love affair."

He stiffened and started buttoning her blouse. "What? How could you tell her something like that? No wonder she's been casting sideways glances at me."

"Don't worry. She knows I'm kidding." She settled back against his body. "If we were, I certainly wouldn't tell her."

Seth relaxed and propped his chin on top of her head. Right now he regretted they weren't having an affair. They'd be in that bed rather than sitting here trying to keep their hands off each other. No, they wouldn't. Not with both their kids here. He was liberal in most ways, but it just didn't seem right with all four of them here, plus the college kids. Not that they'd care, but he sure didn't want it bandied around the Psychology departments at the various universities that Dr. Williams was having sex with one of his employees. Then the question would be, did they while the campers were there? His reputation had to be stellar or donations and recommendations would cease.

He kissed Lynn's temple and she snuggled against him. She was such a delight and so responsive to his touch. When they could actually touch at will, things would be hot and explosive. He grinned. Would she be as greedy when it came to sex as she was to his kisses? God, he hoped so.

This was their last night together. He wouldn't have time tomorrow to say much, so everything would have to be said tonight. "You'll call me as soon as you get home to let me know you made it okay?"

"Yeah, I will. We'll stop somewhere for the night. And with Abby along, I'll probably stop more often.

It'll probably be late Tuesday evening before I can call."

Like a blind man memorizing her face with his lips, he kissed her eyes, her cheeks, and then teased her lips with nibbling, caressing kisses before sealing them to hers. She opened her mouth and he was in, stroking and tasting. He wanted her closer, her breasts flattened against his chest.

Seth broke their kiss long enough to sit up and turn Lynn in his lap. "Come closer, baby." She straddled him. When her skirt twisted beneath her, she rose and pulled it free. It billowed around his knees. She settled on his legs. Oh God, there was nothing between them but her panties and his jeans.

Lynn's eyes closed in passion. The woman was no help at all here. He dropped his head back against the sofa, his breath ragged. His hands found the edge of her skirt and pulled it up until he touched flesh. He kissed the pulse point in her throat and traveled up her neck to the sensitive spot beneath her ear. "Let me feel you close."

She settled against him, and wrapped her arms around his neck. Her heart thumped against his. He caressed her legs, running his hand up and down. Soft, so soft, just like a baby's skin. Unable to stop himself, he molded his hands to the cheeks of her butt and pulled her against his arousal.

Heat and home, that's what she felt like against him. Blind with need, he found her mouth. Open under his, Seth entered and stroked her mouth until the slow burn in his body was too hot to bear. He broke the kiss and dropped his head to her shoulder.

He eased her from his lap and sat her beside him on

the sofa, his arm around her shoulder. "Good God, Lynn. What are we doing?" *I sure as hell know what I'm doing. I'm torturing myself.*

Voice shaky, Lynn said, "When I was a teenager we called it making out."

His laugh ripped through the room. She was stunned at his outburst, and then laughed with him. He drew in a deep breath and exhaled. "Life will never be dull with you, will it?"

"I certainly hope not." With her hand, she ran her finger down his chest, almost to his belt. His eyes followed every movement.

He grabbed her wrist and lifted her fingers to his lips. "Stop that. It just makes me want more. This make-out session will keep me awake for days." With a gruff chuckle, he hugged her tight. Standing, he pulled her up with him. "I've got to go. You need to get some sleep." What he meant was, he couldn't take any more "making out."

"You don't have to go, you know."

He was quiet for a minute. Running his hands up and down her arms, he said. "You don't mean that, Lynn. What would our children think?" His hand moved around to her back, molding her closer to his arousal. "Everyone on this ranch probably knows I'm in here and curious to see when I leave. Especially our kids." Hell, he wouldn't be surprised to look out the door and see them sitting on the dining hall steps. Not that they'd be condemning. They were curious to know if their parents' relationship was serious. Though no one's business but his and hers, he didn't want any of the ranch hands or staff to think less of her.

He nuzzled her neck and growled. "When we make

love, we're going to have all night, maybe days with no interruptions. I don't want a quickie, unless I have time to go back and see what I missed."

"I love you, Seth. I'll be back as soon as I can."

Hands around her waist, he lifted her and buried his face in the V between her breasts, her arms locked around his neck. He lowered her to the floor and tilted her chin. "I love you too." Lowering his head, he placed a sweet lingering kiss on her lips. "Goodnight, love."

A loud pounding sounded on the door.

"Mom, you in there? Can I come in and talk awhile?"

Seth grinned. "You think the kids are keeping an eye on us and planned this?"

"We could always ask."

"Hell, no." He walked to the door, his hat in his hand trying to inconspicuously hide his arousal. Abby stood on the porch. He held the door open for her. "Come on in, Abby. I was just leaving." He looked at Lynn and winked. "See you in the morning."

* * *

Lynn woke with Seth's kisses fresh on her mind. With a smile on her face, she stretched like a cat. A giggle bubbled from her throat when she recalled the look on Seth's face at Abby's untimely intrusion. And a flush rose to her cheeks at the memory of his hands on her breasts.

An hour later, she stood at the pasture fence talking to Beauty and Rosebud. Sam sat by her side. She fed the horses sugar cubes and laughed as Beauty pulled on her shirt pocket to see if there were more.

"You've had enough, girl. Don't you know too much sugar isn't good for you?" She leaned over and placed her cheek on the mare's forehead close to her ear.

"I'm going to tell you a secret, girl. I'll be back soon, back to stay. So, don't forget me."

Beauty tossed her head and nickered.

Promptly at eight o'clock, Seth knocked at her door.

"Come on in, Seth."

"You all packed and ready?"

She stepped into his arms. He held her and kissed the top of her head, but broke away when he heard Brian's footsteps on the porch.

They carried her bags and boxes out to the Suburban. Lynn took a last look around and closed the door behind her. It felt so final. Yet, it was also the beginning. One door closes and another opens. That's what her mother used to say. She might be leaving in one capacity today but she'd be returning in another before long. Of that she didn't have a doubt.

At the SUV, Sam was in his usual spot, the front seat, just as he'd been the day she came to the ranch.

Standing with her door open, Seth wrapped her in his arms. He placed a kiss at her temple and whispered. "I'll be expecting to hear from you before too long."

Sobs clogged her throat. She tried to smile and but could only nod. He chucked her under the chin and mouthed, "I love you." He helped her into the vehicle and closed the door before walking around to hug Brian.

"Let me hear from you, son."

Brian saluted. "Okay, Dad."

* * *

The trip to Mesa Flats went by in a blur. When

they reached the highest point in the road, Lynn turned in the seat to look back at the ranch. The tall dry and faded ocotillo plants, merged with the colors of the desert. When the buildings grew smaller and blended into the terrain, she faced forward with the future in mind.

Next spring, she'd be here when the ocotillo bloomed. She and Seth could drive up here, better yet ride their horses, and watch the sun, as it set behind the mountain and washed the basin in red.

At the small building where she'd left her car, Abby stood in the shade of the carport. She'd ridden in with Brandon and Jared. Her luggage was already loaded in the dust covered Taurus. Jared sat in the driver's seat as Brandon tinkered with something under the hood.

She slid out of the Suburban. "Brandon, is something wrong under there?"

He grabbed a rag off the bumper and wiped his hands. "No, ma'am. It's got oil, radiator's still full of water and coolant, and it started right up. Everything looks good."

She breathed a sigh of relief. As much as she'd like to stay longer, there wasn't a repair shop within one hundred and ten miles. Besides, she had things to do at home.

"Good. Thank you both for checking things out."

Brandon closed the hood. "You're welcome. We had our orders from Dad. Glad he thought of it."

It felt good to have someone looking out for her.

Lynn turned to Brian and gave him a hug. "Thank you for the ride. And, if you have any trouble with those math courses, you give me a call." She indulged in one last look. "I'm going to miss you guys." Then she slid into the driver's seat.

Just as Abby opened the passenger door, Sam jumped in and sat down.

Oh, Lord. Please, no Sam. Lynn got out and walked back around the car.

"Sam. What are you doing?" She reached in and tried to grab his collar but he sidestepped her. "Come on, Sam. You can't go." This wasn't like Sam. He always minded.

Fighting tears, she turned to Brian. This was too much. She'd held herself together to this point, but she couldn't take much more. Brandon and Jared called Sam, but he ignored them. He sat there like a king on his throne.

Brandon and Jared exchanged looks and shrugged. Brian grinned at their lack of success.

Her voice cracked as she spoke. "Brian. You're going to...have to get him...out."

Lynn watched her distress register with Brian. His face fell. He put his arm around her. "Lynn, I'm sorry. Dad wants Sam to go home with you. I thought you knew."

She looked at him in surprise. "But why?"

He shrugged. "I don't know. He just said, 'Tell her I'll be there at Thanksgiving for her answer.' I guess he'll get Sam then. Didn't make a lick of sense to me, but that's what he said." He handed her a leash. "I put all of his things in the trunk but here's his leash for when you stop on the road."

He turned to the dog and patted him on the head. "Sam, you be good now." Sam licked his hand.

Smiling through tears, she kissed Brian's cheek.

"Thanks, Brian. It makes sense to me." Seth wanted her to make her final decision at home in Fort Worth. The ball was in her court but by sending Sam with her he'd have an excuse to come get her final answer in person.

In a much better mood now, she looked across the roof of the car. "Abby, I hope you don't mind riding in the back. Sam likes the front."

Lynn heard Abby mutter something like, "Taking a back seat to a dog." She ducked her head, but not before Lynn saw the grin and her lips twitch.

Intent on getting home, Lynn took the most direct route, foregoing scenery for speed. From Mesa Flats, she drove to Odessa and hit Interstate 20. From there it was a straight shot to Fort Worth.

She glanced at Abby in the rear view mirror. "Abby, I'm submitting my letter of resignation to be effective as soon as a replacement can be found." Then she'd fax him a letter telling him to come for her. "Seth and I are getting married."

Chapter Sixteen

"Mother, you look absolutely beautiful. Seth's eyes are going to pop out." Abby stood back and beamed at her before kissing her on the cheek. "I'm so happy for you."

"Oh, thank you, baby. I never dreamed I could be this happy." Lynn held her child close to her heart for a long moment. "You run on now. I'll be fine until Art gets here."

Lynn looked around the small cabin she'd called home since returning to the ranch the day before Thanksgiving. Nostalgia hit her at the room's barrenness; all her things had been moved to the main house, everything that is except her wedding dress, accessories, and makeup. And the chrome dinette set was gone, along with some of the Pyrex bowls. She didn't have a clue who had taken them or where.

In ten minutes she'd walk down the aisle and become Seth's wife. Her life would be forever changed, for the better. She had no doubts about the decision she'd made just three months before.

Lynn looked down at the ring on her finger. A round solitaire set in a platinum antique setting. It was lovely, Seth's grandmother's engagement ring. Barbara hadn't wanted it and for some selfish reason, Lynn was grateful she'd never worn it. Today when she and Seth said their vows, they'd exchange plain gold wedding bands. The beautiful solitaire would be put up for special occasions and for Brandon's bride someday.

For the month she'd been at the ranch, she'd stayed in the cabin rather than moving into the ranch house. They were both too old-fashioned to set up housekeeping before the wedding. Plus, Chue and Cookie wouldn't have stood for it. Seth might be the boss around here, but those two were very opinionated and didn't mind letting him know what they thought. And, he respected them.

This was home. Her wedding day had arrived at last. She took deep calming breaths and shook her hands to get her circulation moving. *Nerves, it's nothing but nerves. It's not every day a woman gets married, you know.*

Art knocked on the door. "It's time, Lynn."

When he opened the door, he stopped and beamed at her.

"You look absolutely beautiful. Seth is a lucky man."

She hugged him as she smiled through tears. "I'm a lucky woman, Art. I never dreamed I could ever be this happy. In fact, I'm so happy I've forgiven you for your part in sending me out here."

"Does that mean I can throw that stinky pot out?" He chortled and patted her shoulders, then pulled her into his arms for another hug. "Now, don't you start crying and get those pretty eyes red. Come on, we've got a nervous man waiting at the altar."

She smoothed her dress, checked the short veil held in place by a circlet of pearls and baby's breath, and picked up her bouquet of pink and white roses.

As she walked across the road to the dining hall on Art's arm, the skirt of ivory linen swished just above her ankles. Long sleeves hung from an off the shoulder neckline that dipped to a snug waist. It was very simple, but elegant and Lynn felt like a princess. She knew Seth would love it.

The dining hall would be packed by now with family and friends from neighboring ranches. They'd moved in as many chairs as they could borrow so everyone would have a seat and erected a raised stage so they could see. Since it was December, the room was decorated with white and pink poinsettias. Accents of sparkling silver ribbon wove through the flower-covered archway. On each side stood nine foot tall Christmas trees covered with miniature lights, silver ribbon and doves, and a variety of coordinating ornaments.

On cue, the minute Lynn and Art stepped onto the porch, the sweet refrain of "The Wedding March", played on the violin. Stopping for a minute, Lynn drew her hands, bouquet and all, to her heart and drew in deep gulps of air. Her heart was near bursting.

Art gave her a minute to collect herself. "Are you ready?"

She nodded.

As they entered, everyone stood and turned to watch her progress down the aisle.

Through misty eyes, Lynn saw only smiles. Waiting for her at the end of the aisle, was Seth. He stood tall and handsome in his black tux, his eyes on her as she walked toward him.

Standing beside Seth were his three sons, looking so much like their father. Watching her, they smiled and then turned to watch their father's expressions. Lynn was making their father very happy. She knew they loved her for that.

Abby looked radiant in her rose colored dress, joy evident in the big smile on her face and the faint glisten of tears in her eyes. Maria and Clara, also in rose dresses, beamed at her, both trying hard not to cry.

Corby and Zane stood on each side and to the front of Seth, rose satin pillows in their hands. Dressed in black slacks and white shirts with bow ties, they were adorable. Broad smiles lit their scrubbed faces. They were about to burst with excitement and pride at being included in this adult occasion. Seth put a hand to each of their shoulders to steady them as she approached. They moved aside so she could walk between them.

When she reached Seth, he took her hand and folded it over his arm, turned toward the preacher and drew her close to his side.

Before their family and friends, they exchanged their vows of love and commitment. When the preacher announced them husband and wife, a great roar rose from the crowd. Seth didn't wait to hear the preacher say, "You may kiss the bride." He kissed Lynn thoroughly and soundly, oblivious to the crowd in the room.

* * *

The minute they walked into the barn, the band started playing a slow romantic song. Lynn and Seth danced alone in the middle of the big barn. A hush fell over the crowd and when Seth bent to kiss her, the barn echoed with claps and cheers. They broke apart and each led a loved one onto the floor. Seth danced with Abby and Lynn with Brandon, and they continued to exchange partners until they'd made the rounds.

Lynn was dancing with Cookie when Seth tapped him on the shoulder. "Do you mind if I dance with my wife?" Cookie made a mock face of disappointment but handed her over.

"Who's that young woman Brandon's dancing

with?"

Seth twirled her around until he could locate his oldest son. "Oh, that's Riley Espinoza, Roark's sister. They've known each other for years."

He looked mighty smitten with her. She wondered how Abby was handling this turn of events. Twisting her neck, she located Abby dancing with one of the younger wranglers. She and Seth hadn't been dancing any time at all when Roark tapped Seth on the shoulder.

Seth bristled. "Dammit. It's a sad world when a man can't have five minutes with his wife."

Roark shrugged. "Don't chew on me. I haven't gotten to dance with her yet." He put his arm around Lynn and they started to dance. "I think your husband is going to be a possessive man, Mrs. Williams."

"Roark, I think with the secrets you and I share, we can be on a first name basis."

He threw his head back and laughed. Then his expression grew serious. "I'm not going to be finding you parked alone and crying on the side of the road again, am I?"

Lord, she hoped not. "I think I'm past that."

"Good." He nodded to a couple across the floor. "You have a lovely daughter."

"Thank you. She is, isn't she?" But, Abby didn't look very happy as she watched Brandon dance with Roark's sister. It appeared Abby was going to be hurt.

"Don't worry, ma'am. Brandon won't embarrass Abby. He's been taught better manners. She might be jealous tonight but she doesn't love him."

Lynn quirked an eyebrow. "How can you know that?"

"I just do and I plan to steal her away from

Brandon. Abby's going to fall in love with me." He raised her hand and kissed it. "I'll take care of Abby tonight. Don't you worry about her on your honeymoon."

Lynn couldn't believe what she was hearing. He'd barely met Abby. How could he be in love with her? She tilted her head back to look at his face. The man was serious. "Well, okay, I appreciate that."

When their dance ended, Seth stepped in and took her arm. With a smile, Roark clasped Seth on the shoulder and winked at Lynn. "Congratulations, Seth. Best wishes, Lynn."

Lynn watched him walk away, a million questions on her mind.

Seth slipped his arm around her waist and bent to whisper in her ear. "Is something wrong?"

She shook her head and stepped into his arms.

"Ah, I've got you at last." He leaned down and teased her ear and neck with kisses. His voice was thick with passion and his breath stirred her hair. "And I'm not turning you loose again tonight."

With her hand against his chest, she could feel the steady rhythm of his heart. Was she dreaming or did it just speed up?

She noticed Art and Loretta across the room. "Loretta looks lovely tonight, doesn't she? She and Art look so happy." Art held his wife close and if Lynn wasn't mistaken, he was whispering in her ear. Loretta tossed her head back and laughed.

Seth swiveled so he could see the couple. "Yes, she does." He chuckled. "They act like they're on their second honeymoon."

"Hmmm. Must be their trip to Europe put the spark

back in their relationship."

He cleared his throat. "Speaking of sparks. I'm ready to get out of here, how about you?"

"I'm with you."

"Start heading for the door and go change into your jeans and boots. I'll meet you at the corral. Wear your warm coat." He nuzzled her ear and kissed her cheek as the dance ended.

"Where are we going?"

Seth captured her lips for a quick kiss. "It's a surprise. You'll find out soon enough."

She'd been bugging him for a month to tell her. And he'd wanted to, but stood firm. He was surprised one of the wranglers hadn't slipped and told her. Like a little boy, he couldn't wait to see her response.

Thirty minutes later, they were on their horses riding north. The weather was cool enough to need jackets and gloves, but not so cold as to be uncomfortable. The air was refreshing and invigorating. Did Lynn feel the electricity in the air? God, he was happy.

"By the way, where's my suitcase and where're your things?"

"Everything's been taken care of. Don't worry about a thing. Brandon and Abby brought out everything we'd need earlier today." He couldn't resist teasing her. "You'll have your clothes and those lacy gowns you bought in Odessa. They've become the talk of the ranch."

She gasped. If it'd been daylight, he'd be able to see the color in her face. "What do you mean the talk of the ranch? How'd you find out about them?"

He scratched his chin. "Let me see. Cookie

overheard Maria and Clara talking about them. He told Pete. And there you have it. Pete's a notorious gossip."

The look she flashed him wasn't at all loving. He couldn't hold back the laughter that rumbled from his chest. When he was in control again, he grabbed her free hand.

"Lynn, you have to know I'm teasing. Do you think I'd let the crew go around talking about your lingerie? Cookie and Pete did over hear the two women, but Clara threatened them both with death if they told. And since she was holding a rolling pin at the time, they believed her."

Uh, oh. She had that wicked gleam in her eye. He'd forgotten that she was the queen of pay back. A light in the distance caught her attention, and saved his butt.

"Look Seth, what's that up ahead? She leaned forward in the saddle. It looks like a light."

"Might be."

She turned in the saddle and looked around, trying to place where they were. "Are we somewhere near that natural pool where we camped in August?"

"Might be."

"Okay, I'll quit asking questions, after this last one. Are we almost there yet?"

Remaining silent, Seth just smiled. He was excited. For more reasons than one. Ben and Sally had ridden out tonight to set things up so they wouldn't have to find their way in the dark. He couldn't wait to see Lynn's reaction to what all they'd done. He and the wranglers had worked for over a month in their spare time to make their "getaway" perfect.

"Oh my gosh. It's a little cabin. It almost looks like a play house"

He couldn't help it. She'd played right into his hands. "It is. *Our* play house."

She flashed him a grin. "Really? I can't wait to get inside."

They put their horses in the small lean-to and prepared them for the night. Lynn grabbed his hand, hurried to the cabin, and stopped a short distance away to look. He drew her around in front of him, wrapped his arms around hers and spoke into her ear.

"What do you think of our honeymoon cabin, wife? The guys and I have been working on it in our spare time." Later, it would have other uses, but for now it was theirs. "We can come out here anytime we want to get away for a few days."

"It's beautiful, Seth. I can't believe you did this."

He drew in a deep breath. His surprise had made her happy. "Just for you, my love." She turned in his arms and patted his cheek.

"You're the sweetest, most thoughtful man." She cocked an eyebrow. "I guess I'll have to forgive you and forget about the lingerie tale."

"Thank you, Lord." He dropped a kiss on her lips and pressing his cheek against her hair, held her for just a moment. *Thank you for bringing this woman into my life and for making her such a saucy one, at that. You didn't want me to be bored in my old age, did you?* He lifted his head. "You ready to go in?"

"Lead on, husband."

On the porch, Seth opened the door, then swung her up into his arms and carried her across the threshold. He shoved the door closed with his boot. Letting her feet drop to the floor, he kept her body flush with his, removed her hat, and tossed it onto the bed.

His fingers fanned through her shiny hair enjoying its silky texture, and then cupped her face and angled it up for his kiss. Their lips met in a joining sweet with tenderness and promise. He broke the kiss and groaned against her hair. "You've made me so happy, sweetheart."

Turning her head, she kissed his neck. "Oh, Seth, you can't be any happier than me." Arms around his waist, she burrowed against his chest as if trying to get closer. He sighed with contentment and pressed her cheek closer to his heart.

"You've got exactly two minutes to explore our honeymoon cottage before I toss you in that bed."

She flashed him a saucy grin. "Guess I better hurry then."

Lynn started in the kitchen and peeked into the small butane operated refrigerator, then glanced up. "We've got food!"

When she saw the turquoise Formica table from her cabin, she flashed him a smile and ran her hand lovingly over it. She licked her finger and touched the old coffee pot that sat on the wood-burning stove, and jerked it back. "It's hot."

Like a delighted child, she ran to the opposite end of the room to admire the antique iron bed frame. She sat down and bounced a couple of times. "No feather ticking, huh?"

"A bed is where I draw the line. Comfort wins out over authenticity." He lifted the quilt so she could see the box springs and mattress. "Brand new. Traveled all the way from Odessa in the back of Sally's truck."

From the bed, she could see behind the fabric screen. "Oh my gosh! She's a beauty." He'd searched high and low for the antique claw foot bathtub. He'd been ready to admit defeat, but Clara took over the search and found this one in Alpine at a junk store.

"Oh Seth, this is perfect." If eyes could caress, hers were doing so right now. The love he saw there made his heart constrict.

"Wait until you look out back. Come on." He felt like an excited kid as he led her out the back door and onto a small porch with two rocking chairs. Beyond, the moon glowed on the spring- fed pool.

The look of love she gave him made all their work worthwhile. She was pleased.

"You heard my conversation with Sam that last night on the trail, didn't you?"

"Guilty as charged."

Seth put his arms around Lynn and pulled her back against his chest. Lynn's throat tightened, emotion choking her. The evening she'd sat in the Suburban with Brian, and looked out across the acres of ocotillo, she'd had no idea her life could change in such a short period of time. She hoped she deserved this much happiness.

"It's beautiful, isn't it, Seth? Our special place."

"Yes, love, it is." His kiss on her nape sent delicious tingles up her spine, his breath hot against her ear. "Are you happy, wife?"

Reaching back, she pulled his head closer and turned to reach his mouth with hers.

"Oh yes, Seth. I'm the happiest woman in the world." He was a special man indeed, her man. He'd gone to so much trouble to make her happy. A tear rolled down to where their lips were joined.

His tongue flicked out and captured it. "What's

this? Tears on our wedding night?"

"Tears of joy I assure you." She laughed softly with a sniff. "I guess they're from my overflow valve. I'm just so full of happiness, I can't hold any more."

He clasped her closer and they stood, arms locked, breathing in the fresh air, listening to the night sounds, and enjoying the beauty around them, together.

The heat from his body warmed her. It grew hotter as his hands moved up and eased the heavy down coat open, palms skimming over the tips of her breasts before cupping their fullness.

"Now, where were we in August when Abby pounded on your door?"

Lynn felt the vibrations of his chest as he laughed.

She couldn't resist. "I think you're getting pretty close."

He nipped her ear. "You are one saucy woman."

* * *

Wrapped in a blanket, her feet stuffed in suede moccasins, Lynn stood on the front porch of the cabin watching the sunrise. She held her breath as the sun peeked over the far ridge and cast a glow on the millions of ocotillo plants in bloom that covered the valley floor and marched like soldiers up the hillside. With the combination of the pink morning haze and the red-gold blooms, the area was brushed with a red glow. Beautiful. Lynn hadn't decided if it was prettier at sunrise or sunset. It was the middle of March, Spring Break, and she was off for a week. So, she'd have plenty of time to make up her mind.

Seth stepped outside and handed her a cup of coffee. She took it and kissed his lips. "Thank you, love."

"Mmmm, you're welcome." He put his arm around her and hugged her to his side. "Are you happy, sweetheart?"

She tilted her head and hoped her smile conveyed half of what she felt. "Look out there, Seth. Isn't it magnificent?"

"Yes." He dropped a kiss on her forehead.

"That's a pretty good description of how happy I am."

About the Author

Linda LaRoque is a Texas girl, but the first time she got on a horse, it tossed her in the road dislocating her right shoulder. Forty years passed before she got on another, but it was older, slower, and she was wiser. Plus, her students looked on and it was important to save face.

A retired teacher who loves West Texas, its flora and fauna, and its people, Linda's stories paint pictures of life, love, and learning set against the raw landscape of ranches and rural communities in Texas and the Midwest. She is a member of RWA, her local Chapter of HOTRWA, NTRWA and Texas Mountain Trail Writers.

Linda writes contemporary western romances, time travel historical romances, women's fiction and futuristic romances.

~ * ~

Visit Linda at these locations:

www.lindalaroque.com

http://www.lindalaroqueauthor.blogspot.com

https://www.facebook.com/linda.laroque

http://www.goodreads.com/author/show/649259.Linda_LaRoque

Other Books by Linda LaRoque

Contemporary Westerns
Forever Faithful
Investment of the Heart

Futuristic
Born in Ice

Time Travel
My Heart Will Find Yours—The Turquoise
Legacy Book 1
Flames on the Sky—The Turquoise Legacy Book 2
A Way Back
Desires of the Heart—novella
A Law of Her Own—novella
A Marshal of Her Own—novella
A Love of His Own—novella
A Time of Their Own—an anthology containing A
Law of Her Own, A Marshal of Her Own, and A Love
of His Own
Birdie's Nest

Women's Fiction
Shattered Vows
Wounded Hearts—novella